THE FORGER AND THE THIEF

KIRSTEN MCKENZIE

SSP

This edition published 2020
by Squabbling Sparrows Press

ISBN 978 0995 136922 (ebook)
ISBN 978 0995 136915 (paperback)

Squabbling Sparrows Press

ALSO BY KIRSTEN MCKENZIE

To Andrene and Madeleine
You kept me sane during lockdown.
And you made me finish this book.
Thank you

PROLOGUE

FORCED INSIDE BY THE WEATHER, Nedda's wooden clothes rack sat like an emaciated skeleton in front of the fire. The incessant rain lashing the tiled roof didn't bother her, but the intermittent wailing of the dam's sirens sent her clucking to her husband — that ugly great oaf Enzo, lounging in his armchair.

'How many times has that sounded now? Shouldn't you telephone to check if everything up at the dam is okay? Maybe if you showed some initiative, they would give you that promotion?'

Enzo shrugged and Nedda imagined shoving her husband's shaggy head into the fire — the fire she started, with wood she cut and lugged up the narrow staircase to their tiny apartment. The apartment Enzo promised was only temporary until his advancement to head engineer. That was over thirty years ago now, and she'd long given up waiting for his promised promotion from lowly dam worker to engineer.

Nedda turned the radio off, just as the host announced that Frank Sinatra's 'Strangers in the Night' was number one in the charts, for the seventh week in a row. She tilted her head, certain she'd heard something over the opening bars of Sinatra's hit.

'Was that a wolf?' she asked, as she crossed herself. They rarely heard wolves anymore, but she'd always considered them an evil omen. Enzo didn't answer.

The first raindrops hadn't bothered Nedda, gathering in tiny pools, caressing wanton leaves and splashing stones. But the rain kept coming, chasing her inside, falling in unending rivers of wet, drenching the earth until it became like an overfull sponge, forcing the water elsewhere.

The siren died away, and Nedda shook her head to clear an animalistic rumbling between her ears. She turned to prod Enzo's prone figure, but he was at the window, his belly spilling over his trousers as he opened the shutters.

'You'll let the rain in,' Nedda yelled, tugging the laden clothes rack away from the rain.

Enzo didn't answer, too busy leaning out into the void, his gut pressing against the ancient window frame, his attention drawn by something other than his wife.

'What can you see?' Nedda asked, raising her voice to compete against the roar forcing its way into their living room.

'Water.'

Living near to the dam never fazed Nedda. It was convenient for Enzo's work, and for the husbands of her friends. But tonight the darkness disguised the torrents of water streaming from the crumbling dam, pounding against the stone foundations of every house in their street.

The building shuddered, throwing Nedda against Enzo. She grabbed onto her husband. Any complaints about his snoring or lack of advancement swept away by the churning water.

'What do we do?'

'There's nothing we can do,' Enzo replied, holding her tighter.

Nedda looked into her husband's eyes, mirroring his actions as he crossed himself.

'Mary protect us,' she whispered, tucking her head into Enzo's shoulder

The building shuddered again, and a groan from the waterlogged foundations forced its way up through the elderly walls. The fire spluttered as the burning wood lurched from the hearth.

Enzo stumbled as the floor tilted and Nedda cried out as her husband's body crushed her against the wall, gravity holding them in place.

Enzo's grip tightened around Nedda's own middle-aged waist.

'Now we pray,' he said.

Their prayers followed them as the building collapsed, throwing them into the swirling maelstrom as their beloved home became nothing more than dangerous rubble, destined to fill the picturesque Arno.

Nedda screamed for Enzo as the water engulfed her, filling her mouth, cutting short the prayers she'd known her entire life. They would not help her now.

And up in the Valle dell'Inferno, the Valley of Hell, a lone wolf howled at the moon.

THE GUEST

He'd never wanted to return to Florence. He'd been there once on an ill-fated college trip involving copious amounts of alcohol consumed by underage boys while the tutor slept. As a teen, Richard Carstone experienced Florence with the mother of all hangovers, and remembered nothing good about the place. Although the trip had been not long after the war, so he hadn't seen Florence in its finest glory.

But here he was, drinking as an adult after an eleven hour flight. He tried to avoid flying wherever possible because being inside a cylindrical tube, thousands of feet in the air, under the control of a potentially manic depressive pilot filled him with dread, hence the self medication administered before, during, and now after the flight. And that wasn't the only reason he was drinking himself into another stupor.

His meeting with Julia hadn't gone to plan, which was why he was now sitting alone at the bar. He had her best interests at heart, and knew her better than anyone else, and marrying him was far preferable to marrying a foreigner, an Italian. He'd tried every argument under the sun, even pulling out the spectre of Scott, his brother, but she'd shot that down in flames.

Nursing a drink and positioning his glass so it sat in the middle of the tatty coaster, Richard Carstone once again pondered how he came to be in a hotel in Florence, alone with a shot of whiskey, and a coffee served in the smallest doll-sized coffee cup he'd even seen. When it arrived he'd argued with the barman that no one served coffees that small, but the barman then forgot how to speak a word of English, taking himself off to serve someone else.

Everything was Julia's fault. She'd fallen in love with the Italian guy who'd agreed to marry her as long as they did the deed in Italy, satisfying his elderly mother and ancient grandmother that their marriage was genuine. Why Julia invited Richard wasn't a mystery, until five years ago she'd been his sister-in-law — the type who hosts the family dinners because they have the biggest home, and she has all the time in the world. Her Christmas presents always wrapped with ribbons and sprigs of holly, not just held together with string. Easter was always a production, but not with those mass produced chocolates from the gas station. No, not Julia, she'd handmade her own chocolate eggs. Richard tried hating her, but Julia was the best thing to happen to their family since his pop returned home from the war. His big brother was the luckiest man on the planet, until Julia found him cooling on their manicured lawn next to a ladder, his body twisted in an improbable angle, and Richard had been the one she'd called first.

Richard would never forget the memory of his brother's broken body. His death killing their parents, carrying them off like a hawk with an injured rabbit. Scott had been their favourite, their golden child, the prodigal son, the heir, with Richard the spare. But, in the wake of

Scott's death, and after the death of his parents, Richard became Julia's rock, which suited him.

Until Julia hadn't needed him anymore. The Italian swooping in, sweeping her off her feet with his European charm and his money and his connections to the art world Julia adored, a world closed to Richard. He just knew that he loved Julia. Had always loved her.

Then out of the blue, an invitation to her Italian wedding. The last thing he'd expected, but an opportunity to win her back.

Knocking back the dregs of his drink, he stumbled from the bar to his room, hopeful that the whiskey would do its job and that his dreams would be from happier times. Dreams of Julia, the woman he wanted as his wife.

THE WIFE

As THE UNIFORMED Pan Am air hostess waved goodbye, and Rhonda Devlyn stepped off the DC-8 onto the tarmac at Peretola Airport in Florence, Italy, she stopped to smell the air, tasting the enigmatic scent of freedom, something she only had the ghost of a memory of. Terrified of losing her newfound liberty, Rhonda scuttled through Customs, fully expecting an official to tap her on the shoulder, to send her back to America.

She'd never been to Italy, but Florence felt like an old friend, reminding her of a comfortable quilt stored in the cupboard waiting till winter hit.

In the back of a taxi, she dared offering the driver a smile, exercising muscles in her cheeks long unused. Her sudden freedom so tangible it vibrated in every nerve of her battered body.

The taxi hurtled through the morning traffic; the rain washing the streets clean. Although no different to rush hour in any other city, Rhonda smiled at the faces of the drivers. Their looks so quintessentially Italian. Their cars, their manners, the buildings they passed. Tiny Fiats slipped through miniature gaps between fresh-off-the-production-line Alfa Romeo's and the world's largest collection of Lancers.

Judicious use of car horns appeared to be compulsory, with her driver adding to the cacophony, but even the horns sounded Italian.

They pulled up outside the Palazzo della Gherardesca, the reward of decades of damaged dreams. Dreams about a place seeped in history and held together with the blood of the Medici family. Her own blood almost put an end to her dreams, but she'd left that behind her.

A uniformed concierge appeared with a giant umbrella to escort her inside, and with her heart in her mouth, she approached the building wondering if she would find safety here. Would Florence deliver the peace and the security she deserved?

Rhonda walked through the ornate archway, and Firenze appeared. Not Florence, but Firenze, that place of artists, intrigue, manipulation, love, design, disaster.

The palazzo hummed with its own history, and its elegance spoke for itself, and the staff waited discreetly for Rhonda to pull herself back from the past and into the present day.

Through several centuries of changes of ownership and rebirth, the hotel clung to its history the way a shipwrecked sailor clings to driftwood. The doors opened to a frescoed atrium featuring the last word in decadence, with ceilings adorned with cherubs worthy of the Sistine Chapel. And everywhere she looked, Rhonda's eyes drank in the details. The magic the architects and designers had created was beyond compare, and this restoration was so true to the palazzo's origins, that the hotel's owners must have been Renaissance princes in a former life.

It still surprised Rhonda that she'd made it here. The

life she had endured made bearable by this heaven on earth.

At first glance, her room appeared more opulent than any she'd ever stayed in before, but before enjoying the moment, she checked the door and engaged the privacy chain. Safety first.

Satisfied she was alone, Rhonda sank into the enormous bed, gazing at hand drawn frescoes on the ceiling, wallowing in the impossible luxury of solitude.

THE STUDENT

HELENA Stolar stumbled through her order at the trattoria. After every visit to Italy, she left confident that her Italian had improved enough to make life easier, but she'd been back two days and her tongue still failed at the simplest of words. She'd resorted to repeating prego and grazie, ad infinitum using hand gestures more at home at a football game.

Gazing around, she took in the contented faces of the locals. This trattoria wasn't a tourist trap — charging extra for sitting outside and breathing the air, but a local haunt with a modest menu and a loyal clientele, and near her work. And if she didn't have to eat, she'd already be there.

Helena chose Florence for her work experience, to access the best tutors and base materials, but also to look for the art stolen from her family during the war. An impossible task. Experts she'd spoken with on behalf of her broken family called her labour a fool's errand, warning her off the Herculean task of tracking her father's art. The more time she spent in Italy, the more she realised that if the artworks still existed, they hid in European attics or scattered across the globe. But she never stopped looking.

Known for its great museums and galleries, tiny museums filled Florence's obscure alleyways, hidden well off the beaten track, available to a select few. Helena spent her spare time tracking these down, working through word of mouth, chasing recommendations from bakers and postage clerks, coffee bar waiters and taxi drivers.

This morning she stood outside the Soldanieri Gallery, a private homage to Italian art. And although open to the public, it was almost unknown to the casual tourist, unless they were in the market to buy the art on display.

After shaking the rain from her coat, she entered the Roman Renaissance style foyer, wandering through the elegant halls. With no interest in statues and sculptures, she made her way straight to the galleries. The Soldanieri was both a traditional museum and a gallery. The two sections operating in uncomfortable competition with each other. As everything inside was privately owned, the Italian government had no power to stop the wealthy owner selling any of his art to the highest bidder.

She ignored the large biblical scenes with overblown colours and exquisite religious iconography; she concentrated on pieces similar to those which had formed her father's collection — smaller pieces, with an obvious lean towards maritime themed pieces, running the gamut from three-masted sailing ships to smaller tenders.

There was one piece she knew she'd be able to identify as soon as she saw it — a canvas no bigger than a magazine, oil on wood depicting a small tender wrecked on an outcrop of rocks in a storm with a man and woman huddled under the darkened clouds, their faces turned from the artist showing only a profile of fear. It wasn't there. She never expected to recover the painting and wasn't surprised when she couldn't find it, making a short notation next to the museum's name in her notebook.

'Were you searching for something in particular?' a voice asked.

Helen spun around, dropping her notebook, the pencil skittering across the polished marble floors.

As he bent to retrieve Helena's belongings, a flash of gold winked from his cuffs, a golden eagle, an Aquila.

'I was hoping for *The Wreck* by Nicolae Vermont, my father was very fond of it.' She'd learnt early on that to accuse a museum of holding pillaged artwork was a sure way to receive a swift escort out. Now she kept her enquiries benign.

'And your father saw it here, in this gallery?'

Helena detected something on his face. Recognition?

'It's what I've been told. Sadly, my father has passed, so I can't ask him,' she apologised.

After handing Helena her pencil, the man steepled his fingers at his lips.

'The example you are looking for, is it a couple shipwrecked on the rocks?'

Helena's pulse quickened.

'Yes, have you seen it?'

He nodded. 'That picture was never here though, but nearby.'

'Can I visit there? To see it?' Helena asked, her pulse racing.

The man swept the room with guarded eyes, before nodding.

'Yes, I can take you tonight.'

With arrangements made to meet after the museum closed for the afternoon, Helena all but skipped from the building.

ALFONSO CASADEI, the owner of the Soldanieri, watched Helena leave. It suited him to let visitors confuse him for lowly museum staff. It was an excellent means to gauge feedback for the exhibitions, to identify future clients, and sometimes, to find a lover.

Casadei tapped his fingers against his jutting collarbone, every line on his face detailing a life lived on the edge of civility. She was perfect for his collection...

Somewhere outside a melodious bell tolled the hour and Casadei checked his watch. There was sufficient time to join his fiancée for pre-dinner drinks before his appointment tonight. He hadn't predicted a marriage to an older widow, but she came with such a magnificent inheritance, that it would have been foolish to refuse. And it didn't pay to keep her waiting.

THE CLEANER

STEFANO MAZZI LOCKED the door and dropped the heavy keyring into his pocket as he tried straightening his shoulders. The pain snaking across his hips worsened every day, but he refused to acknowledge it until he reached his home. The wet weather made it worse, and both Stefano and Florence were suffering from under two weeks of non-stop rain. He hated the November weather, when the respite of the summer months was so far away. Defying the agony, he lengthened his stride and lifted his chin. No one must see his pain.

As he shuffled along the narrow cobbled streets, he avoided the tourists. Their eyes glazed over at the beauty surrounding them. He also ignored the lengthening shadows holding the history of the Medici's within its confines, his sights firmly set on the well-trod path to his car he took every night, focussed on home.

Tonight it seemed he'd parked closer to home than to work, but given the scarcity of car parking spaces in the city, he didn't bother looking for a spot closer. He'd been parking here for longer than he cared to remember. Most days it suited him. Even on mist-soaked days, which left his hands invisible in front of his face, the lengthy walk cleared his mind of his troubles. It was the only time there was no call upon him. The drive home wasn't calming; most Italians drove as if they were Mario Andretti, and Stefano's car bore the evidence — with both wing mirrors held on with tape, and more scrapes down the side than a water buffalo in Africa.

After braving the evening's traffic and nudging his way into a parking space nearby, he limped home. Stefano selected a far smaller key than the one he'd used to lock up at the museum, but paused before using it. He stroked the third key on the keyring. It didn't have the heft or the gravitas of the first one, nor was it as common as his house key. He didn't need it today, but soon.

He slipped the smallest key into the lock and opened the nondescript wooden door, worn and battered like him.

'I'm home,' he called out. No reply greeted him, and he shuffled in, sloughing off his shoes and bag. His leather satchel making as many trips as him, a trusty companion. It clunked against the stair rail as he hung it over the newel, silence swallowing the noise.

Old world charm filled every corner of the house. Pedestrians outside would never have guessed the luxury behind Stefano's plain front door. The shabbiness of the man a contrast to inside, where tendrils of hand-painted ivy curled up the walls, the valuable wooden furniture shone, with gold leaf adorning every ornate frame, and intricate mosaics dressed the floor he trod in his stockinged feet.

As he made his way upstairs, his heart slowed as the peace of his home enveloped him. Muted tones, delicate antique furniture, and walls adorned with fine oil paintings by long dead Italian artists from the best of schools. As he climbed the stairs, the portraits looked upon him, judging his deeds, approving of his ways.

'*Ciao, amore mio*,' he said. I'm home, my love.

THE POLICEMAN

ANOTHER DAY, another tourist, another missing wallet. Monkeys took more care of their belongings than the tourists he dealt with every day. Who travels to a foreign country and leaves their handbag hanging on the back of their chair? Those had been Antonio Pisani's first three files this morning before a fourth tourist appeared at the front desk claiming his valuables were missing from his hotel safe. The next tourist had had his wallet plucked from his back pocket.

Antonio Pisani patted the front of his trousers, still damp from the torrential rain outside, and felt the reassuring bulk of his wallet in his pocket. No decent Italian man kept his pocketbook in his back trouser pocket. You may as well hand it directly to the pickpockets. Every tourist guidebook he'd ever read gave the same advice, but every single day, tourists flooded into the police station, livid that someone had robbed them. It was enough to drive him to drink.

'Pisani, have you got that file on the room safe theft?'

Rosa Fonti called out, her voice guttural, marking her as a northerner, not a local.

'It's here, Bella,' he said, holding the file above his head.

'Stop calling me Bella,' Rosa said, snatching the folder from his hands.

He could hear her muttering under her breath as she returned to her desk, but ignored it. Rosa was a peculiar specimen; a woman in a workplace not designed for her kind. Soon she would marry and spawn small sulky children, which meant she was just a passing phase in an otherwise unchanging workplace, so no point trying too hard to be friends. As long as she did her share of work, and made the coffee, he didn't mind sharing the office with her.

'Why do you want the file?' he asked, recognising she'd asked for one of his allocated files.

Rosa looked up. 'There's a report of another theft from the same hotel.'

Pisani frowned. Pickpockets were one thing, par for the course in Florence, but thefts from hotel safes were rare, and the city council would come down upon them like the Ponte Vecchio in an earthquake if it hit them with any adverse publicity. Flailing around in his memory for the hotel's name, he gave in, 'What was the name of the hotel?'

'The Altavilla on the Via dei Leoni,' said Rosa Fonti.

THE GUEST

With a hangover larger than the trash problem in Rome, Richard Carstone awoke to the noise of an army of delivery trucks trundling past his window. And somewhere down the hotel corridor it sounded like someone had set up a nursery and was encouraging their young attendees to cry as often as possible.

Carstone winced as he sat up before lurching over to the grimy window. Housekeeping wasn't a priority here. To be fair, he'd booked into one of the cheapest hotels within walking distance of the wedding venue. He didn't crave taking his life into his hands by driving on roads crowded with mad Italians behind the wheels of dubious quality Fiats. As a starter, he'd lost his licence.

The view from the window as dire as he expected in a city as old as Florence catering to an influx of tourists — an alleyway filled with overflowing bins leading onto the street, a family of rats ferreting through the waste in uninterrupted joy. And rain. It hadn't stopped raining since he'd arrived.

Turning his back on the view, he tried jollying the wall

heater into life by hitting it. Nothing. A shower then, that would at least warm him.

The two toilets in the bathroom confused him, and he chose the one with a seat. Sitting there he puzzled over the extra toilet and his mind strayed from Julia, to Scott, to Italy, to his problems, and back to the second toilet. He hoped the hotel had fired their plumber, or had at least got a refund for the redundant plumbing. Two toilets in one bathroom, the perfect illustration of why he preferred America.

Carstone ignored the hair stuck to a cake of soap left by the last guest and waited for the scalding water. And waited and waited, his skin crawling as the filth became more noticeable the longer he stood there. He couldn't bear it, and climbed under the icy water, which was as sobering as expected. With his eyes closed, Richard allowed the water to flow over his face, washing away the flight, the alcohol, and Julia's rejection.

'*Ciao, servizio di pulizia*,' came a woman's voice from his room.

His eyes flew open, 'Hello? I'm in the shower,' Carstone called out. Who the hell was in there? He wrapped a short towel around his waist to investigate.

A youthful woman in cotton trousers and a white shirt stood in the room. '*Servizio di pulizia*,' she said, staring at him.

'Sorry, but I've got no idea what you're saying,' Richard said, trying to tug his towel closed. Either his stomach was too big or it was designed for a child, because it barely met in the middle.

'Housekeeping,' she said with a heavy accent, turning to straighten his sheets.

'Now's not an agreeable time,' he said, dripping on the carpet. She paid no attention, intent on her poor attempts at smoothing the covers he'd had a fight with during the night. If the soap was a sign as to the cleanliness of the linen, he didn't want to think too deeply about it.

Carstone repeated himself, gesturing one-handed to the open door.

She shrugged, turned on her heels and left. Carstone peered out to check she'd gone, surprised at the lack of any housekeeping trolley in the narrow hallway, yet watched her let herself into another room, calling out, 'S*ervizio di pulizia*,' as she entered the room.

Curious, maybe she was just the bed-making girl? Now shivering in the doorway, Carstone returned to his room, drying himself off and rehanging the towel on the rail, making sure each end was the same length. He couldn't ignore the ancient bar of soap any longer and tossed it in the trash. Laying his toiletries in a neat row on the edge of the basin, a balm to his interrupted ablutions, he forgot about the girl from housekeeping. He had a different girl on his mind.

THE WIFE

DESPITE THE ENTICING view outside of the rain-dappled private gardens of the *palazzo*, Rhonda didn't want to leave her opulent room. She still felt the prickle of someone watching her, despite being five thousand miles away from her husband. Twice she'd tested the lock before running a bath.

After bathing, she rubbed at her unease with a towel, scrubbing her body raw as she reassured herself that there was no way he'd find her.

Rhonda stared out over gardens peppered with statues dotting the paths, waiting to hide lovers and sinners alike. Pressing her forehead to the glass, she reminded herself that this was what freedom felt like and admonished herself to stop fear from clouding this moment.

Rummaging through her case, she pulled out a sundress bought on impulse at the airport. A blue majolica print dress with a simple neckline and fitted at the waist with a slight flare. One of the most expensive pieces of clothing she'd ever bought, with money she'd never had access to until now. But what little remained of her self confidence refused to allow her to dress the part of a frumpy housewife in Italy. The shop assistant had tried tempting her with those new miniskirts everyone was wearing now, and Rhonda remembered laughing at the poor thing. She didn't have legs like Jean Shrimpton; she was a housewife. What would she do with a miniskirt in her wardrobe?

The rain indicating it was not suitable weather for a sundress, and her husband would have called her stupid for wearing it, but he wasn't here, and this was her life. So Rhonda slipped it on and checked the mirror. Perhaps it was the light, or the release from hell, but she looked different — younger, unburdened, alive. Fluffing her hair, she assessed her figure then turned away. It didn't matter how she presented herself, no one would stare at her. That's what she'd been told. No one wants to look at you.

After covering the dress with a sensible jacket, and slipping on her shoes, Rhonda collected her handbag and hat and left her refuge, plastering a smile into place, something she'd had plenty of practice doing.

The concierge greeted her as she appeared in the lobby.

'Have you settled in, *Signora* Devlyn?' he asked.

'Yes, thank you,' Rhonda answered, her eyes skittering over the other guests.

'Is there a tour I may help organise?' he asked.

'No, I don't think so. I will stroll the streets and find coffee, and then I will visit the Uffizi.'

'I can arrange your ticket for the gallery?' he offered.

'No, sorry, I mean I am just going to sit outside and drink it in. That sounds strange, I know, but I need to savour the moment. I'm in no rush,' she said, smiling.

'Ah, *perfetto*, perfect,' he said, handing her a map of the city and pencilling in the best route to the Uffizi Gallery.

'Sadly, the forecast today is for more rain. We can only apologise.'

Rhonda thanked the man and disappeared into the outside world.

It wasn't the concierge's place to question Rhonda's peculiar desires. She couldn't have known it saddened him that most guests only experienced a minuscule fraction of the beauty of Firenze, that the city was much more than the Uffizi Gallery and the Ponte Vecchio. But she noticed him checking her fingers, which still bore both her wedding band and an engagement ring. Perhaps he expected her husband to join her, or maybe she was waiting for an *il innamorato*, a lover.

Rhonda flushed with embarrassment at the perceived judgement as she hurried into the rain, slipping the stubborn rings from her finger and shoving them deep into the recesses of her leather handbag.

THE STUDENT

As PART of the intern programme at the Manzoni Art Institute, Helena would spend the next three months learning advanced techniques for fresco painting and restoration. She'd chosen this speciality despite frescoes being in short supply at home in England. Henry VIII's dissolution of the monasteries had dealt with most of them, leaving only fragments for scholars to examine. Three months inhaling caustic fumes during restoration work was far more desirable than another Christmas at home with the ghosts of her family.

Florence in autumn was so much more bearable than the summer, when tourists clogged the streets and cafes, behaving with unbearable rudeness to the locals. She identified more local than tourist, given this was her third visit to Florence, each trip longer than the earlier one. Her trips to Florence buoyed her through the lonely grey rainy days in England, although it hadn't stopped raining since she'd arrived in Italy, reminding her of the rain which caused the disaster in Aberfan in Wales just last month. And she uttered a muted prayer, grateful that she was in a cosmopolitan city and no where near a coal mine.

After arriving at the studio, it surprised her to recognise students from last year working at their allocated tables. She hadn't realised that they weren't yet qualified conservators, thinking them well ahead of her in the programme.

'*Ciao*, Helena!' Benito enthused from the enormous drafting table, as he threw his arms around her.

Dressed in white lab coats, the students resembled a room full of scientists, and in actuality, that's what they were. They learnt and worked in an environment filled with ultraviolet lights, microscopes, a bulky microliter centrifuge, test tubes, scalpels and other diagnostic machines Helena still didn't understand. She knew what they did, but not how they worked.

'Hello, Benito,' Helena replied, leaning in for the customary double kiss, flushing at her proximity to the attractive Italian. 'Did you just get here?' she asked, pointing to his pristine workspace

'It was difficult getting out of bed this morning, until I smelt the coffee,' he said, running a stained hand through his thick black hair, making it look like he'd styled it with electricity. Girls killed for hair as thick as his.

'Hello again, Helena,' said the other person at the table, lifting her blonde head a fraction.

'Hello, Marisa,' Helena said, swivelling back towards Benito, the social veneer straining under the mutual dislike. She would never forgive Marisa for what had happened last season. It was unforgivable. Girls don't do that to their friends.

'Are you here for the whole three months?' she asked Benito.

'I am and you?'

'Same, but this term they're paying me to be here, instead of making me use my leave.'

'How wonderful!' Benito enthused, oblivious to Marisa's scowl. 'That means it is your shout tonight. Where are we going? To the Rendezvous? You remember the basement bar near the Arno?'

'You Italians are all the same. Drink, drink, drink! Yes, I remember, and I can't believe that dive is still operating.'

'Drinking isn't all that's on my mind,' Benito replied, winking. Despite knowing that Benito DiMarco was an incurable flirt, Helena's pulse quickened at his words. Maybe this time she'd be the lucky object of his attention. Her fantasies had carried her through the past year, and there were few nights she didn't fall asleep dreaming of Benito and what might be...

She stumbled over her answer, Benito's appeal was overwhelming, but her appointment with the curator so unexpected that she'd be a fool not to meet him tonight.

'I can't tonight, but tomorrow, definitely. We'll have a rendezvous at the Rendezvous. Now back to work,' Helena joked, before moving off to her workstation. The outlook for her winter in Florence improved immeasurably now that Benito was there. It was a shame Marisa was back, but she'd deal with that problem if it raised its head again. She needed to remember not to trust Marisa, especially with men.

From her cushioned stool, she greeted her table companions - Vitali, the small Russian man with an uncanny resemblance to Lenin but with less of a revolutionary bend, and Oona - a quiet Irish girl with an accent as broad as the Arno River. She seemed nice enough, but quiet. A fourth stool lay unclaimed.

Today's assignment was an unsigned portrait of a Renaissance noble. Their first task was to clean away decades of dirt clinging to the discoloured varnish, before they began any actual restoration work. The careful removal of the varnish was next, always tricky, but there were several patches of paint loss on the canvas, and any haste might lift more paint. An extra pair of hands would have been helpful, otherwise it could take them days to lift the varnish.

As they worked, the pile of soiled materials next to them grew along with the stench of fumes. Helena's mind wandered as she considered how best to handle tonight. Should she demand that they hand over her father's artwork? Should she ask the police to go with her? Her hand slipped.

'*Merda!*'

Their tutor - Feodor Sim loomed above Helena, ripping her hand away from the canvas, his firm grip pinching the tender flesh of her wrist. His eyes narrowed to slits.

'You're ruining the canvas. Concentrate,' he yelled, before releasing her and throwing his hands up in despair.

Helena tugged her sleeves over her reddening wrist, the flush inching up her cheeks giving her gawping classmates even more to stare at.

Feodor Sim, a renowned tutor, and artist in his own right, ruled with an iron rod and expected greatness from his students, and they rewarded him with such. When he wasn't peering over their shoulders and tutting in their ears, he worked on private commissions — mixing ingredients to replicate the paint used by the original artist, mimicking recipes and techniques long since lost to the modern artist. But he was mercurial, prone to screaming at the slightest infractions, threatening to expel students who disappointed him more than once. Helena had never endured his anger until now.

Helena stumbled over a heartfelt apology, holding back the reasons for her distraction. Should she tell him, ask for his help? She bit her lip, thinking she'd burnt that bridge now.

'You will concentrate or you will leave,' Sim said, with utter finality before retreating to his alcove — his private inner sanctum.

Sim's lab resembled an alchemist's lair — stocked with vials of crushed gemstones, powdered beetle carcasses, and foreign seed pods. Like Ali Baba himself, Feodor Sim collected rare ingredients from around the world. After analysing paint samples from Byzantine, Renaissance, Elizabethan and Napoleonic art, he painstakingly collected samples of the authentic ingredients with the goal of recreating the paints applied by long dead artists, both famous and forgotten.

It had fascinated Helena to watch Sim mix his concoctions, sampling them on tiny pieces of prepared canvas or board, depending on which artist he was mimicking. He would make a superb forger with the attention to detail he gave every sweep of the brush. But to be on the end of Sim's anger… it wasn't something she ever wanted to repeat. She couldn't afford to upset him.

'I'm sorry,' she said to his retreating back. She had to focus and would worry about her appointment later.

THE CLEANER

STEFANO KISSED his wife on the forehead, but she didn't move from staring out the bedroom window. Not a good day then, Stefano thought as he changed out of his overalls, folding them before laying them on the chair ready for tomorrow.

He left his wife to her hidden dreams and made his way to the kitchen. Once his wife's domain, he'd taken over but changed nothing. The basil still grew on the window ledge and ripe persimmons sat like sun-burnt buddhas in a bowl, threatening to explode. But in the corners, dust gathered, stray crumbs hid under benches, and desiccated carrots lay rotting at the bottom of the vegetable basket. But Stefano was oblivious to the surrounding decay.

He pottered around the kitchen, pulling apart yesterday's leftover ciabatta, roughly chopping radicchio leaves and prepping the artichokes for steaming. After dicing a small red onion from the bowl, he added it to the radicchio, and threw in a handful of capers. He sliced the still hot artichokes into thin slivers, adding them to the bowl, followed by a splash of vinegar, olive oil, and shredded basil. The herby scent perfuming his gnarled fingers.

Stefano tossed the salad together, mixing in the stale ciabatta, and serving it onto two plates. He poured two glasses of red wine — a *vino novello*, and loaded everything onto a wooden tray before carrying it upstairs. If it was a good day, she'd eat and drink with him, bringing such joy, but those were rare.

'I'm coming, my love,' he called out.

He placed the tray on a small table under the window. The mahogany and walnut table's delicate surface still held the vestiges of inlaid flowers and leaves, hidden as soon as Stefano set his tray down, obscuring the centuries-old beauty.

His wife refused to look at the food, her silent rebuke punishing him.

He chose his words carefully.

'Please, Carmela. Nonna made it, downstairs. She asked me to bring it up because she's up to her arms in flour and didn't want to trek powder up the stairs.'

Despite Carmela's grandmother having been dead for thirty-odd years, mentioning Nonna settled her. He'd resorted more and more to subterfuge and half truths to keep her happy. But tonight he would face another night of angry silence. Nothing he did drew her away from the window and the waiting.

THE POLICEMAN

SPREAD OVER THE DESK, the files made for sobering reading. Twelve reports of thefts this year from hotel rooms, with no one linking them until now.

'All from the Altavilla?' Pisani asked, slurping his third coffee, missing the flash of disgust on Rosa's face, oblivious that his coffee breath was worse than the stale air inside the meeting room.

'No, the last three are from the Altavilla. They left their passports and most of their valuables in their rooms while they were sightseeing, but when they checked out in the morning, their cash had vanished—'

'And their passports?' Pisani interrupted. A brisk trade in stolen passports had sprouted in Italy, with the market for new identities almost as lucrative as the burgeoning heroin business run by the various Mafia families.

Rosa nodded, 'Gone too. Passports and cash.'

'And the others?' Pisani probed, ignoring the information laid out in Rosa's report, and her sigh. He leaned back in his chair, eyes closed, as he listened to Rosa read from her report.

'There were five reported thefts from hotel room safes at the Primavera, all from foreign tourists, with another four reported at the Prati. If you look at the dates you'll see that they are consecutive, the Primavera first, the Prati, and then the Altavilla—'

'One thief targeting different hotels,' said Pisani.

Rosa's loud sigh stopped Pisani, and he stared at the woman, surprised at the frustration on her face. He hoped she didn't expect any credit for arresting the thief. What did she expect, to make the arrest herself? The file was his and the glory would be too. As it should be.

'Yes, that's my thought—'

'Easy to pick him up at the Altavilla, if he's still there,' Pisani prophesied.

'It could be a woman,' Rosa said.

'Unlikely, too clever for a woman. Get the staffing records from those other hotels, and we'll go to the Altavilla to check their files. Yes? Right, lunchtime.'

PISANI LEFT, leaving Rosa open-mouthed at the table. The man infuriated her more than any other person she'd ever met, yet sometimes he would leave the newspaper on her desk, open at the sports results, especially if her team had played particularly well that week. Those moments were few and far between, but they happened frequently enough to stave off the hatred threatening to boil over.

'Idiot,' Rosa muttered, clearing away the empty coffee mugs and discarded papers, including a crude cartoon depicting her entwined with a leaning tower — a crude play on Pisani's name. She lobbed it into the bin before returning to her desk to prepare for her trip to the

Primavera Hotel, a cesspit catering to budget-conscious travellers.

Rosa refused to allow Pisani's sexist remarks to colour her opinion when she arrived at the Primavera Hotel, and she adjusted her uniform jacket and hat before entering the tepid establishment.

Although set a few streets back from the tourist strip, the Primavera sat close enough to the Arno River and the key tourist destinations to appeal to backpackers and recent arrivals from the countryside. Its foyer was clean, in the way that a place always has one room cleaner than the rest, and apart from the recent thefts, the only other complaint on record was the arrest of a drunken guest causing mayhem.

The hotelier kept her records on site, although there wasn't much to see — a family-run hotel meant they used few non-family members apart from over the busy season, and even then, those extra staff were the children of friends, students working the holidays.

After running her finger down the list, Rosa asked about each of the staff, 'What about this one, Serena Zetticci, she didn't last long and worked here when the thefts occurred?'

The nervous hotelier shook her dyed black hair, 'No, not her, she is the daughter of a friend. I checked these lists after the thefts. None of them would steal from here.'

'None that you'll tell us about?'

The woman coloured, 'No, not at all. This hurts all small hotels, which is why I am helping you. I want the thief caught.'

Rosa noted the woman's shaking hands as she passed the sheaf of papers back. 'Run off copies of these for me, and I will be in touch if we have more questions.'

Rosa stuffed the still-warm copies of the staff records into her satchel, hoping to keep them dry during the long walk back to her car. Her scheduled visit to the Prati Hotel - another low budget hotel accommodating the poorest of travellers, could wait until the rain eased.

As she sat in the car, drying out in front of the heater, she went through the names again. None of the employees sounded familiar, and the hotelier knew the part-time staff and vouched for their honesty. That was the nature of life in Italy, everyone knew everyone else, or at least someone knew someone who knew your family. Someone must know the identity of the thief.

THE RIVER

SHE REVELLED in the seven inches of rain, frolicking like a lamb in a meadow, dashing and crashing, teasing the gods until they threw their hands up in anger, unleashing even more rain to placate the irksome water, taunting them with her earthbound form.

The River slid back as the side of the hill tumbled into her clutches, delivering a ton of delectable earth, left naked by decades of rampant logging unfettered by rules or regulations.

She clapped her watery hands, dancing in circles until she herself was dizzy with glee. Scooping up handfuls of mud from the riverbed, she dashed the heavy mud against the walls holding her course, knowing that the pressure would weaken the bank until it joined her on her merry path of destruction.

Water poured down the valley, through farms and houses, pig pens, and poultry cages, past towering trees, and struggling saplings, saturating graveyards and devastating crops. Egged on by The River, the water stole away washing and chickens and carpentry tools, tossing them wantonly into the churning torrent.

Thirty miles upstream from the city of Florence, the *Valle dell'Inferno* - Dante's Valley of Hell, was living up to its name, as The River curled through the valley, her tendrils swirling around the telephone poles, ripping them from the sodden earth and slinging them into the deepening chasm, leaving the citizens of Firenze with no warning of the impending inundation.

THE GUEST

Carstone walked to the breakfast buffet in an even fouler mood than the night before. The shower hadn't worked; the heating didn't work, and at first glance the breakfast looked as bad as the stray pubic hair on the shower soap.

Julia wasn't at breakfast, typical. He didn't blame her though, given the hotel's poor breakfast offerings. A bowl of apples — last seasons from the look of it, single serve sachets of cereal - American style, and a platter of croissants with an array of three types of jam. No eggs or pancakes, bacon or mushrooms.

He tapped a croissant — as solid as the marble statue of David. All around the room, Richard noted other guests picking at their croissants with the grim determination seen on climbers clinging to the icy sides of Mount Everest.

The joyless dining room revealed the shy coffee pot, tucked inside a servery adjoining the barren kitchen. His plan of filling his stomach with bacon and eggs as ethereal as Julia. In the beginning, she'd needed him for everything, begging him to move into the guest bedroom in his brother's house. He'd even encouraged her to get out, to visit the galleries she loved so much, and like an idiot he'd been ecstatic when she'd followed his advice. What a fool he had been slaving over finalising his brother's estate, when she was busy being wooed by the Italian. The Italian was about to have access to all his brother's money, leaving Richard with his brother's old suits and leather shoes, when he should have been sleeping in the arms of his brother's wife.

After pouring a coffee, he studied his fellow diners, who ignored him as they reread their guide books. Richard didn't need a guide book; he was here for one reason - Julia's wedding. The statues and churches and bridges and galleries were nothing more than old stones, and the genuine tourists were welcome to them.

Carstone tapped his wristwatch — the only valuable article he owned, everything else sold to pay off his debts. It would have been nice for Julia to turn up for breakfast. She'd invited him to this hellhole, so the least she could do was have the decency to join him.

He toyed with the condiments on the table, lining them up, equidistant from all four sides of the table. Carstone checked the time again. She wasn't coming. After everything he'd done for her. He slammed his hand against the table, making the other guests jump in alarm.

Throwing back his coffee, he eyed the weather outside. Rain. Torrential rain. If it weren't for his gnawing hunger he'd go back to bed with a glass and a bottle of whiskey. Some things never changed. Still, he would not sit at the table waiting for a woman who no longer needed him. That she'd replaced him again, filled him with an irrational anger that he was having more and more trouble controlling. She had supplanted him once, with his brother Scott, and now she'd done it again. He'd recovered from the humiliation once and would do it again. With help from the alcohol.

Carstone strode from the dining room, out into the rain, walking past English tourists moaning about the weather, and garrulous Australians, as he searched the streets for a cafe serving proper food to normal people but the only cafes he found featured locals slurping from enormous cups of froth and dunking biscuits, reminding him why he hated travelling. In America they knew how to serve a decent breakfast, like the waffles at Uncle Bill's Pancake House in Manhattan Beach, his favourite.

A wooden crutch toppled into Carstone's path. A legless man sat huddled on the path, wrapped in a grubby army coat, with a smattering of coins in the tatty hat by his side. Carstone returned the wayward crutch to its spot, then tossed a 500-lira note into the hat. He hated to see veterans begging on the street. Carstone's father had also lost a leg in Europe, but had returned to a stable job and a loving family. He nodded at the old Italian soldier before walking away, guilt gnawing at his rumbling gut.

Forced into the nearest cafe by the worsening weather, the waiter directed Richard to an empty chair in the grimy front window, thrusting a menu into his damp hands — a menu all in Italian.

'Excuse me,' he called out, wanting to ask for a menu in English, but the waiter ignored him.

Regardless of how many times he tried reading the menu, Carstone couldn't find any mention of eggs or bacon or waffles. How the hell was he meant to read Italian? Wasn't it obvious he was American?

The waiter reappeared to show another customer to the last empty seat in the place, the one next to Carstone.

Carstone tried ordering breakfast, but the man had

disappeared into the throng of customers inhaling their coffee and cigarettes at the counter.

'Christ,' he muttered, scanning the menu once more, ignoring the stares of the woman sitting next to him.

'Can I help?' she asked.

'You speak English?'

'Yes, most Italians can speak a little English, some more than others.'

'Can you explain why there aren't any eggs on this menu? Am I missing something?'

She laughed, 'You won't get eggs for breakfast here. Cino would rather stop cooking than serve eggs. For lunch, yes, but for breakfast, no. If you want something more American, order the ham and cheese toast,' she said, leaning over to point it out on the menu.

'Thanks. The hotel breakfast was dreadful and all the other cafes only offer cakes or biscuits.'

'Biscuits? I don't understand.'

With his hands, he tried explaining the size and shape of the biscuits he'd seen the other patrons eating.

'Ah, the *fette buscittate*, they are a twice-baked *brioche*, a sweet biscuit. Good with jam,' she explained. 'Shall I order for you?' she asked, but ignored his answer, firing off in quick Italian her own order, and one for him.

'And a strong coffee too,' Richard Carstone directed.

'I've ordered you a coffee, it's all good. Cino's coffee is the best, which is why this place is always busy. You're lucky he let you in, usually he turns away tourists saying that he is full.'

'If you're a regular, how come he put you up here with me?'

'Because I like to sit where I can see the world, and to supervise you,' she said, grinning.

Despite her laughter, Richard couldn't decide if she was joking, but suspected there was a dash of truth to it.

The food arrived, putting an end to their conversation. Richard watched her from the corner of his eye as he ate. It wasn't bacon and eggs, but it wasn't bad. Perhaps the company had something to do with the food tasting better than expected? She was a strange one, always watching the stream of people outside.

'Are you keeping an eye out for someone in particular?' Carstone asked.

'An eye out? Sorry, I speak English, but some sayings I don't know.'

'An eye out means are you looking for someone.'

'No, I just watch,' she replied, sipping her macchiato, eyes flicking over the tourists.

'Why are you in Florence?' she asked, turning her gaze towards him.

'For a wedding,' he said, and for some inexplicable reason adding, 'not mine.' As if she even cared.

'Pleasant place to get married, I suppose.'

Richard didn't want to be in Italy but assumed anyone from this historic town would have thought it the perfect place for a wedding. As he was about to ask her to elaborate, she checked her watch and stood up, 'Thank you for the company, but my shift is about to start,' she said. '*Ciao.*'

And like a gust of wind, she left, without even sharing her name. If Richard had asked, she would have told him it was Rosa, Rosa Fonti.

THE WIFE

Away from the hotel, Rhonda huddled under her umbrella, the rain beating in tandem with her racing heart.

This was a far cry from the unending laundry pile at home and a release from the umbilical attachment to her appliances. Her fingers went unbidden to twist her wedding rings, a nervous habit, forgetting that she'd buried them deep in her purse, the freedom from those gold shackles more liberating than anything she'd ever known. She scanned the surrounding faces, which elicited nothing to worry about — just nameless faces hurrying about their day.

Stepping forward, she waited for divine retribution for abandoning her sacred marriage vows, but nothing happened. She took a second step, then a third. She pulled her hat from her head, examining it in her hands. An inoffensive fedora with a beige ribbon. A classic, but no longer in vogue and in desperate need of repair or replacement. Like her, slipping unnoticed into middle age, losing her looks and youth against a backdrop of ironed business shirts and matching black socks. Hidden under aprons at fundraisers and dances and church services and award nights. There was no one moment when she'd changed, more like several life vignettes, each occasion pushing her towards sensible heels, a manageable chin-length bob, and a life of servitude.

Somewhere deep inside a tiny voice whispered that she'd be harder to recognise without her hat, a hat he'd chosen.

As the streets encircled her with their history, surrounded by buildings embracing their age, Rhonda threw her hat into a gutter running with water, and started walking. In a city which didn't know her, she could be the woman she wanted to be and not a woman escaping from her past.

Rhonda lost her breath outside the *Cattedrale di Santa Maria del Fiore*, the Cathedral of Santa Maria del Fiore. The peppermint colours reminiscent her of childhood candies, and for a moment she could almost taste them. Groups posed for photos outside the famous cathedral, couples too, their arms draped around each other's shoulders, their bodies close together. Rhonda hurried past. Famous monuments didn't interest her as much as the hidden history of a city did. Secrets held behind high walls and bolted doors.

The colours of Florence reminded her of Arizona's Painted Desert. All oranges and a hundred unique shades of beige with burnt terracotta. Despite the rain and the chill in the air, the colours of the city warmed her, and she could only imagine how glorious it must all look under a Tuscan summer sunset.

At an unknown square, she searched for a sign to show where she was. Life flowed around her as tourists wandered about wide-eyed and old Italian men meandered past immune to the beauty of the historic buildings.

Papering the walls were the same posters she'd seen outside her hotel — all featuring the face of a young woman, her inky hair tucked behind her ears. The blurred black-and-white image highlighting the innocence seeping out of the paper, the girl's eyes focussed on something beyond the photographer's lens. With no children herself, Rhonda couldn't imagine the pain of the missing girl's family.

As she walked the perimeter of the square, Rhonda ran her hands over the rough stone of the buildings. What mysteries did they hide? She was like these buildings, holding secrets within herself. Would she be able to keep them safe? Which was why she was here, to escape from her secrets. Secrets that threatened to kill.

THE STUDENT

HELENA DIPPED her head to one side, then to the other, the pain in her neck unbearable.

'I'm done for the day,' she announced, massaging her painful neck for Vitali who looked perturbed at the disruption to the lab's serenity.

'Me too,' Oona agreed, running her hands over her own neck.

Helena started packing away her materials, leaving her brushes soaking in jars of mineral turpentine and securing her sharp blades beneath their protective covers, before slipping off her stained lab coat, slinging it over the crowded hooks on the wall.

'You leave early?' queried Sim, stirring from behind his canvas to peer at the girls. A great teacher when he taught, but mostly he hid behind canvases he refused to let his students see. The work was for private clients, his constant refrain.

'Sorry, Feodor, the travel has caught up with us both,' Helena countered, more for Oona's benefit, who looked like a deer caught in headlights at Sim's question.

'After today though…' Sim left his sentence unfinished, his dissatisfaction obvious. 'You should stay, and clean up after the others,' he stated, his tone unequivocal.

Helena's face flushed as indecision tore at her. She couldn't stay, not after she'd arranged her appointment. But Sim's temper was the stuff of legends. The next three months were the last part of her degree. She needed to pass. She had no choice.

One by one her colleagues left, casting sympathetic glances her way. They'd all been in her shoes. All of them except Marisa. Helena bristled at the smile Marisa threw towards her as she sauntered out behind Sim himself. There was always a teacher's pet every year. Marisa had that role nailed down tight, same as last year, although Helena suspected she knew how Marisa achieved those lofty heights.

'I'll stay and help,' said a voice behind her.

Benito, in all his Italian glory, stood with a broom in one hand and a polishing cloth in the other, looking so out of depth that Helena laughed.

'Do you even know how to use those?'

'I'm wounded that you mock me,' Benito said, his plump lips forming a ridiculous pout.

'Pass them here,' Helena laughed. 'You do the brushes and I'll take care of this side of things.'

'Excellent,' Benito replied with a sigh of what Helena assumed was relief, which is when Helena knew her suspicions were correct — he was clueless about cleaning. Maybe, one day, she'd be tidying his apartment.

She daydreamed of life with Benito as she swept, not noticing that she'd entered the inner sanctum of Feodor Sim until she nudged a painting drying on its easel. Helena dropped the broom to catch the painting and froze.

'Benito,' she whispered, unable to tear her eyes from the canvas.

'Helena, you shouldn't be in there,' Benito warned, his voice low.

'Just look at this.'

'Helena, that's Feodor's, leave it. You know how angry he would be if he discovered you were in here. It is unforgivable.'

Instead, Helena grabbed Benito by the arm, dragging him to face Sim's easel.

The easel featured the study of a sailing ship caught in a storm, the faces of the crew and passengers in supplication to an uncaring God.

'That's Rembrandt's *The Storm on the Sea of Galilee*,' Helena whispered, tracing the ridges of the paint, 'and I don't think it's a copy.'

'Of course it is, they lost the original years ago. Feodor is practising his technique. It is a passable reproduction. Come on, let's lock up,' Benito said, dismissing Helena's concerns, nudging her out of the alcove and away from the easel.

Despite the fresh smell of oil paint, the canvas looked old, as if it had been languishing in damp storage for a hundred years.

Helena ducked around Benito to return to Feodor's canvas. The one unbendable rule Feodor Sim had was that his workspace was off limits. Maybe this was why?

'Leave it,' Benito said, anger rolling through his voice.

Engrossed in the sailing ship's detail, Helena didn't move. The white-capped waves rendered so lifelike that she could taste the salty spray.

'Helena.'

At once both shaken by what she'd seen, and conscious that she should take advantage of her time with Benito,

Helena casts one last glance at the painting before succumbing to Benito's implied warning.

Benito all but shoved her outside, and with her arms shielding her hair from the rain, she waved goodbye to Benito, dashing down the streets to her soulless accommodation. Helena pined for a night in an ancient palazzo, or at an artisan's house, full of history and hidden crevices, but didn't have the funds to stay anywhere else. She'd been told how well off her family were before the war, with enough money for long summer holidays and elegant jewellery for her mother. She remembered nothing of those days. Most of her memories started in England, with a mother who may as well have been a painting herself for all the attention she showed Helena. There was no love left for Helena, her mother reserved that for the memories of Helena's twin sister and father and brother and aunts and uncles. After she completed her training, she would apply for a proper job here in Italy. A clean start.

She didn't have time to dwell on Benito's anger. He was just as afraid of Sim's reaction if he found out they'd been in his inner sanctum. Tomorrow she'd ask him if he wanted to have a drink with her. There were three long months ahead of her to woo the attractive Italian, and to apologise for her behaviour tonight.

Helena checked her wristwatch, enough time to clean up before meeting the curator. The butterflies in her stomach raced faster and faster until her entire body vibrated with excitement, and tugging the cuffs of her shirtsleeves as far as they'd reach, she carried on to her room, mulling over her options if the piece of art was the one her mother reminisced most often about. Helena couldn't recall it, she had been a toddler when their lives changed forever, her father's collection seized for the Führer, the war scattering her family across Europe. She couldn't remember her sister any more than she could remember the art. Only ethereal feelings remained — the ghost of a touch, a lingering scent whipped away, snatches of words in a foreign tongue. Her life before the war as mythical as Atlantis, but the art was a tangible fragment of her missing father.

HELENA HOPPED from one foot to the other, the incessant rain keeping pace with her impatience. The curator was late.

'I did not think you would come, not in this weather.'

Helena turned to find the curator emerge from the evening's gloom.

'I've waited a long time to see this painting,' Helena replied. 'The weather could never be a deterrent.'

The man nodded. 'Alfonso Casadei,' he said, extending his hand.

His name drew no sharp intake of recognition from Helena. Although an art student, her station in life meant that the gulf between them couldn't have been wider. She would be no more likely to dine with the Windsor's than socialise with Casadei, apart from tonight.

'Helena Stolar, thank you so much for meeting with me tonight.'

'The entrance is a little way from here, keeps the curious at bay,' Casadei said.

Helena pulled her collar up and followed Casadei into the squall. There was no point using her umbrella, so she tucked her head down and hurried after the well dressed man, his cologne heavy with notes of bergamot — a bittersweet citrus scent, not unpleasant in the rain but she suspected it would overpower in an intimate setting, and she felt sorry for his wife.

In the darkness it was impossible to gauge her surroundings. She would never find her way here again, not without Casadei as a guide and a map book.

Anticipation warmed every inch of her body. What she'd do after confirming it was her father's painting was a question she hadn't allowed herself to consider yet, disappointment a familiar companion.

Casadei fumbled with a keyring, choosing an old iron key before sliding it into the keyhole of the battered door. He stood back, allowing Helena to enter first. The darkness inside taunting her insecurities, but she swallowed her fear and stepped into the blackness.

Casadei flicked a brown bakelite switch on the plastered wall and light flooded the room.

It wasn't a traditional museum by any stretch, despite everything displayed in cabinets around the room and on freestanding panels groaning under the weight of the artwork hanging upon them. The floor was uneven, with different levels stepping up and stepping down, so some pieces seemed posed on a stage, designed for viewing from below, paying homage to the art itself.

'Amazing,' Helena whispered.

The deep corners of the space remained in muted darkness, their treasures hidden from sight. Even more paintings hung on the reverse sides of the panels, but Casadei hadn't flicked on any further switches, leaving the other pieces up to her imagination.

'All this…' she said, feasting on the extravaganza. 'How is it… what is this place called?'

'It doesn't have a name. It is more a repository of... how to describe it? Things?'

'Things, yes,' Helena agreed.

'Shall I take your jacket?' he offered, his manicured hand reaching out.

Helena passed him her jacket, her mind trying to process what she was looking at. She tugged at her shirt sleeves, pulling them over her slender wrists.

'May I?' she asked, pointing to the cabinets nearest her, excitement tickling her nerves.

'Be my guest,' Casadei replied, hanging her jacket on the coat hook and tidying the array of shoes abandoned by earlier visitors, all ladies shoes.

Helena took her time, examining surfaces covered with art and the cabinets filled with curiosities. One cabinet groaned with old pottery adorned with gladiatorial battles or writhing figures entwined in the throes of erotic ecstasy. Any museum in the world would kill to acquire his collection of Roman-era pottery.

A waist-high cabinet featured decorative belt buckles and ornate brooches, a hundred unique designs covering a millennium of human activity. One enamelled piece took her breath away — circular-shaped, it resembled a wheel with coloured spokes picked out in blue and white enamel. Perhaps it was once a pendant or the centrepiece for some larger piece lost to time? With nothing labelled, she drew upon her own reservoir of knowledge to puzzle out the origins and uses of the things on display.

Helena moved towards the art on display. Some pieces picked at her memories, as if she should recognise them. Others looked like undiscovered masterpieces which should be in the Uffizi Gallery.

'This art?' Helena said, turning towards Casadei.

'Yes?'

'Who owns it and where did it come from?'

'It belongs to Italy,' Casadei replied, his wide smile revealing rows of perfect white teeth.

'But how is it here, and not in one of the big museums?'

'This is Italy. This is how things are,' he replied, his hands shuffling yellowed sheets of paper.

Helena turned back. With the poor light, it was impossible to examine the artwork with any certainty. But she was sure she was standing in front of a maritime piece by Johannes Schotel and a self portrait by French artist Henri Fantin-Latour.

'Is this by Schotel?'

'Perhaps, there are so many pieces that sometimes I forget the details,' Casadei shrugged before turning his attention to a bottle of champagne he'd pulled from a cabinet.

'It is, I'm sure of it,' Helena muttered.

'Did you find the piece you were looking for?' Casadei asked, releasing the cork with a soft pop.

Helena abandoned her study of the seascape, the heaving waves so lifelike that she could almost feel the icy spray of the waves slapping at the hull of the boat.

'Over by the window, I think that it where it is hanging,' Casadei said, concentrating on pouring two glasses of fizzing liquid.

Helena crossed the room to a panel standing below a window, black paint flaking from the inside of the glass. Art jostled for space, as if Casadei had given up displaying things properly, focussing instead on filling the space with no regard to exhibiting his art with any cohesion. Hung this way, the collection lacked clarity, leaving the viewer unable to appreciate the artist's intentions or feelings when their brush worked its magic on the canvas.

Her eyes darted from one piece to another, her brain struggling to comprehend the value of everything. Millions or even tens of millions. And then she saw it, her father's pride and joy. The gilt frame, tattered and scarred from its travels, still featuring the tiny plaque identifying it as *The Wreck* by Nicolae Vermont.

Helena caressed the gilt frame, her world shrinking to a shadowy memory of a man's sad eyes as he said goodbye to her and her twin. Where, from the safety of her mother's arms, she took one last look at the crying man before black-shirted soldiers separated them. Then her memories stopped and didn't begin again until after she and her mother had made the journey to England.

'Is that the one you meant?' Casadei asked, appearing at her shoulder, passing her a glass.

'Yes,' Helena replied, wiping her misty eyes.

'Your father had a fine eye; a delightful piece,' he said, clinking his glass against hers before taking a long sip.

'I don't remember it growing up, but my mother told me how she and my father used to joke that the couple in the painting represented them, shipwrecked on a rock in the middle of the ocean with only each other. She used to threaten to move it into the bathroom instead of leaving it above the fireplace.' Helena smiled at the memory, oblivious to the look of horror on Casadei's face.

'It belonged to your father?'

'My mother said so, yes, part of my father's collection of maritime art. He had an art gallery before… you know, before.'

'Your father was Jewish?'

Helena nodded.

'And you're a Jew too?'

'What does that matter?'

'The gall of you, coming to my gallery, and now you are trying to thieve this art? Art which belongs to Italy?'

'Pardon?' Helena stepped back, his words a slap to her face.

Instead of replying, Casadei grabbed her by the wrist, pulling up her sleeve, revealing a line of inked numbers which would be with her for the rest of her life. Helena pulled away, stumbling on the uneven floor, her champagne spilling on the floor.

'You're all the same. But you'll not get your hands on this, no. You're just like all the others, and we showed them the door. Oh yes we did, the door to hell.'

Helena cowered beneath him, her breath coming in short agonising bursts, his hatred too much to bear.

'Now get out.'

THE CLEANER

STEFANO TRUDGED the early morning streets, his bag hanging on his shoulder. He'd packed a lunch of goat's cheese and boiled eggs, with fresh bread from the baker.

This was his favourite hour of the day, the calm before the ignorant tourists emerged from their gilded cages. Tourists were an essential part of Florence, but he preferred his city without them; without their harsh voices and grubby habits, their discarded brochures and ticket stubs, and their preoccupation with photographing the exhibits. Couldn't they just appreciate the art without touching, or taking a photograph? Were their eyes incapable of taking in the beauty?

Stefano unlocked an unobtrusive side door, and slipped into a darkened hallway, his wrinkled hands flicking the light switch, years of practice guiding his way. The worn stones in the service hallway as ancient as the marble floors in the public spaces, but less appreciated, and never admired. His boots traced their usual path through ancient corridors once trod by the ruling families of Firenze.

Once in his workroom, he prepared his materials for

the day. Nothing required his attention first thing in the morning. There was no mess, no spilt drinks or blocked toilets. That would come later. For now, time allowed him to prepare his espresso and to savour the bitter brew. There was never time at home. Dealing with Carmela took all his energy, requiring so much of him, he'd started taking his morning coffee at work, in peace.

With an espresso in hand, he wandered the galleries, surveying his domain. The security staff still bleary-eyed, gossiping about their night. They greeted him warmly, not straying far from their little heaters, idle until the museum opened. No one worried about the staff stealing the museum's artefacts, or damaging the ancient frescos. No, it was the public they couldn't trust. The public were as light-fingered as a concert pianist. Anything not tied down or hidden behind glass was fair game. It was a constant battle for the curators between entertaining the crowds, and a traditional purist museum experience.

Their new director was all about experiences, which felt a thousand kinds of wrong, and meant more of the exhibits were out of storage and on show, breathing in the open environment.

It filled Stefano's heart to see Italy's cultural treasures on show. As he stood in the darkened reception rooms, he imagined hearing the voices of the past — plotting and planning, scheming and salivating over secrets and lies. His life was nothing like that of the families who'd lived within these walls, but he didn't envy them their lives. His was a simple one, one he enjoyed living. He lived for art, and knew he appreciated it more than the visitors who traipsed the halls, ticking off another museum on their grand tour.

He stopped in front of a family portrait — a mother with two children, painted in the religious style with the mother stylised as the Virgin Mary; with Jesus and John the

Baptist depicted as children. Reminiscent of any family, the emotion in the mother's eyes a mirror to the love all mothers held for their children. His own mother had pressed upon him the power of art, filling their home with canvasses she'd painted or collected. Those pieces still hung in his home today, the home of his childhood. A daily reminder of how fleeting life can be and how timeless art is.

Distaste filled his mouth as he approached the museum's newest installation — a Baroque table set with pewter tableware, including candlesticks older than some countries. The scene roped off with velveteen ropes between brass poles. They'd made him drill great ugly holes into the tiles to hold the poles in place. It turned his stomach to defile history this way. This new director wouldn't last long. Residents were already writing angst-filled letters to the newspapers, decrying the director's obsession with entertainment over culture. This was not Disneyland, and art was not for parading under fireworks every night.

He moved the dull candlesticks one inch to the left for better balance. Art was balance. But this balance wouldn't last. The security guards could not watch every inch of the museum, even with the cameras the new director had installed. Stefano didn't trust those anymore than he did the tourists. And knowing the habits of their guards, they wouldn't keep their eyes glued to the surveillance screens. They were probably using the monitors to watch that new American TV series about a crime fighter dressed as a bat - *Batman*, an imbecilic idea for a television series. No, they needed to walk around, their physical presence more of a deterrent than cameras covering the exhibits. In his heart, he knew the candlesticks wouldn't stay in situ; any moment now and they would disappear into the deep pockets of an opportunistic thief, forever lost to Italy.

A horn-handled knife lay alongside the pewter plate, time blunting its blade, but the glorious carved handle remained — a skill given over to machinery now. Stefano stepped past the velvet ropes and stroked the curve of the handle, following the lines made by a master carver long dead.

The bone felt warm under his hand, at home within his weathered palm. His pulse quickened. The knife would go missing too, if not today, then tomorrow. Stefano returned it to its place in the tableau and took a sip of his coffee, the last mouthful cool on his tongue. He shuffled from the hall and back to his workroom to await the masses and hours of answering frantic summons to clean up a spill, unplug a blocked toilet, and conduct systematic maintenance from the top of the museum, right to its hidden basement, where they stored the balance of the collection, waiting for space or a surge of interest. Eight hours of being on his feet with the glorious art the tourists came to see, but never really saw.

Carmela used to marvel at his dedication to his work at the museum, his ability to focus on the smallest detail, where even the tiniest crevice couldn't escape his ministrations. At home he would collapse into bed, oblivious to even the largest cobwebs marching across the wall, but at work he was renowned for his fastidiousness — always the last employee to leave, mopping his own footprints as he backed out at the end of every day. Tonight would be no different.

Stefano collected eight hours worth of sandwich wrappers and paper napkins, shoving each article into a rubbish sack. For a museum which forbade eating or drinking, a mountain of rubbish associated with those activities accumulated every day. Sometimes he heard the guides admonishing a tourist for consuming food in the gallery, but only sometimes. The museum didn't pay them enough to care. They valued the prestige of the job more than the art, infuriating Stefano. Which is why, when he reached the room with the pewter display, it was of no consequence to slip the horn-handled knife into his garbage bag, leaving it to mingle with soiled napkins and torn museum brochures. No one watched the security cameras after the crowds had left. And why should they? Everyone trusts the cleaner.

THE POLICEMAN

PISANI PULLED his collar tight as rain trickled down his back. Forced into a task so far beneath him his teeth were grinding of their own accord, giving him a headache, another one. The girl should do this and he should be at Fiorella's, drinking *cappuccino*, listening to the jukebox and chatting to the locals and absorbing the vibe of city life. His days of interviewing hoteliers about thefts from tourists were long gone.

Why Pisani was back in uniform on the streets was a complicated story and still made his bowels gripe. Professional jealousies formed part of the fabric of the town and ruined his life. He vowed he would never let that happen again, which was why he was here, off the main strip, in a torrential downpour, interviewing a nicotine-stained hotelier in a two-star establishment.

'I'm telling you now to show me your personnel records,' Pisani repeated, massaging his temples. Perhaps he should see a doctor about his worsening headaches? Time to think about that later.

The man behind the scuffed wooden counter threw his hands up in the air. 'They aren't available, we don't keep them here,' he pontificated, as a parade of humanity scurried through the lobby, chins tucked in, avoiding any eye contact with the uniformed Pisani leaning against the counter.

Pisani took it in, despite appearances otherwise.

'I'll see the staff records now or I'll be back with more police and immigration. I am thinking most of your guests here do not have the right visa's, no?' Pisani smiled as his last comment hit home.

The hotelier paled and began pulling open cupboards and drawers until he found a file full of loose papers and torn notes, dog-earned and coffee-stained. 'I just remembered where they were. It's very busy here and these things get beyond me sometimes,' he said, his words stumbling over themselves, saying anything to avoid trouble with immigration.

Pisani leafed through the files, mumbling to himself as he scanned the register of employees, the hours they worked, and the meagre salary paid to each staff member. The list longer than he'd expected, with some names only appearing once. A scam? An attempt to get government employee benefits? Pisani doubted about the veracity of this business, but that wasn't his concern. Let someone else investigate whatever fraud this cretin was committing.

'I'll have a copy of these,' he said, waving the papers at the proprietor, whose worried eyes never left Pisani.

The hotelier looked as if he wanted to argue, until Pisani's head swivelled to watch a pair of gypsy-like characters emerge from the stairwell, before vanishing back the way they came after spotting Pisani in his uniform. The hotelier nodded and turned to the ancient copy machine.

As the photocopier whirred into life, Pisani examined the lobby. Adorned with the usual plethora of tourism brochures and a poor assortment of dying plants, it also featured with a packed bookcase leaning in the corner. Pisani wasn't a big reader, but he enjoyed having a book on the go to help him relax, and wasn't fussy about the topic, reading both fiction and non-fiction in equal amounts, making him well read for a man of his background.

'Your guests, they leave these here?' he asked the hotelier as he skimmed the titles of the paperbacks, almost all in English. He got a grunt back in reply.

Pisani ran his fingers over the spines. No point pulling out one in English. That was too hard. He spoke enough to get by, but reading that infernal language was enough to try the patience of a saint. He lingered over a paperback of Alberto Moravia's latest novel, in Italian. After picking it up, he walked back to the counter and slipped it inside the folder holding the photocopies, the cost of doing business in Italy.

With the papers in hand, Pisani glared at the hotelier. 'The paperwork for your staff, get onto sorting that out as soon as possible, you wouldn't want a visit from immigration,' he said, installing a healthy fear of his power over the man.

Pisani rubbed at his temples as something tickled his memory and he glanced toward the Arno River, his view obstructed by the surrounding buildings. He could only imagine the speed of its flow after the two weeks of rainfall they'd experienced, and his body shuddered in response. Pisani shook off the premonition and strode into the rain, recoiling as a sodden sheet of paper slapped him in the face.

Ripping it off his face, Pisani dropped it into the gutter,

but not before recognising the haunting visage of Lucia Nicastri on the poster. It wasn't his file, but every officer was looking for the girl. The daughter of one of Florence's most famous archaeologists, who came from old Florentine money. Old money meant the police worked harder for the Nicastri's than they did for most other victims — it was the way things worked in Florence, in Italy. Like most of his colleagues, he doubted they'd ever find Lucia, but they kept searching for her, and so ignored the illegal papering of posters on every city wall. Nature would take care of them, sooner rather than later given the weather.

Back at the station, he dumped the folder, sans his new paperback, unannounced onto Rosa's desk. Her hand jerked, spilling coffee over his trousers.

Pisani yelled, the hot coffee soaking through to his thighs and pooling at his feet, his dishevelled wardrobe now resembling that of a drunken vagrant. 'Stupid woman.'

Rosa shrugged, ignoring his tirade as she read through the folder he had thrown at her. Her indifference ratcheting up his blood pressure even further.

'These are employee records,' she said, looking through the papers.

'So you can read. At least that's one thing you can do,' Pisani said, swabbing at his legs with a handful of tissues.

'What a mess,' Rosa mused, shuffling the papers into a tidy pile and offering them back to Pisani.

'They're all yours, I've no time for paper chasing. I've got far more important enquiries to make,' Pisani postured, lobbing the tissues into the bin. 'When I come back, I expect you to have checked all their employees against our files. It's like the United Nations there, one will be the thief. All wrapped up by the end of the weekend, perfect.'

With that, he left her to it, feeling like his head would explode if just one more person spoke to him, or asked anything of him. Pisani stumbled, his leg unresponsive for a heartbeat before returning to normal.

'Stupid girl,' he muttered, rubbing his thigh again.

THE GUEST

BREAKFAST SAT like a solid lump in Carstone's stomach. Once he left the cafe, it felt like he'd run straight into a group of marathon runners at the start of a race, given how many people were loitering in the streets. Not just loitering, but walking in circles. Richard thought he'd seen the same two tourists, complete with sandals and backpacks, walk past for the third time. Either that, or there was a tribe of huge blonde men, who shopped at the same khaki uniform and discount sandal store.

He had no plans since the waiter had made it apparent that he needed to move on, that staying until lunchtime wasn't an accepted course of action. More than anything, Richard wished he'd ignored the waiter's polite attempts to move him. Being outside, without an umbrella or full length oil slicker, was madness, and bad enough for Richard to find a museum to escape the god-awful environment. And Julia wanted to get married here? She should have done that in Texas, where everyone spoke English and served decent food. She should have been marrying him. He had to survive two more days until her wedding to someone else and suffer through a dinner tomorrow night with her Italian fiancé's family. Life couldn't be any worse.

A brief thought of Scott flashed across his mind. Would he have wanted me here? Richard didn't know. Ever since Julia's engagement, he'd been asking himself the same thing. Julia chose the Italian over him, the same way she had chosen Scott despite dating Richard first, leaving Richard with nothing — no girlfriend, no wife, no job. He scuffed his soaked loafers through another puddle as he realised that after the wedding, if he vanished from the earth, he had no one to notice, or care.

Absorbed in his own world, he was blind to the stream of humanity around him until he walked into a crowd of people, accidentally knocking a girl to the ground.

'Jesus, I'm so sorry. Are you okay?' Leaning down to scoop her up, someone shoved him from behind and he landed on top of the girl.

Struggling to push himself off the now hysterical girl, splashing around as if at the seashore, he tried apologising to the girl, now screaming foreign obscenities at him.

'I'm sorry, it was an accident, sorry,' Carstone yelled, trying to make himself heard over the avalanche of angry voices. And then, like mist dissipating in a breeze, the crowd vanished. The girl's screaming voice shut off.

Carstone stood there like an idiot surrounded by bemused onlookers staring at him. He hadn't been dreaming. Turning in a circle, he couldn't see any sign of the woman he had knocked over, or the group she'd been with. Reality hit. His hands checked his pocket. Empty. Robbed blind. It had all been a con.

Carstone spun around. The onlookers were moving off, the entertainment over, focussing instead on frescoes and their soggy guide books. None of them cared that he had been robbed. They would be next, they just didn't recognise it yet.

At the nearest cafe, he asked where the police station was, grateful he'd left the bulk of his cash and his passport in his hotel room safe.

After several attempts and wrong turns, he found the station — the ubiquitous blue light, a shining beacon. His soaked shirt and ruined shoes matched the mess of his hair plastered to his head, creating a pseudo monk-like tonsure. He tried running his fingers through it, which made him look deranged. He'd achieve nothing standing outside, so entered the station.

It was easy to spot the counter he required. The sign above it was in English - Tourist Police. If a country needed police for the tourists, then the country needed help.

At the desk, Richard Carstone cleared his throat to attract the officer's attention at the front desk.

'I've been robbed.'

THE WIFE

RHONDA SLIPPED into an empty chair in the crowded cafe, the slats of the chair still warm from the previous occupant, the inclement weather forcing Florence's tourists inside where they huddled next to the struggling heaters.

Rhonda almost ordered a juice, but checked herself. Given the time, it could be a late lunch, which called for a wine. No more waiting until it was wine o'clock like the other women she knew. She ordered a glass of wine and a simple *gnocchi*; she settled down to people watch. Even with the torrential rain, the Florentine streets were full — young and old, fat and thin. Elderly men supported by younger men, their faces echoing each other. Backpacks and designer handbags, trilby hats, and elegant women sheltering under funereal black umbrellas, admonishing the rain for its existence.

Her *gnocchi* arrived, accented with truffle oil and slivers of fresh basil. Twinned with the chilled *chianti*, the meal was sublime, enough to keep the panic at bay, stabbing at it with every forkful of her meal. But it crept up on her, its insidiousness twisting her insides. If he found her, she would have to return home.

After travelling to Italy on her married name, using her maiden name sat tight across her shoulders, like an ill-fitting coat, chaffing at the collar. She rolled the syllables of the name over her tongue, tasting the anonymity. Witnesses might have assumed she was saying Grace before her meal, her maiden name as unfamiliar as the Italian language, yet that was her, and had been for nineteen years of her life. She had been much too young, which she had realised the moment her foot crossed the threshold of the church. The wedding hadn't been her idea; she was a reluctant player in the farce and had been reaping the consequences.

'Excuse me, is this seat taken?'

A voice interrupted her solitude, and Rhonda looked into the lined face of a typical American, pale complexion, sandy hair, lean, polished brogues, collared shirt and jacket. An anomaly amidst the easy casualness of the other diners.

Yes, she wanted to scream. Yes, yes, yes.

'No,' Rhonda said, as she gathered her cutlery and napkin and wine glass, moving them closer to her side, a deep flush staining her face.

The *gnocchi* turned to dust in her mouth. Socialising was not part of the plan, but her manners took charge. She couldn't turn them off on cue. Rhonda sipped her wine, silently chastising her lack of confidence.

'You are eating alone?' he asked, the drawl of his accent marking him as a Texan.

Rhonda nodded, taking another sip, not wanting to engage.

'It's so good to get off my feet. I admire these historic streets, but at my age they are tiring to walk,' he said, summoning the waiter, and ordering a wine in flawless

Italian for himself and another for Rhonda, without asking if she wanted one.

Rhonda focussed on the jungle of legs walking past her table.

'Paul, Paul Tobias,' he said, offering her his hand.

Rhonda shook his hand, the action reminiscent of the shaking of her heart. What name to give him? At the hotel, she'd used her maiden name. Her married name was on her passport, but she would never be that person again, and had flung the accursed document into the river, letting the flow of the Arno wash away a lifetime of purgatory.

'Rhonda Devlyn,' she replied, the words flowing from a mouth still sticky with wine.

'Lovely to meet a fellow American. Sometimes America seems like it is on another planet, so far away.'

'Mmm,' Rhonda replied, avoiding any verbal intimacy with the stranger.

'Have you been in Florence long?' he asked, charm dripping from his words.

'This is my first day,' Rhonda managed, glancing towards him. He was staring at her for far longer than what was polite. She slid her eyes back to her food, moving it around her plate, wishing he'd disappear.

'For your first day,' he exclaimed, 'you must let me be your guide, it would be an honour to show you the places the sheep never see. The herd is so obsessed with the statue of David and Giotto that they miss the hidden gems. The Soldanieri Gallery, the Bargello. There are so many options.'

Rhonda wiped her palms on her dress. What would it take to make him disappear?

'Thank you for the offer, but sadly I have plans,' she stuttered, trying to stay calm.

'Surely not?' he protested.

Rhonda missed the anger between his arched brows as she sipped from her glass, desperately trying to extricate herself from this social interaction. What was wrong with eating alone?

'Sorry, but I am booked on an organised tour,' Rhonda said, abruptly standing up, accidentally knocking over her chair, sending it crashing into another table, smashing their carafe of wine.

Mortified, Rhonda stammered out an apology as the waiter materialised.

'Please it is okay,' the waiter tried calming her.

Rhonda pulled a handful of notes from her purse, pushing them into the waiter's hands. Too much to cover the meal and wine, but her desire to escape was overwhelming.

Panic sent her pulse racing and a roaring in her ears drowned out everyone's words as she bolted from the cafe. If she'd looked back, she may have seen the man watching her flee, before jotting something in a notepad.

THE STUDENT

HELENA CURLED TIGHTER INTO A BALL, her eyes squeezed shut as the memory of the previous night replayed. How could she have been so wrong?

Her world oddly silent, bar the soothing rainfall outside, trying to lull her back to sleep. The hallway should echo with the thunderous footfalls of everyone bustling off to their tutorials, and the familiar tick of the ancient heating system should have been keeping time with her heartbeat, an accompaniment to the rain beating against the small window of her bedroom. But silence her only companion.

Helena checked the watch beside her bed with the sinking knowledge that she'd slept in and would be late. Flicking the light switch only added an impetuous clicking noise to the falling rain. The power outage wasn't unusual. Florence's antiquated utilities could not handle the hoards of tourists and the sheer number of the rural population streaming into the crowded city looking for employment.

No power meant no hot water for a bath or for coffee, but it also meant she didn't need to go to the lab this morning. No electricity meant no light to work by — a necessity for their basement laboratory. So Helena pulled the covers around her shoulders and stared at the barren ceiling, attempting to forget last night.

But the memories of yesterday, and the lack of heat, made the compact room as appealing as an icy coffin dug into graveyard soil. Combined, they drove her from bed and into the communal bathroom, hoping that there might be a vestige of warmth somewhere in the antique water pipes. With a deep breath, Helena submerged the lower half of her body into the bath, managing not to scream with shock. She finished in less than a minute, a quick rinse sufficient for the day ahead.

With chattering teeth, she dressed. She couldn't abide the cold and often wondered if that harked back to early childhood, where warmth was an impossibility, and extra clothes or blankets an imaginary luxury.

To defend against the cold she wore too many layers, and paint stained most of them. Today's ensemble no different. The red pigment adorning the hem of her jersey came from a modest restoration at St. Botolph's Church in Hardham. The blue on her woollen trousers from the near complete reconstruction of St. Catherine of Alexandria's beheading in St. Peter's and St. Paul's Church in Pickering. As long as she wasn't cold, she never noticed the paint splotches. They formed as much a part of her life as souvenirs did to tourists.

Outside, heavy clouds threatened to continue yesterday's rain. With no point in going to the lab, there was only one other place she'd rather be — the *Biblioteca Nazionale Centrale di Firenze*, the National Central Library of Florence. As a student, she had almost unlimited access during opening hours, and prayed that their electricity was still working.

The library answered her prayers.

If the streets of Florence were heaven on earth, the cool interior of the library was Florence's heart, pulsing with memories long gone, holding the collective knowledge of centuries of scholars. Even the wooden reading desks were works of art in their own right, crouching next to polished shelving which stretched up to the ceiling. The 62,000 miles of shelves held everything she needed. Every obscure text and tome, every reference article and ancient book. The genuine treasure of Florence.

In a seat under the top window, Helena settled a folio into the support cradle and began reading an old treatise on paint composition used by Byzantium artists. Modern diagnostics disproved much of the information, but many pages still held nuggets of gold, and references to its application. In the Byzantium era, the saying everything that glistens is not gold was incorrect. Almost everything was gold.

Helena's skin tingled, and she tugged her sleeves down over her hands, both a defence and an attempt to get warm. Last night she'd been too hot. Her host hanging her coat and scarf on a hook inside, so courteous and suave. Even now she could smell his lemony aftershave in the folds of her scarf. Helena yanked it away from her face, the scent making her dizzy.

It had been so hot inside, and he'd been so polite, and so interested in her and her questions. And she'd asked so many questions about the art, the museum. In the beginning she didn't realise who he was, and that it was his museum, and that this was another of his galleries, one for private customers. That realisation came later.

Bile rose in her stomach and she wrenched the scarf from her neck, dumping it on the ground. Still the odour of lemons clung to her, seeping into her, infecting her with its cloying poison.

Adrift with her memories, Helena didn't notice the changing light in the window above her. Florence shivered after the sun set, the temperature dropping further as the wind whipped discarded ticket stubs through the air, sending hats flying down historic streets, bouncing off tourists struggling with umbrellas, maps and sensible woollen skirts.

And further up the Arno River, more rain pummelled the already sodden earth, before dancing through tiny cobbled streets hand-in-hand with the winter gale, hauling disaster towards the city.

THE CLEANER

STEFANO IGNORED the tourists watching him mop up the tea they'd spilt, his ears deaf to their apologies. Yes, yes, time was short, and they only had another hour before they were due back at the bus, and they hadn't seen the art their guide had told them they must see. It wasn't a Da Vinci or a Michelangelo, but by an artist they'd never heard of. But their tour guide had recommended they visit, so here they were, and they'd just taken a minute to drink tea from their thermos, and they hadn't meant for it to spill.

From here they'd go to the Uffizi - the primary reason they were in Florence. Rome and Venice, the highlights of their trip, only detouring to Florence to view Michelangelo's statue of *David* in his naked glory, then Botticelli's *The Birth of Venus*, followed by Caravaggio's nightmarish render of Medusa's head. They saw almost nothing else of Florence. And Stefano preferred it that way.

The tourists moved on, laughing self-consciously, their mess already forgotten. Stefano watched their retreating backs. He held no opinion about them or their inability to adhere to the museum's rules about no drinking or eating inside. Instead, he mourned that they lacked any culture themselves, soulless heathens.

With his mop and bucket, he slipped unseen past the tour groups. He could walk through a hundred tourists and not one would acknowledge him — he was one of millions of invisible service workers around the world who did the cleaning, removed the rubbish, tidied the public spaces, but without them, the world's monuments would disappear under a mountain of trash and writhing nests of rats. But there were advantages to being invisible.

Stefano tipped the garbage sack into the sink, blinking at the clatter of the pewter knife as it tumbled from the bag. He pulled a polishing cloth from his pocket to dry the ancient object before wrapping it in another cloth and slipping it into his leather satchel.

It was as he'd predicted. The foolish museum curator should never have left such valuable and portable things on display. They always went missing, and like always, it was his role to rescue them from the clutches of ignorant tourists.

Shuffling once more through the service corridor, he nodded at the security guard coming the other way.

'Busy day, Stefano?' the guard asked.

'Busier than normal for this time of year,' Stefano agreed, his hand tightening around the mop handle.

'Bet you'll be mopping the entrance again this afternoon,' the guard continued, consulting his wristwatch, a war relic.

Stefano stopped, fresh water sloshing from his bucket, 'Why?'

'The weather. You haven't been outside yet, have you?

The rain is getting heavier, and you know what that means?'

Stefano knew too well. When it rained in Florence, the architecture outside lost its lustre, with every man diving for shelter as if he were Noah searching for salvation from the Great Flood. Muddy shoes, discarded coats, lunch wrappers, sticky fingers, crying children. He would not get home until late tonight.

'It always rains like this in November,' Stefano replied. 'Nothing changes.'

Stefano uttered a silent prayer, *let nothing change his plans*.

THE POLICEMAN

'THERE'S another tourist at the counter, says he's been mugged.'

Pisani's head sank to his desk. The third one today. The bane of his life, although the tourists brought it upon themselves, flaunting their wealth with their bundles of cash and flashy jewellery.

'Where's this one from?' Pisani sighed, knowing full well that interviewing a stupid tourist would go nowhere. There was never enough evidence. Their local gangs were like a winter mist, slipping through cracks in the walls before disappearing into thin air. They'd once rounded up dozens of them, chasing them like squirrels and squeezing them for confessions, but there'd never been enough evidence to arrest a single one for theft and it galled him.

'Show him into the interview room. Fat lot of good it will do, though,' Pisani said, slamming his pen down.

With his notebook and a coffee, he ambled towards the interview room, his mood fouler than the weather. What an end to a rubbish day. First, he'd wasted his morning interviewing the slippery hotelier, then his extended lunch had given him bad indigestion, which started off another headache. He would rather be at home dreaming of retirement.

The room held a dishevelled man tapping his fingers against the tabletop. His youngish face a surprise to Pisani - it tended to be the older tourists who were targeted. Younger tourists didn't have enough to steal.

'*Ciao*, good afternoon,' Pisani started.

The man looked up from the criminal graffiti adorning the desk. Although he smiled at Pisani, with a mouthful of bright white teeth, there was no mistaking the disdain for Pisani that flashed across the man's face.

Pisani swallowed his instant dislike of the man, thumping his notebook down and slumping into the opposite chair. No doubt the tourist was judging Pisani's age and girth, wondering why he was still in uniform and not running the place. Pisani asked himself those same questions every day.

'Please, tell me you name and talk me through what happened to you?' Pisani said, leafing through his notebook for a blank page.

'Richard Carstone, I'm an American citizen—'

'Of course…'

'They robbed me of my wallet, using a girl to distract me. I tripped over her and she started screaming. Gave an award-winning performance.'

'Did you lose your passport, sir?' Pisani asked, steepling his fingers. No point writing anything else. It was a familiar story.

'No, my passport is in my room safe. So I have that at least.'

'Which hotel are you living at? We will need a photocopy of your passport for the file.'

'I'm staying at the Altavilla Hotel, do you know it?'

Pisani's head jerked up. 'Yes, I know it. How many nights do you stay there?'

'Three. I am only here for a wedding. It would have been less if I could have managed it with the flights. It's a dump. Does it even have a licence to operate as a hotel? Is that something you check in this city?'

Pisani's jaw tightened. The Altavilla wasn't one of Florence's better establishments, but this gauche man, with more teeth than sense, had no right to criticise. He was a guest in their city.

'Being a hotelier is tough and sometimes standards slip, probably a minor aberration.'

The American tourist laughed, his eyebrows disappearing into his hairline.

'I am there tomorrow on other business, so will call on you for the copy of your passport for the file. I'm sorry, Mr Carstone, but these gangs, they are ethereal, like the wind, and just as impossible to catch. If you had a photograph of the girl, that would be helpful. Or if you'd got another witness to give a statement,' Pisani said. 'But without those, I am sorry…'

'That's it?' the American exclaimed. 'You aren't even going to ask around yourself? My wallet has just gone? And its contents?'

'Mr Carstone, the tourists, they are too encouraging to the criminals. It is a tide of crime that we cannot push back—' Pisani started.

'Too encouraging? If you can't keep your criminals in check, you are in the wrong job. The sooner I'm back in the States, the better. It's not like I did anything to encourage them. I hadn't even spent any money save what I gave to one of your beggars.'

'How much did you give him?'

'500 lira, that seemed about fair seeing as he didn't have any legs. It's a shit way to treat your veterans, that's for sure.'

Pisani sighed. He agreed with the American, but there were other ways of supporting the down-at-heel veterans. Flashing cash like that was only ever going to result in a visit to the police station. The American had himself to blame and Pisani had nothing to add. He shrugged, leaving Carstone to interpret it a hundred diverse ways.

'I will see you tomorrow at your hotel. Perhaps you may have remembered something more by then, that can help us?' Pisani stood, rubbing at a sauce stain on his sleeve.

The tourist followed Pisani, defeat replacing his cocky smile. But he ignored the hand Pisani offered, walking out into the deluge.

Pisani shook his head, Americans. He had to trust the gods that the thief at the Altavilla wouldn't strike this tourist.

Feeling the fingers of a headache, Pisani turned away from the retreating tourist, and addressing the nearest officer, he said, 'I'm finished now. Tell the girl I will meet her tomorrow morning at the Altavilla, first thing.'

Pisani had to think hard about where he'd left his car, as he tried staving off his looming headache. The headaches were becoming more frequent, more debilitating, although he refused to believe that they were anything more than a byproduct of the wine he consumed most nights.

Dante's hell couldn't have been worse than Florence's roads, and by the time he found his car, Pisani's windscreen wipers were incapable of coping with the water the sky threw down. Ignoring the honks from other drivers, he hurried to get home before the pain incapacitated him.

Already his vision was narrowing, and he needed to be somewhere silent. Sometimes even the sound of a dripping tap sent needles through his brain. He prayed that tonight would be different. Perhaps the rain would wash away the pain erupting from his temples.

THE RIVER

An icy shiver ran through The River as the melting snow joined her rampage. Welcoming the melt, she let it slide into her flow, encouraging it to weave its way amongst the debris, caressing the livestock carcasses floating feet up in the maelstrom.

The River encouraged the Mugnone tributary to race through the man-made canals created to control her path, a poor attempt to tame her cousin. Nothing could tame them, as she was about to show them.

As she waited for her relative to join her, The River trumpeted her anger at her treatment. They'd choked her with the runoff from factories and heavy industry, destroying the wildlife who'd entertained her for centuries with their tiny chicks and wriggling spawn. Species she'd loved and supported, vanishing overnight, leaving her bereft. Nothing tasted as sweet as revenge.

As the innumerable streams and tributaries wound their way down hillsides, creeping through sewers and storm water systems, she cheered them on — utter devastation within her grasp. Already she felt the bridges quivering above her as she rattled their foundations, teasing them with the power she'd unleashed further up the valley.

At 150 miles long, Dante once called her "the cursed and unlucky ditch". His callous words still hurt. Was she not the most important river in Italy? Had she not provided for the people living on her shores for over two millennia? Dante's thoughts were of no consequence, for his bones were dust and yet she remained. And today she would wipe his legacy from Florence.

THE GUEST

CARSTONE'S EXPERIENCE with the police a low point in his life, and he left the station with the bitter aftertaste of bureaucracy in his mouth.

To add to his woes, the skies opened only twenty paces from the station, drenching him in seconds. With no money for a taxi, he trudged through the sodden streets trying to find his hotel. He contemplated throwing himself upon the mercy of his sister-in-law, Julia, but given the chilly reception he'd received when he first arrived, he thought it unlikely that she'd risk angering her fiancé to help her former flame.

It took over an hour before he found the hotel. In the rain, the Altavilla looked like it had given up, mirroring how Carstone himself felt.

He shook himself off like a dog after a swim and tried explaining to the receptionist about the theft of his wallet. Her pencilled eyebrows didn't even move.

'These things happen,' she said, cackling like an ancient hag.

'The police want a copy of my passport, so they will be here tomorrow,' he added.

That made her eyebrows lift, and she scanned the room, as if she expected a mob of gun-toting police to storm the counter.

'My husband, he will deal with that. I… you must… not the police,' she mumbled, before lapsing back into Italian, the fear on her face genuine.

'It's for their file,' he reassured her. On one hand, they didn't care about his robbery, but mention the police, and it was as if Stalin himself was still in charge. Carstone wanted to ask about the hot water, a puddle forming at his feet, but she was busy wiping tears from her eyes, blaming him for bringing the police to the hotel. No wonder the Roman Empire collapsed.

Trudging back to his room, wet footprints marking his path, Carstone struggled to find anything worthy of gratitude. A dry change of clothes would be a start, then he'd ask Julia for a loan, and dinner. A last supper before she became Julia Caesar, or whatever her Italian husband's surname was. Something like Caecilius or Caesar. No, it was Casadei. A stupid name for a man she shouldn't be marrying. She should have been his wife.

And that bloody baby was still crying somewhere nearby. He would bring that up that next time he was at reception. This place was a dive, but guests deserved a level of peace. And they weren't getting it with that racket. The damn thing just needed feeding.

Carstone unlocked his room, which looked just as he'd left it. The useless maid hadn't been back to replace his damp towel or to change the sheets. The wrinkled linen disgusting him as he imagined an army of previous guests sleeping in his sheets before him.

After straightening the towel on the rail, he eyed up the

bath and spun the taps, praying for the water to heat. He turned his back on the anaemic flow and stripped off, warmer without his clothes than he was wearing them.

The mirror showing him as dishevelled as the bedroom he'd just walked through. No surprise that the woman on reception hadn't shown one iota of interest. Carstone's brother Scott, Julia's husband, had been the poster child of the family — blonde and blue-eyed, a hit with the ladies. Richard lived in his shadow, only ever excelling at being average. His hair had an average amount of grey for his age. His face boasting normal age lines apart from the deep furrow between his eyes. That had developed as Scott lay dead on his lawn.

No matter how hard he searched for Scott's face in the mirror, he would never be there. Tearing himself away from his reflection, he tried the water — warmer than before, but still not hot enough to thaw a snowball.

After attempting to dry himself off with the sodden towel, he checked the wedding invite, rereading Julia's additional notes detailing the pre-wedding dinner, her contact details in case anyone needed her, and directions to both the wedding venue and the reception. Carstone double checked Julia's notes and the map. The reception was nowhere near the venue, or the hellhole of his hotel.

'Damn it, Julia,' he cursed, flinging the papers onto the floor.

In a pair of dry slacks and a sweater, Carstone sat down to pull on his socks. At this rate, he would run out of clean clothes, turning up to the wedding more crumpled and grubby than he normally looked after an all night bender. There wasn't a washing line in the bathroom, and no sign of laundry facilities, although he assumed a wizened old woman was out the back, stirring dirty sheets in a tin bathtub with a hefty wooden stick.

He'd just smoothed out his second sock when his stomach dropped. This angle provided a perfect view into the open wardrobe, his eye at the exact height of the room safe — the safe which held his passport and emergency cash. The safe which stood wide open. Open and empty.

THE WIFE

RHONDA SHOOK BEHIND A CHURCH PILLAR. The solace she thought she'd find, absent. The brief interaction with Paul Tobias enough to make her hands shake, her heart flutter.

She'd come to Florence to escape, to be no one, but recognised the inevitability of her husband finding her. She wasn't an expert at covering her tracks. But she had time on her side, and distance.

As she caught her breath, the hush of the church enveloped her and she fell into one of the polished wooden pews. Softened with embroidered squabs, it provided a welcome respite from the stone columns which gave the church its strength but no warmth. Frescoes adorned the walls, the faces of a thousand angels, infused with peace and love, reflecting on her.

With her eyes closed, she pretended to be an ordinary tourist, but it was no use, she didn't deserve the salvation provided to the faithful. God was not her saviour, not now that she had forsaken her marriage vows.

Rhonda leapt up from the pew. She didn't belong here. From the doorway, she surveyed the rain-swept palazzo outside. Devoid of tourists, life outside mirrored that of the middle of the seventeenth century. Da Vinci himself could have walked into the palazzo, a woollen cape protecting him from the rain, and not looked out of place. In her daydream, she almost mistook the man hurrying through the square as the artist. Rhonda drew back into the shadows as she recognised her lunch companion. Had he followed her? She stopped breathing as he hurried past, his head swinging from side to side, the rain washing away his footprints.

She waited until he disappeared before rushing back to the safety of her hotel. Back behind locked doors. But even they wouldn't keep the demons out of her head. Had she ruined her one chance of freedom?

Rhonda pulled the covers over her head, her whimpers muffled by the pillow. The man was no one, a Lothario preying on foreign women. Her sobs subsided as she rationalised her overreaction, with sleep soon following.

Terror filled her dreams as hoards of faceless men pursued her through featureless streets, the tolling of bells the only sound other than her laboured breathing. Rhonda fought them, her sheets twisting around her sweat-drenched body, tightening like hands around her throat, pulling her down, down...

Gasping, Rhonda woke disorientated, scrabbling to disentangle herself from the sheets. The remnants of her dreams slipping from her subconscious as she tried to calm her nerves. One face she couldn't wipe from her dreams was that of her husband. He was coming. That she knew.

THE STUDENT

HELENA STRUGGLED WITH HER STUDY, her mind clouded with nightmares she couldn't control. She forced herself to concentrate on the old texts. Absorbed in her struggles, Helena didn't notice the time until the librarian asked her to leave.

She rolled her shoulders, releasing hours of tension from struggling over the archaic language of the texts in front of her.

'Is it still raining?' she asked the librarian, her voice croaky from lack of use.

'*Sí*, and getting worse,' he answered, picking up Helena's discarded volumes. 'Don't forget this,' he added, scooping up the knitted scarf.

Helena flinched.

'It's not mine, sorry.'

The librarian examined the scarf in his hands, before walking away, winding the scarf around his own skinny neck.

Bracing herself for the weather, Helena shoved her notebook under her shirt and waited for the librarian to open the locked outer door. An arctic blast hit her. The rain tore at her legs, scaring away the last of the lingering tourists faster than an outbreak of the plague. Helena hesitated, jumping in fright as the wind slammed the door shut behind her. There was no going back.

Head down, arms wrapped round her middle protecting her precious notebook, she dashed through puddles bearing abandoned maps and half eaten slices of pizza — the rain too dire for even the rats to bother ferrying it away. Her stomach grumbled with emptiness.

Helena passed another lamppost dripping with posters appealing for news about the missing girl. She didn't stop to read them, too focussed on getting out of the rain. But these posters were for a girl with longer hair and wider set eyes with a soft mouth. A girl of similar age to Helena. A girl who strolled the same streets, eating at the same cafes after visiting the same museums, marvelling at the same pieces of art and sculpture.

Ducking into the nearest open cafe, she shook herself like a dog, water running from the tip of her nose. It would be stupid returning home in this weather. She had enough cash for a meal while she waited for the rain to ease. She couldn't risk her notebook getting any wetter, since it contained three years of thesis notes — the Changing Depiction of Women in Frescoes in the Italian Renaissance. A topic she'd poured her heart and soul into. She wanted to restore frescoes, true restoration, not the bizarre crosshatch infill so many conservators thought appropriate.

Her notebook also held the list of places she'd searched for her father's stolen art. The list was extensive. She needed to write up her notes from last night, but couldn't find the words. Casadei's anger had terrified her. There was a blackness within the man, and she didn't want to face it again on her own. Tomorrow she would ask Sim for his advice. Helena has heard that there were organisations who were helping Holocaust survivors retrieve their stolen art. Perhaps she should approach them for help as well?

Around her, other weather refugees were doing the same — shaking out coats and stowing umbrellas under their chairs. Helena pushed her way to an empty chair, after first grabbing a handful of napkins and wiping herself down. She pulled her notebook free from her waistband, sliding extra napkins through the pages.

'Research notes or the next prize-winning novel?' a voice queried from behind.

Spinning, she spied Benito, looking just as bedraggled, with water dripping from his overlong hair.

'My thesis notes,' she replied, smiling.

'Your notebook fared better than mine,' he said, holding up a sodden sketch book.

Helena handed him a pile of napkins, 'Split these apart, and weave them between the pages. It's the best you can do until you can put it somewhere to dry, if you want to save what's in there.'

Benito fumbled with the napkins, struggling to separate the leaves of paper. Helena reached over to divide them, her fingers more nimble than his stained digits. She wasn't trying to look at his art, catching only glimpses — a sketch of a woman's shoe, hints of a woman's eye, the curve of a shoulder, a fragment of cascading hair, noting that he had a sympathetic eye for proportion.

'I didn't know you sketched,' she said, motioning towards his sketchbook.

'Sometimes I try. I have a tutor, but,' he shrugged, 'it is hard to live up to his standards. So now I drink,' he said, the sodden mess of the sketch book mirroring his emotions.

The waiter appeared to take their order, a flash of irritation on his face at the pile of soggy napkins.

Shifting in her seat under his judgmental stare, Helena ordered a *Gorgonzola and Porcini Mushroom Risotto*, hoping her order would placate the waiter.

'Two of those, *grazie*,' Benito said, before adding two glasses of the *Brunello di Montalcino*.

Helena protested, the wine far exceeding her finances, but Benito allayed her concerns.

'My shout, for the wine at least, to drown my sorrows with a friend. The perfect opportunity to know you better, yes? Without the others here to intrude,' Benito said, winking.

Helena's heart gave a leap of joy, and she couldn't wipe the smile from her face. Their food arrived, the fragrant *risotto* turning several heads as it made its way to their table.

'I wish I ate this way at home,' Benito said, shovelling a forkful of the *risotto* into his mouth, 'But without my mother cooking for me, I am doomed.'

Helena sipped her wine, savouring the chocolate and raspberry flavours on her tongue, letting nearby conversations wash over her, the warmth of the other diners filling the air with a miasma of perfume, damp clothing, garlic and tomatoes. Not an altogether unpleasant aroma, and enough to chase last night's demons away.

'When will this rain stop?' Helena asked, peering through foggy windows smeared with rivulets of water flowing into the pulsating drains of the city.

Benito didn't even bother looking outside, 'Maybe by tomorrow,' he suggested. 'It always rains this way in November.'

THE CLEANER

Stefano cursed the weather. Whenever it rained, regardless of how heavy or light it brought back the worst of his wartime memories. Long hours marching to nowhere important before marching back to somewhere less important. Shooting. Losing friends. Replacing friends. Abandoning friends.

Rain meant longer work hours, it meant getting home later; it meant she would be difficult and that he would get no rest tonight, and that there'd be no opportunities for him to duck out to visit his workroom. And that worried him.

Most homes in Florence leaked, the rain an unavoidable burden people lived with. One day someone would fix their home, one day. Until then, they set bowls under leaks, moving beds to other parts of the room. It was part of life as a Florentine, but it didn't improve his mood. If he could have afforded a better apartment, he would have moved in a heartbeat. Soon, he told himself. Soon.

Perhaps he should go to his workroom first, to make sure nothing sat on the floor? He didn't want to go to sleep only to wake to find his beloved city under water again. He also had the knife to consider.

After mopping the last of the wet footprints, he left his mop dripping in the sink, squeezed out his cleaning cloths, and tidied his workroom. He took great pride in his work, and would never consider leaving his work space messy. He'd been doing this job for so many years now, every action as comfortable as breathing, yet parts of him ached and didn't work as they had when he was twenty. He still felt lucky to have a job, a home, and a wife.

Locking the door, he opened an umbrella as old and as weathered as himself, pulling his satchel closer. Stefano bowed his head, as his boots trod their weary way homewards, until he changed his mind mid-step. His wife could wait. Just thinking those words crushed him, and although her need of him was great, it was preferable for her to stay at home staring out the window, watching for someone who was never coming. His workshop... he picked up his pace, his satchel banging against his aching hip.

Rain slashed at his legs, trying to tear the umbrella from his grasp as he reached what he called his workshop. Someone had slapped a poster of a missing girl on the door, and he ripped the sheet away, tearing the soggy face in half, swearing at whoever had defiled his door. No consideration for the property of others, just like at the museum. He tried not to think about the missing girl, arguing with himself that there were always missing girls, too many of them. Stefano fumbled with his keys under the umbrella, exposing his body to the elements, drenching him in seconds.

Slamming the door shut, he flicked the switch.

Light from a handful of naked bulbs filled the cavernous room as he navigated the steps down from the doorway — a regrettable design flaw in a city prone to flooding. He had plans to move everything into larger premises — away from the city and into the countryside, with bees the only noise instead of the incessant hum of tourists. The time to move was close. After years of planning, it was all coming to fruition. He could count the days on one hand.

Stefano walked the perimeter of the space. To call it a workroom would have been a disservice to what it held within its walls.

Set back from the walls were a museum-worthy collection of small articles of furniture, gleaming with love and polish, a rainbow of different woods — pale yellows, deep browns, iridescent reds, and others as black as the night. Some woods were rare, extinct, milled from existence to make tables and chairs.

Stefano ran his hand over a 19th century mahogany and satinwood table, adorned with gilt and inlaid tulipwood marquetry. A marvellous piece, more at home in the rooms of Louis XVI or in Catherine the Great's Winter Palace. Perhaps a piece passed down through generations of the same family? And next to it was another exquisite piece, older than the first, a lacquered cabinet in the Genoese style of the 18th century with a luxurious golden crown at the top.

Systematically he checked the furniture, moving one or two further away from the walls, protection from any leaks. And then he examined the art which hung on free standing panels of his own construction. Each panel heaving with framed representations of the Madonna, unnamed Italian nobility from centuries past, benign landscape studies, and more modern depictions of children at play.

Satisfied his treasures weren't at risk, he surveyed the cabinets of curiosities, before remembering the package in his bag. Stefano withdrew the cloth package and slid out the carved pewter knife. At his workbench, which stood centre stage on a raised platform, he laid the knife down. The museum hadn't done it justice; the knife needed a proper clean and polish to bring out its beauty. To the average person it was just a knife, used like a puppet to entertain the uninitiated. But to Stefano it formed part of Italy's history, and in his workshop he could protect it from wandering hands, secure from the scavengers who fed upon Italy's cultural heritage.

Under the watchful eyes of the surrounding portraits, he buffed the blade dulled by time, a slow polish the best option because of the carving on the handle. This was a labour of love, one the museum didn't understand or chose not to understand because of the costs of proper conservation and restoration. Management believed the museum existed to entertain the tourists, and not for the love of Italy's cultural treasure.

Immersed in his work, he lost track of time, the paint on the top windows restricting what little light the rain let through. There were rugs cushioning his feet, but nothing helped his cramping hands, and he slowly flexed his swollen fingers. Cocooned in his workroom, it was only the pain in his hands which dictated that it was time to stop.

Before locking up, he reverently removed a drop cloth covering a painting leaning up against the workbench. Stefano suspended the painting from an empty hook beneath a stylised bronze eagle, its gleaming wings outstretched. He stood back to stare at the painting. Delivered by the artist while Stefano was at work, the last thing he needed was for it to suffer any damage. Perfect and irreplaceable, it was waiting for its reentrance into the world, at a price which would allow him to move to the countryside with all of his treasures, and his wife, if he could persuade her to leave her window.

Reluctantly he locked up, preparing himself for the journey home and the consequences of tonight's detour. He justified his digression; he had to check that that the rain hadn't slipped inside like a thief to destroy his life. Carmela would forgive him. Nothing he did could be worse than what he'd already done.

THE POLICEMAN

PISANI WOKE, not to his jangling alarm clock, but to the jarring sound of a telephone. Normally he left it off the hook at night to avoid situations like this. He'd accepted the early morning calls in his youth, but he didn't need them now. Let someone else deal with night time emergencies, he was beyond that. Lifting the handle, he dropped it straight back into the cradle, cutting short the annoying noise.

The phone rang again. This did not bode well. The creeping edges of dawn trickled in through his window, but that didn't mean that there weren't still another two pleasant hours of sleep available.

'*Si?*' He nodded to the man on the phone. '*Si*, yes, I will be there, *ciao.*'

Pisani sank back into his pillow as the tentacles of last night's migraine slithered back. Today would start with painkillers with his coffee. He'd been told to hurry, but there was always time for coffee.

Flooding was hardly a reason to get him out of bed, that's what they paid the municipal staff for — to deal with flooding, not the police. But as he was still clawing his way back to his original position, so he would go.

He struggled out from under the covers he'd pulled around him as the temperature dipped into negative numbers overnight. He opened the shutters. Concealed by a sheet of water falling from the grey sky, Florence looked distorted, off kilter. In the streets below, people hurried by, disguised by umbrellas hoisted above their heads. Pisani wondered if they were worrying about the date - November 3rd, the anniversary of the devastating flood of 1844. Tomorrow of course would be the anniversary of the 1333 floods. If the city had listened to Leonardo da Vinci or even Michelangelo, Florence wouldn't have to worry about rain in November.

Pisani spat his morning breath outside, and slammed the window shut, grumbling under his breath all the way to his kitchenette. With coffee brewing on the stovetop, his mood improved, and he changed into fresh clothes, discarding last night's clothes on the floor. His cleaner would sort that out. With no wife to do these chores for him, he relied on Sophia to clean up behind him. The arrangement suited him well. There was no need to put up with a woman's inane chattering at night, or when he was drinking his espresso. No perfume to tickle his nose, or toiletries cluttering his small bathroom. Sophia came when he was at work and finished before he came home. If he needed things, he left a note, confident she would replenish whatever he was missing. He left money on the table for her and she returned the spare change. The perfect relationship, better than a marriage.

Sipping his coffee, he dropped a handful of coins on top of a brief list for Sophia; coffee beans, *biscotti*, shaving cream. He should have added toothpaste to the list, but the state of his breath never crossed his mind. He had no one to point out his toxic morning breath.

On the drive to work, he could barely see the road through the rain, almost driving into a roadblock — two damp Municipal Officers standing at the barrier, hands hidden in their heavy jackets, forbidding any further passage.

Pisani gestured that they should let him pass. They ignored him. He honked his horn.

One of the officers walked over, his arrogant swagger grating on Pisani's nerves. 'The road is closed. Closed to everyone, unless you are driving a boat.'

'It can't be that dangerous,' Pisani argued, pointing to a pair of students cycling in the rain, their faces belying any concern about the weather or the condition of the roads.

The officer shrugged, 'Roads are closed.'

'Fine,' Pisani grimaced, backing the car into a questionable space, before storming off into the torrential rain. He squelched his way through torrents of water gushing down the streets like racers at the start of a marathon. At the station, he spied Rosa Fonti talking with another female officer — the short one with the dyed red hair. She reminded him of a miniature version of Botticelli's Venus, and he wouldn't have minded seeing her naked in a scallop shell, but for now he felt as bitter as if he were chewing on a thistle leaf.

'Morning, Pisani,' Rosa said, her face impassive. The redhead turned away, suddenly fascinated by an old notice pinned on the wall.

Pisani stormed past them and into his office, peeling off his coat. His shirt was just as wet, and clung to his body, a physique stretched beyond its natural shape by too many glasses of wine and enormous meals. He was rubbing at his shirt with a wad of tissues when the door opened.

'Pisani, pleased you made it,' said the gaunt grey man in the doorway.

Chief Inspector Fausto Nucci had been a peer of Pisani's until Pisani's spectacular fall from grace, and now it felt like Nucci couldn't stomach being anywhere near Pisani in case the taint rubbed off.

'We need everyone today, and even you can imagine the number of tourists who will need help. Get some dry clothes on and tidy yourself up, we're going out.' Nucci turned on his polished heel and walked out, leaving Pisani wallowing in his damp misery.

His position was a woman's fault, it always was. If she hadn't used her sneaky feminine wiles on him, none of this would be happening. The vixen had inveigled herself into his world, innocently at first with little requests — a lift here, a package delivered there, a search through the files to track down a cousin she'd lost touch with, a parking ticket she'd like him to make disappear because she was only a few minutes late. And then, not just one ticket, but dozens of tickets. Such an irresponsible girl. The parking outside her home was appalling. Then a subtle shift. He'd been so enamoured with her attention, he hadn't seen it coming when she'd asked him to intervene when they'd charged one of her cousins with a contravvenzione, a misdemeanour. And he'd done it. After a cursory glance at the file, and with her whispering sweet nothings in his ear, he'd called in some favours, had the charges dropped.

And so it went on, until the day she'd come to him in tears, mascara running down her cheeks, crying about her uncle's arrest, claiming mistaken identity. He'd had nothing to do with the crime they had charged him for. Her tears had tugged at his heart. He'd persuaded himself that her love for his weathered face, and his foibles, was genuine. But when she'd given him her uncle's name, a criminal known as Lupo the Wolf, he'd paused, but he'd still become involved. They were in love.

From there it was only a matter of time before it burst like a rotting corpse, leaving the stench to follow him for the rest of his career.

Once he had made himself as presentable as possible, he emerged from his office. He needed another coffee and then he'd start the day.

He stomped over to the coffee pot where Rosa joined him, her floral perfume overpowering the aroma of coffee Pisani had dared enjoy for a moment. She fiddled with the radio's volume, listening with rapt attention to an interview with Fiorentina's Ricky Albertosi as he once again rehashed the team's Italian Cup win.

'Do we have to listen to that?' Pisani grumbled. 'It is old news.'

'But it's Albertosi. With him in goal, we could win the Championship.'

'I don't understand why you love football so much. Fiorentina have not won the Italian Championship for ten years, not since nineteen-fifty-six, and probably won't in my lifetime. What would a woman know about this?'

'Shall we go through the lists today then, till we're needed to save the hapless tourists?' she asked, ignoring his dire predictions and pouring herself an extra large coffee, filling it with three teaspoons of sugar too many. Their conversations about football as predictable as Florence's weather.

'Lists?' Pisani asked, distracted by the quantity of sugar Rosa spooned into her cup.

'For the thefts from the hotel room safes,' she replied, sighing.

'Fine, let's do that, might keep us out of the rain,' he agreed, recognising he had a legitimate reason to avoid assisting the foolish tourists with their overfilled suitcases and appalling children.

It didn't take them long to chart and cross reference the names of the workers.

'These only account for the workers on their books, but doesn't cover the employees they pay under the table, or an opportunistic thief trying their luck at the lower end places,' Rosa theorised.

'Or it could be this person,' Pisani replied, smugness writ large on his face. It wasn't often he scored one over his colleague. Not that he was lacking in the mental faculties department, but on a deeper level, he recognised that his policing skills weren't on par with the younger officers coming up the ranks behind him. He'd got through on bluster and good luck, and a complete lack of qualms about claiming the credit for work by those beneath him. His fundamental problem was that he was lazy, the type who, like cockroaches, survived every effort to get rid of them.

One name stood out on all three lists, Bianca Zito. Twenty-six years old, with an address in the Santa Croce area of Florence, which wasn't a surprise to the two officers.

'Does she have any previous charges for dishonesty?' Rosa asked.

Pisani wondered if she was cursing herself that she hadn't spotted the link first. A foolish mistake and one Pisani would never let her forget.

Nucci leaned in, interrupting them to summon everyone to the briefing room, leaving the potentially light-fingered Bianca Zito to live another day.

THE GUEST

Richard swore. This was the absolute last straw. With no money or passport, he couldn't even leave this abysmal country. They may as well take his bloody legs as well while they're at it.

He hammered on the abandoned reception desk and hollered for help, but to no avail. Richard considered his options. The police were coming tomorrow to get a copy of the now missing passport, so he didn't need to ring them. He could plead with Julia for help, since she owed him a thousand favours, but given their last conversation at the bar, he doubted she'd be open to helping him. She had tried revoking his invite to the wedding, explaining that inviting him had been a mistake, breaking his heart again.

Back in his room, Carstone pulled up short upon finding the same housekeeping girl back.

'Can I help you?'

'*Non capisco*,' she shrugged, dusting the bedside table.

'You spoke English yesterday. Speak English today, damn it.' Carstone lost control, his hands balling into fists as he stood over her like an angry football coach admonishing his team, but she just looked at him with blank eyes, her dusting cloth hanging by her side.

Carstone grabbed her arm and dragged her to the open wardrobe, gesturing towards the barren wasteland of the empty safe. She struggled against his grip, before breaking free. She ran from the room, throwing her bottle of disinfectant and polishing cloth at Carstone's head.

Carstone had sunk to a new low, not the best behaviour for a surgeon. He was lucky she hadn't sprayed him with the bleach. He imagined the headlines back home "Eye surgeon loses sight after assaulting hotel employee". Odd, the spray bottle was empty. He picked up her cloth — bone dry and cleaner than the rest of the hotel. Carstone put two and two together, and came up with one word, thief. He ran after her, scanning the hallway. Gone. He tried the emergency exit. Locked. She'd vanished.

Back inside his room, he slammed the door, no longer caring if he bothered the other guests. With nothing else to do, Carstone climbed into his unmade bed, exhausted, exasperated and angry. Things never went well when he lost his temper. Like that last time with Scott, and the argument over Scott lending him enough money to settle his debts. Scott had the temerity to ask him what he was planning on spending the money on and refused to lend him a dime if he was going to spend it on women and alcohol. Damn it, he just needed a small loan to tide him over whilst he sorted out the surgery. Yes, there was a woman on the periphery who needed paying, a patient he'd become too involved with, another one. But Scott didn't need those details. For gods' sake, he was Scott's only brother, it should have been an easy yes to lending him the spare cash Scott had.

MORNING CAME, and Carstone crawled out of bed, the new day providing ammunition to his simmering anger and the remnants of last night's hangover. He needed his passport back, to leave this country before he did something he would regret. He blamed Julia for the position he found himself in, it was always Julia's fault. He hadn't started drinking until after she had married his brother. That was the start of his problems, and they'd only escalated since then.

In the dining room, Carstone surveyed the detritus of left over breakfast dishes. The scene as welcoming as vomit on the pavement. After clearing a space at a table, he waited for the police, sipping the dire coffee and tearing at a stale pastry, looking for any sign of Julia or the other wedding guests. He assumed she'd warned them away from him. Another blow to their relationship, if they still had one.

A face appeared around the corner — an older woman in an apron, cleaning the tables, her headscarf the colour of rancid butter.

'Do you speak English?'

'No,' came her succinct reply.

Carstone ignored her answer. Everyone knew English, and if they didn't, they shouldn't be in the hospitality industry.

'Someone robbed me yesterday, stealing everything from my safe. I have to speak with the manager.'

'*Non parlano Inglese.*'

'Yes, you bloody do. A girl was in my room yesterday, twice. She's the one who stole from my safe, and I want to speak to the manager.' Carstone's voice rising with every word, his anger too. He ended the sentence by hurling his coffee cup to the ground, smashing it to smithereens.

The woman screamed and fled the room, the other

diners freezing in shock, their conversations halting mid-sentence as if the ventriloquist pulling their strings had vanished.

Carstone poured himself another coffee and sat watching the dark coffee soak into the floorboards, staining an already weathered floor. He flexed his knuckles and smiled at the other diners, enjoying their discomfort. He wasn't here to make friends, just to win back the woman who should have been his. Now that wasn't an option, he didn't care about taming his behaviour.

Beyond the dining room, a babble of raised voices floated towards him, a high-pitched wailing and banter. Carstone placed his cup in the centre of the table and wandered out to investigate.

In front of Richard Carstone stood the woman from the cafe, this time wearing a masculine black uniform, rendering her almost androgynous. 'We received a complaint about the assault of a staff member here—'

'You're a policewoman?'

'Yes,' she said, and looked like she was appraising Carstone, assessing his risk.

'You've received a report that I what? Assaulted someone? Rubbish, I've done no such thing. And I thought you were here about my stolen passport, or the mugging I endured yesterday, but now that useless cleaner is claiming that I assaulted her?'

'I know nothing about a mugging, but I am interested in hearing more about the theft from your safe,' the officer said. 'But in the meantime, we'll take you back to the station to process you for the assault. There are thousands of other things I am doing today, so I can't guarantee how long it will take. Everyone is busy supporting the genuine tourists, instead of dealing with a visitor to our country who terrorises old ladies going about their legitimate business. Come,' and she turned away, her heavy boots clomping on the wet tiles.

Carstone pocketed two extra pastries and hurried after her. He'd ring Julia from the station to ask her to rescue him. Her boyfriend was a serious player in town, with plenty of family money and influence. If he couldn't get him off these ridiculous charges, then there was always the consulate. No one treats an American citizen like this. No, the consulate would help him, even if Julia's lover didn't.

Outside was like walking into an apocalypse — with water bombarding them from every angle, defying gravity as it reached up from the cobbled street, drenching his shoes and socks.

'Is your weather always this bad?' Carstone asked.

The policewoman had pulled a man-sized jacket on over her uniform before leaving the hotel and if she heard him, she didn't say, slipping into the front of a marked police car, with her brutish looking colleague locking Carstone in the back of the dry car, before clambering in behind the wheel. How he fit behind the steering wheel was a mystery — he should have been on a farm deep in the countryside crushing walnuts with his bare hands.

Driving through the roads of Florence was like shooting the rapids at Niagara Falls - rivers gushed from every pipe, dislodging drain covers, leaving them bobbing in the violent flow of water.

'Is it safe to be driving in this weather?'

'This is fine, normal for Florence. Tourists worry but we Florentines know it is just rain,' the policewoman threw over her shoulder, keeping her eyes on the road, hardly providing any assurance that the weather wasn't concerning her as much as it was Carstone.

It wasn't until they drove into a cavernous rear entrance that Carstone realised that driving into the back entrance of a police station was a terrible sign. When the engine died, and the officers got out, leaving Carstone stewing in the back seat, he knew he was in trouble. He banged on the window, but attracted less attention than a rat in a sewer. Five minutes later the driver returned, releasing Carstone from his confinement.

Carstone gagged on the stench of unwashed criminals permeating through the underground garage and felt the judgemental eyes of the officers assessing him. He wanted to yell, 'I'm a respected surgeon,' but even that was a lie.

'Come,' came the imperious command from his former lunch companion standing in a nearby doorway.

'Are you going to charge me?' Carstone asked, trotting along behind her, the brute following behind. 'No one has given me my Miranda Rights.'

'Maybe,' came the not so reassuring reply. 'I am unfamiliar with Miranda, sorry. First tell us about the theft from your room safe.'

They reached a grubby desk covered in papers and manila folders, and she showed him a chair.

Carstone considered educating the woman about law enforcement in America and the introduction of Miranda Rights, but the look on her face suggested that wasn't the best idea. He still had to organise a new passport. So, swallowing his pride, he sat down. He also had a wealthy ex sister-in-law to woo back before she married someone else, and time was running out.

THE WIFE

AT THE ENTRANCE to the hotel's dining room, disappointment swallowed Rhonda as she saw a room awash with diners, with nary a spare seat available.

A waiter hurried over, flustered at the high numbers of diners who'd descended upon him at once.

'*Signora*, I'm sorry but I have no free tables. May I suggest breakfast in your room?'

'No tables at all?' Rhonda craned her head past the worried waiter.

'Unless you will share?' he offered.

Rhonda squirmed, she didn't want to share, but walking to another cafe didn't appeal given the sheets of water cascading outside, obscuring the elegant gardens. If she ate in her room, the voices in her head would send her mad.

'Yes, I can share, but maybe choose someone who has almost finished?' she suggested.

The waiter exhaled and lead her to a table for two by the window, the remains of a meal in front of the man seated with his back to them. As he cleared the table, he asked the guest if he minded sharing. The gentleman responded in agreement and turned to greet his impromptu breakfast companion.

It was the man from the cafe, Paul Tobias.

Thrown, Rhonda searched for a way out, but the waiter was standing by her chair, a linen napkin hanging from his arm, and Tobias stood waiting, a smile on his face which didn't reach his eyes. Rhonda slipped into the proffered chair, immobile as the waiter draped the starched napkin across her lap.

'Coffee, *Signora*?'

'Please, yes, thank you,' Rhonda stammered.

'So we have our drink, *Signora*,' the grey-haired gentleman said, toasting Rhonda with his espresso. To anyone looking their way, they would have looked like the quintessential empty nesters.

'So it would seem,' Rhonda replied, avoiding his eyes. She'd seen something in them, something familiar, and she swallowed, her throat threatening to close.

'I can recommend the omelette. Not at all Italian, but they won't judge you here for ordering it,' he added, firing off an order.

Rhonda held her tongue. He was a stranger to her, so what entitled him to order for her? Her skin crawled. 'Did you just order me an omelette?' she asked, reaching deep within herself to question him.

'Yes, I hope you don't mind. Service has been slow this morning. So many unexpected guests because of the weather, I thought it prudent to get in quick,' he said, inclining his head towards the restaurant entrance, where a group stood arguing about the seating arrangements.

Rhonda couldn't dispute his logic and lapsed into intense contemplation of the condiments.

'Shall we continue our conversation from yesterday?' her table companion asked. 'I'll start, I am Paul Tobias—'

'Yes, I remember,' Rhonda interrupted. Unconsciously, her right hand reached to fiddle with her wedding rings, forgetting that she'd slipped them from her finger.

'Are you married?' Tobias asked, a tart snap to his voice as he took in her nervous habit.

She froze, losing the power of speech until the waiter appeared, carrying the silver tray high above his head as he navigated the crowded dining room. Her omelette's arrival saved her, and she relaxed. Food she could talk about, throwing around hundreds of adjectives to describe the taste in her mouth and the artwork on her plate with no effort. Even if the meal contained the most vile conglomeration of flavours, bringing her to the point of gagging, she could discuss it. This was the only part of her life where she was at ease. Her recipe books were her bibles and the kitchen her favourite room in the house, the safest room despite the sharp knives resting in their blocks.

Rhonda turned her attention to her plate and the first forkful, which proved to be a delicate balance of the ordinary served with a side of genius. A sharp cheese, the heady scent of shavings of garlic, the finest slivers of red peppers, and the yellow yolk only seen with the freshest eggs. She hesitated before adding a twist of cracked pepper, but her second mouthful confirmed her decision. Perfection.

'It was the right decision then?' Tobias asked, observing her reaction.

Like a startled deer, Rhonda moved her eyes from her plate to those of Tobias. Blinking, she found her voice, 'It is one of the best omelettes I've eaten for a long time, yes.'

'Good, I am pleased that you are enjoying it. I read the

pleasure in your eyes. It's just as well I ordered for you then. A woman needs a man to care for her.'

Rhonda's enjoyment of the meal soured at his rank words. Those were the same words someone else said to her, hundreds of times over the years. 'I appreciate the omelette, but I can manage myself, thank you.'

'But you must let me show you around today. With this weather, only a few places are suitable to visit, and I know them all. You'll be safe in my hands, I promise,' Tobias said, his tone that of a man used to getting his own way.

'No,' Rhonda retorted, louder than she'd meant to. Several diners turned to look. Her companion's face turning to stone, his coffee cup lowered to its saucer, his free hand clenched into a fist.

'Sorry, I didn't mean... sorry, I have other plans. Thank you for you letting me share your table, but I must go,' she stammered, rushing away.

Like knives, Rhonda felt Tobias's eyes watching her until she disappeared from his view. There was no such thing as coincidence. He knew who she was.

THE STUDENT

Benito and Helena spent the evening bonding over *risotto* and wine, comparing notes about their vagabond lifestyles, chasing restoration work in the smallest churches in even smaller towns, refining their skills and practising their craft. Tonight, the complete opposite of the previous one. Helena forgot about Casadei and his unpleasantness, and it wasn't until the waiter cleared his throat for the third time that they noticed the cafe had emptied, with them the last two diners.

Laughing self-consciously, they both begged a bag from the uptight waiter to protect their notebooks and left. Sheltering under the awning outside, they surveyed the near apocalyptic weather.

'This will be hell to clean up in the morning,' Benito observed.

'Will it get worse, do you think?' Helena asked.

Benito shrugged. 'This is as bad as I've seen it. But it will be better in my apartment, I swear,' he winked. 'A liqueur, some candles, a little music. Come, we will get wet, but we won't die.'

Helena's heart soared, and they ran laughing through the empty Florentine streets, dodging puddles which threatened to swallow them whole, street corners echoing the red lights of firemen pumping out basements or police directing drivers around weather-related accidents until they reached Benito's apartment.

Despite being built post-war, Benito's apartment building looked as if it had been a casualty of German bombing, with the entire building blanketed in darkness.

'It's not looking good, is it?' Benito admitted. 'It is just as well I promised you candles.'

With no inclination to walk the unfamiliar streets home alone, especially after passing at least twenty sodden posters appealing for information about the missing girl, Helena had no choice but to follow Benito into the chilly building, his hand tightly clasping hers.

They trudged up the stairwell into an inky apartment. Benito fumbled his way past furniture shrouded in midnight black, and moments later a match flared and the comforting scent of beeswax wafted over the room. More candles leapt into life as Benito moved around, the flickering flames encouraging the shadows to dance in the corners.

As she slipped off her wet shoes, Helena wondered if Benito would have still lit the candles if the power was on. Were they an attempt to create intimacy, or were they just emergency lighting? She smiled, hoping it was Benito's romantic side. If only Marisa could see them now. Dreams do come true.

Benito fluttered about like a caged canary, wondering aloud whether to boil the water for coffee or to find her dry clothes.

'Clothes,' Helena directed through chattering teeth.

There wouldn't be much romance if she caught hypothermia.

'*Sì*,' Benito nodded, and disappeared through a gloomy doorway.

Helena looked around — two couches, a small table pushed against the wall piled high with paint tubes, an empty easel by the window with a dozen canvasses leaning inwards against the sideboard. She considered sneaking a peek, but before she'd made a move, Benito returned with an armful of blankets and a cocky smile. He'd shed his wet clothes, changing into silk pyjamas, but ruined the overall look by adding a bulky jacket.

Helena laughed.

'Not quite the response I was going for, but I was cold,' Benito said, the dim light obscuring his petulant pout. 'Best I can do,' he offered, handing her trousers and a woollen jersey.

Helena stripped off her clothes in the dark bathroom and struggled into the oversized clothes. Searching for a towel to dry her hair, her hand closed over a silk shirt on the towel rail. She brought the sleek fabric up to her nose and inhaled. The shadow of sweet lemons remained, and Helena thought she recognised the perfume. Unable to locate a towel, she had to dry her hair with the shirt. She felt a twang of guilt. Was it his mother's fragrance? No, Benito's mother was no longer alive, hence his daily espressos and pastries at Piero's Bar. And as she draped the shirt back over the rail, the overt citrus scent nudged at her memory, Marisa. Was it Marisa's shirt?

Benito had built a cushioned cocoon between the couch and the floor, and Helena hurried across the floorboards, slipping under the blankets. With the curtains open, the city stood bare before them. The failure of the aged Florentine power supply let through the light of a million stars.

'Sightseeing from the floor,' he joked.

Helena laughed, squashing her unease about what Marisa was to Benito. She squirrelled further under the covers, pulling them up around her ears. She wrinkled her nose at the peculiar smell of the blankets. If she pushed aside the odour of stale sweat and man, she swore she could detect the same lemony scent. Helena ignored it. She was here, and Marisa wasn't. Benito had chosen her.

Benito handed her a strong coffee and Helena warmed her hands around the mug as she watched the shadowy city, Benito's shoulder rubbing against her own. Helena imagined this was what it must have been like for Italy's brilliant artists, held captive by the night, the stars stoking their creativity.

The scene teased her senses as she let her mind wander, allowing it passage through her cupboards of thoughts, dreams and fears, into a world where her own art adorned chapel walls, filling the souls of worshippers.

Someone knocked on the door.

Benito froze against her before slipping free of their cocoon, hurrying to answer the incessant hammering.

The candles jumped and shuddered as Benito stepped into the hall, not fully latching the door behind him, allowing Helena to catch snippets of their conversation.

'I didn't expect you tonight… it's not convenient… he should have told me… I didn't know he said you…'

Moments later Benito reappeared, and, ignoring Helena's questions, rifled through a stack of canvases, selecting one before leaving the apartment, slamming the door shut.

The discarded paintings fell over in the gust. Helena

jumped up to rescue them. The last thing any artist wanted was their art damaged.

Candlelight illuminated a portrait of a woman in a green dress in the style of Bartolomeo Veneto. Hues of ruby, topaz and emerald leapt from the canvas, vivid but subtly different from any of the Veneto's Helena had studied. She propped the canvas up against the fish tank, before lifting the second piece — a study of the same woman. Her gaze challenged Helena - an impetuous tilt to her head, her hand poised above a scrap of parchment.

With the pieces side by side, they could almost be original Bartolomeo Veneto paintings. Although Helena was sure that in the daylight the colours would be wrong, lines not as certain. But for a moment she wanted to believe they were real, and that these were two unknown masterpieces unearthed by a brilliant young art restorer.

When Benito came back, he was shoving a handful of lira into his pocket. He pulled up short as he saw Helena staring at the canvasses.

'What are you doing?' he asked, wrenching the pieces from her.

'They fell over,' Helena said, flustered at his reaction.

'Keep out of my things. I didn't invite you round here to snoop.'

'They're very good—'

'You should go,' Benito said. 'I'm tired.' His anger wiping away his earlier pleasantries. 'You can return my clothes another day.'

Helena stood speechless as Benito motioned her out. After shoving her feet into her soaking shoes and gathering her wet clothes, she left, shaking. She rushed home through sheets of relentless rain, posters of missing girls slathered on every surface. She didn't understand what she'd seen at Benito's apartment, or why he'd reacted the way he had.

But his behaviour was inexcusable. And when she saw him again, she'd… she would tell him how she felt, maybe. She didn't know what to do. She started crying as she tried making herself smaller on the empty streets, the darkness pressing into every inch of her body.

THE CLEANER

'I'M HOME,' Stefano called. No response, not that he expected one, but calling out a habit borne from many years. There had been a time when his words resulted in a flurry of skirts, slender arms wrapped around his waist and his face papered with kisses. Dim memories now, her arms wasted away, lips drawn tight over worn teeth. Lips which had lost the knowledge of love.

Stefano stripped off in the hall, no need to traipse water upstairs he'd have to mop. Easier to bundle everything into the old tub in the kitchen — his way of minimising the housework later.

Once dry, he entered his wife's bedroom.

'*Ciao amore mio.*' Hello my love, three words he'd uttered every day since their wedding.

No reaction. Carmela stayed seated at the window, gazing at what, he didn't know. But it wasn't at him. She gazed into a past which no longer held him.

If she was hungry, she gave no sign. Stefano returned to the kitchen and prepared a simple *bruschetta* with tomato and basil, pouring them both a small wine. It would help settle her tonight. Rain always made things worse, bringing back memories of shivering in winter, of babies born and babies lost, of bullets flying.

He picked at his meal, drinking the wine faster than he had planned, babbling about his day. His anecdotes about the tourists used to make her laugh until she doubled over, her cheeks turning red, tears streaming. Tonight there was nothing. Carmela never wavered from the window, watching for someone who would never return.

'Goodnight, my love,' he said, placing a kiss on her forehead, resting his head against hers for a moment. He thought he heard her whisper the same words back to him. Some nights she did, some nights she didn't. Tonight, he wanted to believe that she still loved him.

Light-headed from too much wine, he retired to his bedroom. Sparsely furnished compared to the rest of the apartment, a calendar above his chest of drawers the only decoration. Circled in bright red pen, two days from now, were the words *vendere l'arte*, sell the art.

THE POLICEMAN

Rosa Fonti lead Richard Carstone through the police station to a chair piled with folders.

'Please tell me about the theft from your safe, and then we can discuss the assault-'

'You can't call it an assault—'

'Don't interrupt the officer, just answer her questions,' Pisani thumped into a chair next to the man across from Fonti, before recognising him as Richard Carstone, the unlucky American tourist from the day before. 'Oh, it's you,' Pisani commented, taken aback by the sight of the man at Rosa's desk.

'You have met each other?' Rosa asked.

'He reported a mugging yesterday. I should have taken a copy of his passport this morning, but things came up—'

'Impossible for you to see my passport when someone stole it from my hotel room safe,' the American interrupted, his voice rising.

'Calm down Mr Carstone, there is no point making things more difficult for yourself—'

'More difficult? This entire thing has been an

abomination. You should question the hotel staff instead of grilling me and putting my life at risk, driving through flooded streets—'

'A slight exaggeration,' Rosa interjected, shuffling through folders. 'So this theft—'

'Which one? The one where they assaulted me and stole my wallet? Or where they emptied my room safe of all my belongings, including my brother's cufflinks I'm to wear to his wife's wedding? That one?'

'The theft from the room safe, please.' Pen poised, Fonti waited.

'Fine,' the American snapped. 'After they mugged me, I returned to my hotel to find the housemaid in my room. And after she left, I noticed the safe was open in the wardrobe. I ran out to find her but couldn't see her for dust, the dust from the cash she'd swiped.'

'Did you see her take your money and passport?' Pisani asked, his interest piqued by the mention of the maid.

'No, I didn't, because I'd wasted too much time here giving you a bloody statement. If you'd been more efficient, I would have been back at my hotel before they fleeced me there too.'

'You don't know that for sure, Mr Carstone. They could have emptied your safe in the morning. Please focus on the housemaid. Did she wear a name tag?' Fonti asked.

'It's not the place where they pay for name tags, or air conditioning or hot water, or towels designed for adults. You've seen it. Look, you should be speaking to the manager of the place, not me. The girl was in my room yesterday afternoon, and I saw the same girl the day before, when I'd stepped out of the shower. Darkish hair, skinny, in her twenties. You're thinking, that's not enough to go on, but that's bullshit. Go there now, question everyone—'

'And that's what we plan on doing,' Pisani interrupted, 'as soon as we get your statement, and sort out this assault.'

The American threw back his head and sighed.

They went through his statement, teasing out what he could and couldn't remember about the housekeeper, whether she'd had piercings or tattoos, hair colour, length. Was her voice high or deep? Her accent. Each question building a picture of the thief.

'Why aren't you there now, looking for her?' Carstone asked.

'We're following strong leads. We have enough to conduct our investigation, so let's go,' Pisani said, bored with the rude American but eager to do some actual police work, before being tasked with herding damp tourists.

The annoying Fonti tried raising the assault, arguing with him. He had no time for this, and launched into her, waving his hands around, working himself into a mock rage, putting on a show for his superiors and the stupid tourist.

'You should have dealt with this when you were there this morning. Look at the delay you've caused with this false accusation. Mr Carstone has been the victim of two crimes, and you've dragged him out in the worst weather we've seen for years, a crime. We need to go, now.'

With satisfaction, Pisani noted a flush on Fonti's face. Pisani was about to say more, but Nucci appeared, slapping a folder onto the desk.

'Fonti, there's been a theft from the Bargello Museum. You need to get over there, I've got no one else available.'

'I'll go,' Pisani jumped in, a theft from a museum far juicier than a missing passport. Let Fonti deal with that.

'Fine, I don't care which of you go,' Nucci replied.

'What did they steal?' Pisani asked, imagining the glory

of recovering a stolen Donatello, or a Michelangelo sculpture.

'A knife,' Nucci replied, a smirk on his face.

Pisani's mouth fell open, caught in a trap of his own making. There was no glory in recovering a stolen knife. No headlines or promotions.

'A knife? You want me to investigate the theft of a knife, in the middle of our worst flooding in years?'

'Don't over-dramatise things, Pisani. This flooding isn't a catastrophe, more a minor inconvenience to traffic and tourists. So yes, a missing knife is what you will investigate, to the full extent of your abilities,' Nucci said.

'Fonti and I are investigating a hotel sneak thief, in fact I've just interviewed a key witness, which has led to us identifying a prime suspect. We were about to leave to—'

For an Italian, Nucci never moved much, his hands often clasped motionless behind his back. But for now, they were steepled at his chin. A dangerous sign. 'Our priority is this missing knife. Fonti is more than capable of arresting a petty thief,' Nucci said, his tone broking no further discussion.

Incapable of speech, Pisani stood there, certain that somehow this was Fonti's doing, so she'd get all the prestige from arresting a prolific thief. It wouldn't surprise him if Fonti and Nucci were having an affair. Fonti was just Nucci's type. It was always the women, with their slippery ways, making his life miserable.

'Fine,' Pisani said, before stomping out of the office and leaving watery footprints in his wake.

AFTER MISINTERPRETING the instructions from the crone in the ticket office, Pisani spent the best part of twenty minutes wandering the vast halls and staircases of the Bargello, until he coerced a cleaner to escort him to the museum director's office.

Pisani arranged his face into a mask of competence and entered without knocking.

Marco Seuss, the director of the Bargello Museum, swore, pushing the secretary off his lap, sending the junior man tumbling to the carpeted floor.

Amused, Pisani waited as the Seuss tidied himself away, his secretary slipping past into the hallway, adjusting his shirt and trousers.

'Yes?' Seuss asked, making no attempt to explain away what Pisani witnessed.

Pisani filed the information about Seuss and his predilections, information was a tradable commodity in Italy. 'You called me here,' Pisani replied, a smile lurking on his lips.

'No, you are mistaken—'

'I am not,' Pisani said. 'You called about a theft.'

Seuss relaxed, as if Pisani's employment and his knowledge of the director's dalliance were of no consequence.

'Ah yes, the theft, although I suspect it's not the only one. We provide authentic experiences for our visitors, and they repay us by stealing our exhibits. So we hide everything behind glass and they complain that they can't things. So we replace the exhibits with replicas but then scholars write to the newspapers claiming we are stifling their studies, calling us a cultural jail instead of a reference library for the people. A thankless job. We have thefts, yes, all the time, but we keep them quiet. If the public knew what went missing, they'd never allow another tourist into the city and tourism would die. And our country with it, no?'

Pisani wet his lips to reply, but Seuss continued.

'Italy can't afford to lose its tourists, any more than it can afford to squander its artistic treasures. I wouldn't have bothered calling you over one knife, no, but it isn't just a knife. More like the entire knife block, or the kitchen itself.'

Intrigued, Pisani sat down.

'Coffee?' Seuss asked, before filling Pisani in on his suspicions.

'It's hard getting good staff, yes?' Pisani quipped, sipping on the espresso delivered by the slender man who'd most recently been in the director's lap.

The director's eyes narrowed. 'Not all the staff are under suspicion,' Seuss replied, offering a list to Pisani. 'I've narrowed the suspects down to half a dozen possibilities, based on the dates of their employment, and from what I know of their backgrounds—'

'What they want you to know about their background, you mean?' Pisani clarified.

'We are a small family here, and I attempt to get to know my staff on a personal level—'

'I saw that,' Pisani smirked, taking the list from the man's manicured hands, noting that the names had several things in common — all men and all foreigners. 'But I still need the employment records for your staff and a list of everything which is missing,' Pisani said, dismissing the worthless list from his mind.

'That is unnecessary, I have prepared this list of suspects. We have a big gala next week and we must tidy this up before then. And as for a list of the missing articles, impossible. The museum doesn't have a register of everything on exhibit, let alone in storage. I have only been here for two years, an inadequate amount of time to fix the disaster I inherited.'

Pisani allowed Seuss to rant about the inequalities in

Italy's museum sector, how hard it was finding good Italian staff, and how difficult the budget made his job, before realising Seuss didn't want the thief found or the stolen exhibits returned. Calling the police was the director's method of protecting his position. If they couldn't find the thief, the fault would be the police's. And if they found the thief, it would be the conscientious museum director who'd identified the discrepancies, bringing it to the authorities for further action. Either way, Seuss would come out of it as untouchable as the Madonna herself. Pisani wouldn't win regardless of his results. The coffee in his stomach soured.

Seuss was like Romulus and Remus, suckling from the government's coffers. Pisani felt used. Fonti misled him, Nucci hated him, and now this investigation, where the possibility of any glory faded with every breath.

Pisani and Seuss walked through the public galleries, sidestepping tourists mingling in clumps around the artworks, damp jackets steaming in the warm, close air of the museum. Pisani never bothered visiting the cultural heart of Florence, save what they had required him to do as a child. He knew the art was here; that it was priceless, and that it belonged to Italy. And as a policeman, he recognised it needed better protection, but he also knew that there was never enough money for that.

When Seuss stopped at the latest exhibition, Pisani's jaw fell open at the scenes of opulent daily life spanning the Baroque and Renaissance times, moving into more modern times and showcasing the Reformation and the Age of Enlightenment. All of which lay within easy reach. Any semi-competent thief could pocket almost anything on display, barring the furniture, although thinking of all the thieves he'd arrested, he thought of a few of them would give the enormous tables and sideboards a try.

'You leave all this out in the open?' Pisani asked, shaking his head at the stupidity.

'Yes, our visitors want an experience. All the best museums are like this.'

'How do you monitor everything?' Pisani asked, taking in the long hall, thronged with tourists.

Marco Seuss pointed towards the ceiling and two boxy cameras.

'Who monitors the footage? How many cameras do you have?'

'It is the new world officer, we have the best cameras which monitors everything that happens.'

'I assume you don't see everything or I wouldn't be here now would I?' Pisani said. 'Take me to your security room, show me this technology you have, that missed seeing the person steal the artworks the Cultural Ministry entrusted to your care.'

Pisani hadn't thought to keep his voice down because no one was near them. He didn't notice the cleaner mopping up a spilt thermos of tea nearby, listening. No one ever sees the cleaner.

THE RIVER

THE RIVER LUXURIATED in the anguished screams of the panicked horses. Rushing beneath the locked door of the stable, forcing her way through gaps in the stalls, she rose around them, splashing their thumping hooves, tickling their throats and entangling their glorious manes. The River revelled in the sight of her reflection in their pearly white eyes as they tried fleeing her embrace.

Seventy thoroughbred horses succumbed to The River's watery embrace, drowning in their well-appointed stables. Entombed for eternity, they joined Enzo and Nedda and countless others destined to become victims of The River's unstoppable rampage towards Florence.

The River slunk through the cellars of the homes clinging to the edge of the valley, soaking the olives plucked just days earlier, adding to their bitter taste with pollution gathered upstream, rendering a whole season's harvest worthless, and uprooting hundreds of gnarled olive trees, destroying future harvests. Karma for the way they'd treated her.

Soon, she'd be throwing 120,000 cubic feet of water per second into the ancient stone city. And she couldn't wait.

THE GUEST

AFTER HOURS of the most convoluted questioning, cross-examination, interview and processing, Carstone decided they weren't charging him, although he wasn't a hundred percent positive. The female officer, he finally got her name - Rosa Fonti, announced he could ask Julia to pick him up from the station. Not an ideal solution. Julia had been picking him up from police stations since before Scott died. He couldn't ask her again, not now.

'Can you drop me off at the Altavilla?' Carstone pleaded, the whine in his voice making him despise himself. No wonder Julia despised him. 'Since you're not arresting me,' he tried, frustrated at the ambivalence of the situation.

The policewoman shrugged, speaking with her colleague before nodding.

'Ludo will drive you to the Altavilla, but you must say sorry to the woman you assaulted,' Fonti said, sounding like his mother used to, extolling him to apologise to Scott for whatever misdeed he'd done, and there had been many.

The entire thing as much of a Mickey Mouse

operation as a Memorial Day weekend at Disneyland, and Carstone would have agreed to anything at this stage to get him back to the hotel without Julia finding out.

The odd threesome trotted back into the garage, now suffering from its own flooding issue — small tsunamis erupting under each footfall. Carstone clambered into the car, grateful that the threat of an assault charge had evaporated.

Tucked up inside the concrete fortress that was the Carabinieri's headquarters, he'd been oblivious to the sheer volume of rain which had fallen while Fonti and her colleagues questioned him, and then questioned him again. Fonti's supervisor frustrated with the answers and ordering Fonti to question him again about the mugging, the missing passport, and the assault. As if they were accusing him of fabricating the whole thing.

Carstone noticed the glee in the man's face when he thought he would be prosecuting an American. Foreigners so jealous of his country, that they liked nothing better to get one up on the Americans. That was as plain as day on the man's florid face.

The police officers had stopped to talk to a group of firemen, their helmets pushed back from their heads, all of them smoking, the water in the parking basement already near the top of their high rubber boots. Carstone guessed they were there to pump the garage out and wasn't surprised to see them taking time out for a cigarette. Symbolic of everything else in this country.

Carstone shivered in the back of the police car, his toes shrivelling in his waterlogged shoes. He would have to replace them. There was a time when the cost of shoes never concerned him, ordering half a dozen pairs of handmade shoes every year. He'd had more than enough money to last a hundred lifetimes. But two misconduct charges from the Medical Council, an expensive payout to a patient after a procedure went wrong, and an illicit affair with a client which made the papers, drunk and disorderly tickets, the list was never ending, and his cash reserves vanished, his staff resigned, he lost his licence and then his surgery. Scott chose not to step in and help.

Whilst Carstone had been at the station, the autumn sun had set, covering the city in a damp blanket of night, creating untold difficulties for the brute driving now that some roads had become impassable and since they'd left the station, they were detouring or backtracking every few hundred feet, leaving Carstone disorientated.

'Do you know where you are?' Carstone asked from the back seat.

No one replied.

'Are you lost?'

In the front passenger seat, Rosa Fonti gesticulated, suggesting directions to Ludo the driver who peered through the spasmodic windscreen wipers, shaking his head, his silence betraying his concern over the conditions. Although Carstone didn't understand a word of their conversation, he got the distinct impression that the woman wasn't confident in her driver's abilities. Carstone wasn't either. The man might be a muscle-bound god, but there wasn't much going on upstairs. On more than one occasion he'd almost lost control, taking corners too fast, planing on the oil-stained water caressing the narrow streets.

His hands gripping the edge of his seat, Carstone tried focussing on the scenery as they drove — graffiti, rubbish bins, compact cars and transit police directing the few cars foolish enough to venture out. A dismal scene and one he couldn't wait to escape. If he never returned to Italy, it would be too soon. So much for the picture perfect postcards of searing blue Tuscan skies and brilliant oranges, and lemons so yellow that they seemed make-believe, as if the orchardist had painted them just for the photo. All nestled against woven baskets of delectable baked goods and handmade pasta served by barefoot maidens, riper than the grapes on the vines.

The few street lights still operating cast their glow on the now familiar face of a youthful girl plastered to every lamp pole they crawled past. A young woman, missing in a city, like so many other girls in so many other cities. He wondered what had happened to her — either dead or working the streets, too embarrassed to return to her family.

'Who is the girl?' he asked Fonti, pointing to a poster flapping in the wind and rain.

The policewoman twisted her head, momentarily taking her eyes off the road.

'That one? That is Lucia Nicastri. One year she's been missing now, and still her family keeps putting up those posters.'

'What do you mean? Are there posters for other girls?'

'Some, yes, they come for work, but work is difficult to find without family to help, so they…' she shrugged, which said more than her words.

Carstone stared out the window, trying to spot a poster which wasn't the missing Lucia, but they all looked the same, sad eyes, pretty faces, dark hair. It was as if it was a certain type of girl who was vanishing — dark haired, slender, doe-eyed. His type. Almost like the girl from…

'I'm sure I've seen her,' he said.

'Who?'

'That Lucia girl, from the posters. The missing girl.'

He had Fonti's full attention now.

'Where did you see her?'

It had taken the entire ride for the memory to click into place. He'd seen the posters everywhere. But now he was sure he'd seen her, at the Altavilla, in his room. The girl from housekeeping. The thief.

'She's the girl from my room, the thief.'

Fonti stared at him, mouth gaping wide.

Then Ludo the driver, distracted by Carstone's announcement, lost control of the car in a spin around a corner. A solid thump as the car collided with another, flung Carstone into the security screen, slicing his head, and silencing Fonti.

The two cars lay kissing in the street, fuel bubbling from their ruptured bellies, adding to the avalanche of liquid flowing through Florence.

The blow to Carstone's head knocked him out, but as he came round, his old anger returned. 'Holy hell, you bloody idiot, what the hell just happened?'

His skull was thumping, and Carstone checked his head, his hands coming away sheathed in red. He hammered on the grill, smearing his blood against the scratched metal cage. 'Help, I'm bleeding back here.'

Panic set in as he realised his cries for help would make no difference to the people in the front. With the driver slumped over the steering wheel — his head forming a human skull sized hole in the windscreen, and the unresponsive policewoman held tight by her seatbelt, her car door crushing her legs, neither were in any position to help him.

'Help,' Carstone screamed, despite knowing with utter certainty that the driver of the other car couldn't help — impaled as he was on the spiked metal railings on the building next to them. Blood running from the new cavities in his stomach.

Carstone kicked at the rear window, then the side

windows, but nothing short of a bomb blast would break them. Flipping onto his back and bracing himself, he kicked at the side window — over and over and over, swearing at the reinforced glass. The policewoman moaned, and Carstone hammered against the partition, relief sweeping over him as she moved her head.

'Are you okay?' Carstone asked, pressing his palms against the screen.

The policewoman closed her eyes again.

'No sleeping, wake up now, you're okay, just wake up. Don't go to sleep.' Carstone's long unused medical training taking over.

Instead of kicking the window, Carstone concentrated on kicking the door. Weakened by the accident, it gave way, leaving Carstone's legs flailing in the rain.

Slipping in the wet, Carstone raced to the other side, ignoring the driver's unblinking eyes. Using every ounce of strength he could muster, Carstone pulled the Herculean-sized driver from the car, dumping him on the ground before crawling into the front seat. His rusty skills returned unbidden as he checked Fonti's vital signs.

'Can you hear me?'

He probed her legs, hips, ribs. A broken arm, and he suspected internal injuries but couldn't tell for sure, not while she was still in the car.

'Come on,' he cajoled, releasing her seatbelt and dragging her across the centre console and into the street, grateful she was on the shorter side of average.

Carstone stood in a commercial Florentine street with an unconscious woman in his arms, in an apocalyptic rainstorm, without a clue what to do next. He desperately needed a drink.

Spying a covered doorway, albeit as wet as everything else, he carried her over, his own blood dripping into his eyes, every footfall more precarious than the last. After laying Fonti in the doorway, he returned to check the other car, but the driver was toast — their face as shattered as their windscreen. Why didn't people realise seatbelts saved lives? Nothing would bring the driver back.

Carstone draped his jacket over the policewoman and tried quelling his rising panic. Where was everyone? Had the accident occurred anywhere in America, a dozen do-gooders would have materialised, offering advice and help.

After moving Fonti's legs, he prepped himself for what he was about to do. Once upon a time he would never have considered charging the door for fear of injuring his hands, hands he needed for delicate surgery, but those old concerns had no validity here, and channelling his panic and anger he charged the lock, shoulder first.

Pain shot through his arm, radiating out through his fingers. The gash in his head reopened, rain washing fresh blood into his eyes. He ignored the tingling in his fingers as he tried again. The aged wood around the lock started to give, and with a last kick to the left of the lock, the door crashed open.

Unable to carry her with his damaged shoulder, he hooked his arms under her and half-dragged, half-carried her inside. The water followed, champing at the bit to find a fresh path of destruction.

The temperature inside colder than outside, the old stones holding the icy temperature. If he found a telephone, he could ring Julia, ask her to sort something out and explain to the emergency services why he'd broken into a museum, and had an unconscious policewoman on the floor and a dead one outside.

TWO DEAD BODIES, an unconscious policewoman, a broken lock, no electricity and a storm which sounded like the apocalypse. The equation wasn't good. On the plus side, Carstone wasn't under arrest and wasn't drowning in the backseat of a police car. All things considered, his day had improved.

The rain forced its way inside, wasting no time in making itself at home. Carstone's arm and shoulder surged with pins and needles as feeling returned. A small mercy he wasn't a surgeon anymore, as he suspected his arm would be out of action for weeks after the battering he'd given it. His entire body felt like Henry Cooper must have after going five rounds with Cassius Clay. He ached, his body was sluggish, bruised.

In the darkness he found a workbench and dragged Fonti onto it. She was still breathing, and from what he could tell, her pulse was steady. She just wasn't conscious. A grave sign.

He was freezing, his clothing soaked through. Everything the policewoman wore was just as wet. He needed to get her out of her heavy pants and shirt, or she would be in a worse state. And he'd be up for killing two police officers.

She wasn't the type Carstone went for, not that there'd been any women for years. Being struck off the medical registry ruined a man's social status. No one wanted to date a pariah. But he couldn't help noticing her athletic body underneath her heavy masculine uniform.

Carstone marvelled at his situation. It seemed more than likely that he'd miss Julia's wedding, and he wondered if she'd forgive him or even notice his absence? He couldn't help laughing. It was his fault Julia was marrying again. If it wasn't for his fight with Scott, his brother would still be alive, married to Julia. And he wouldn't be here, cuddling a half-naked Italian policewoman, going into shock. Regardless of everything, of his situation, of his personal feelings for Julia, he still didn't want Julia marrying someone else when she was still Scott's wife.

The cold and shock lulled him to sleep, together with the drip, drip, drip of the water keeping time with his slowing heartbeat. Slipping into an eternal sleep had never seemed so enticing.

THE WIFE

Rʜᴏɴᴅᴀ ʜɪᴅ ɪɴ ʜᴇʀ ʀᴏᴏᴍ, like a child scared of the monster under the bed.

With cold analysis, she knew the man downstairs wasn't after her and knew nothing of her life but still the familiar fear pressed down, crushing her windpipe until she gasped for breath in the room's corner.

She needed to escape. Perhaps being outside would wash away the demons? And then she'd find a gallery or museum and indulge in the culture forbidden to her for so long.

Before leaving the room, Rhonda checked inside her suitcase, the canvas still in place. She had two days until the appointment she'd flown to the other side of the world for. The sale of the canvas, her ticket to a new life.

Oɴᴄᴇ ᴏᴜᴛsɪᴅᴇ, she pushed through the gushing weather, head down, hands deep in her pockets, she walked, following no map other than the one her feet chose.

The flooded streets filled with debris, but Rhonda carried on, flitting around the rubbish, her mind awash with flashbacks — dancing with her father, balanced on his feet, uncomfortable dances at school, her ill-fated wedding dance.

Rhonda tried rubbing away the watery thoughts, but like stalactites the memories had taken root, stabbing at her heart. She stopped to get her bearings. Up ahead was a sign pointing to the Bargello Museum, and underneath the sign, the now familiar poster of the missing girl.

Ducking in through the open door, Rhonda's footfalls were the only sound in the near empty museum. The sleepy ticket collector fumbled with Rhonda's coins and the entrance ticket fluttered from her hands onto the ancient cobbles, looking much like Rhonda felt, once useful but now worthless. Rhonda ignored it, doubting anyone would challenge her for a ticket today.

Hugging the walls of the open courtyard, Rhonda ignored the statuary on display, and it wasn't until she was inside the old building that she gazed in awe at her surroundings. Art crafted by the hands of the world's masters filled every nook. Greek gods, the Madonna, a wolf guarding its kill, a story lay behind every statue.

Another tourist meandered past, a small suitcase in her gloved hands. Rhonda watched her, remembering how she had walked out of her marriage with nothing more than her passport and a similar-sized bag containing a change of clothes, cash from the safe and a small canvas cut from its frame, leaving behind photos of her parents, the dining room suite carved by her great grandfather, her favourite coat, her pots, pans. Her knives.

Rhonda had always known her husband kept cash in the safe for emergencies, but it had never crossed her mind to use the money, until... She tried not to think about it.

Amiable women travelling alone didn't entertain thoughts of murder.

THE STUDENT

Helena spent a fitful night dreaming of a nameless Renaissance woman reaching towards a shadowy figure on the banks of the Arno, pleading for help as her heavy brocade gown dragged her under the surface of the swollen river.

Weak morning light struggled to push through the heavy rain battering the city as Helena woke. The icy morning left her shivering in bed and she pulled the blankets tighter around her shoulders, her fingers stroking her neck, massaging away the lingering choking feeling. She coughed, trying to clear the sickly sweet bergamot clogging her mouth.

She wondered if she'd dreamt the quality of Benito's work, or whether what she saw was a reality. They were his canvasses, yet from memory they looked to be mid-sixteenth century, or even older. Benito couldn't have painted them, but if he was Sim's protégé... She'd always assumed Benito was a student like her. There was little she was certain of anymore.

He liked no one looking at his art. Their tutor was the

same, Feodor Sim. Like two peas in a pod, neither liked people examining their unfinished pieces. Thinking back on it, she couldn't remember ever seeing any of Benito's finished work other than the pieces he restored for the lab.

Outside, rain still stabbed at the window, beating against the thin glass with increasing pressure.

Helena couldn't stop thinking about Benito's reaction to her seeing his art. Something nudged at the edge of her mind, a memory she couldn't quite grasp. Two men, two nights, two disastrous experiences. Yet the experience with Benito hurt the most. Of Alfonso Casadei, she'd put his grasping fingers and sneering derogatory comments behind a sturdy wall. She wouldn't think any more on the words he'd used once he'd seen the mark on her arm. His vile comments so filthy, nothing would wash them from her skin.

After Helena returned from the bathroom, she found a note slipped under her door. From her tutor Feodor Sim, urging her to come in despite the power outage, for an urgent commission, all hands on deck.

She sighed. That meant seeing Benito again, and Marisa. How would she last the next three months?

THERE WAS an ocean outside her building — a turbulent, heaving ocean rebelling against the gravity of earth. Water grasped at Helena's ankles as she dashed through the squall, intent only on getting to the lab before the others. That way she could set the narrative as the others arrived, instead of walking into the hostile enemy.

As she navigated the flooded streets, she noticed she was almost the only one out on foot. Cars lay abandoned at weird angles in the middle of roads. An ID card floated past in the bloated gutter, a stranger's face smiling up at her. And everywhere she looked, more posters pleading for information about the missing woman. She picked up the pace, disturbing a flock of pigeons frolicking in the deluge. Even with the streets empty of tourists, the pigeons remained hopeful of crumbs from her bag and followed her down the road before giving up and moving on.

Upon reaching the lab, she found the door locked. Although already drenched, she didn't fancy spending any more time outside, so knocked harder and longer. She was about to leave when it opened, Benito's hand holding it steady against the piercing wind.

'Oh, you're here,'

'Feodor asked me to come.'

'Did he?' he said, before stepping back to allow Helena inside, an uneasy look on his face, as if they didn't know each other.

Benito had coffee warming above the small crucible kept for melting the beeswax they used for restoring the encaustic pieces in their care. She hadn't seen it used for coffee before.

'Coffee?' he offered, already pouring the thick liquid into a cup, ignoring the strict rules around liquids in the lab. There had never been rules around smoking, and he had a half burnt cigarette hanging from his lips. She couldn't believe she'd ever found it attractive. Now it just made him look like a common labourer.

'Thank you.'

Helena sipped her strong coffee, still incredulous at Benito's behaviour. He'd thrown her out of his apartment late at night during a raging storm, yet acted as if it had never happened. Half a dozen times she started speaking, but clamped her lips shut, not trusting herself to stay civil.

Devoid of the other students, the lab had an eerie

quality to it, as if it were waiting. For what, Helena didn't know. She tried to avoid looking at Benito, pretending herself that nothing had happened. The thing with Marisa made more sense, if something similar happened to her last year.

Helena tried shaking off the depressing thoughts about Marisa, and Benito, and the hellish experience at the gallery. Like always, luck was not on her side, and she'd been an idiot to think it was. She finished her coffee and slipped off the stool, splashing into a thin film of water on the flood.

'Benito, there's water coming in,' she called out, certain now he was avoiding her.

No answer.

With a handful of white lab coats, Helena rushed down the hall to stuff the coats around the doorframe to soak up the water dribbling through the gap at the bottom. She shuddered to think how bad the rain must be outside now.

The awkwardness of the morning all but forgotten as she approached Benito's workbench.

'We have to get the art off the floor.'

'Why? It'll be fine,' he said.

'But the water?'

'It is Italy, everything leaks. It will be okay.'

Helena balled her hands into fists. Everywhere in the lab, pieces of precious artwork stood leaning against benches, or were stacked like playing cards, half restored, or awaiting attention, or appraisal. The lab was a riot of unfinished work with little rhyme or reason to how things were stored. And water was inching its way down the hall, closer to the art.

'We need to get everything off the ground and onto the tables,' she said, moving closer to Benito, her hand on his arm.

He paused in his work, the slender paintbrush in his hand hovering over the golden halo of a peaceful Madonna.

'Best we wait for Feodor,' Benito said, dipping his brush into the tiny pot of gold leaf.

'Wait? There's no time to wait. We don't even know where he is.'

'He left early to deliver one of his private commissions to Alfonso Casadei. You have met him, I understand?' Benito's voice lowering to the sly silk of a fox with a rabbit in its sights.

'I've met him once, but we aren't friends.' Helena blushed, the red inching up her chest, inflaming her neck and cheeks.

'He's a powerful man in Florence. You shouldn't have accused him of stealing your father's art. An accusation like that can cause many problems…' Benito said.

Helena tried regulating her heartbeat. Pushing her hair from her face, she swallowed hard.

'Do you feel the same way, like Casadei, about Jews? About the art the Nazi's stole in the war?' she asked.

Benito stared at her, his gaze hammering against her until she lowered her eyes to the floor.

A loud crash outside echoed in the silent room, making them both jump.

'Was that someone knocking?' she asked.

Benito shook his head, averting his intense gaze from her. Why on earth had she harboured romantic thoughts about the man? It was almost as if she could smell the rot inside him, seeping through his pores.

He would not answer her question, she realised that now. So instead she began the arduous task of lifting the artwork off the floor, stacking everything on the empty workbenches in case the water reached the lab. There was something else she was missing. Something that didn't add up, like, why was she the only one here this morning.

'Why is no one else here?' she muttered, stomping around the lab, slamming frames down harder than necessary, her temper impeding her judgement.

'Because Feodor told them not to come in.'

'What?' Helena hadn't expected that explanation. It made no sense. 'I don't understand. He told me to come in.'

'That's because of Casadei and your background,' Benito replied.

'Pardon?'

There was another thump outside.

'Not that I mind,' Benito added. 'I don't necessarily agree with his thoughts about Jews. Although I agree that it's better not to dredge up the past. You can't change what happened. Sometimes it is best to let things go, move on. Can you move on, Helena?'

But Helena wasn't listening anymore. At first she thought it was the sound of rage she could hear, the cries of six million slaughtered Jews surging through her veins. She heard them, but she could also hear the rush of water, and not just the gentle drip of rain leaking through the bottom of the door frame. Water gushed into the lab, gravity pulling it into the building not inch by inch, but in giant leaps and bounds.

Helena gasped and Benito broke off his monologue, his face changing from evil personified to worried artist.

'We've got to lift everything off the ground. Come on.'

They splashed about the lab like demented mermaids until they'd removed all the art from the floor; the benches threatening to give way under the weight of centuries-old plaster and wooden frames. Together they wiped the damp frames, frantically trying to save everything from irreversible water damage.

'What now?' Helena asked, perching on a stool to keep her feet clear of the water, her teeth chattering and her arms clasped around her.

Benito surveyed their efforts, his scuffed boots as waterlogged as Helena's shoes. 'We stay here,' he answered, swinging himself onto a stool.

'Are you crazy? I'm freezing, I need some dry clothes, and the water is still rising.'

'It's not safe to go out,' Benito replied. 'And if we abandon the lab, the vultures will strip the place bare,' he said, his arm sweeping across the jumbled piles of art.

Helena stared at the art, the water and the man in front of her, shivering as she remembered his words. 'I'll take my chances outside, and you can defend the art against the marauding masses,' she said, leaping off the stool and splashing towards the exit.

'Have you stopped to consider that if there's this much water inside the lab, how much there is between here and your apartment? At least we are dry in here. We have coffee and there's food in the kitchen. Change into one of the dry lab coats and you'll warm up.'

As much as she wanted to escape, she knew Benito was right. At least he was trying, and maybe this was his way of making amends? Perhaps she had misunderstood his words? She so wanted that to be true. But while changing into a dry coat, she recognised that she hadn't misinterpreted Benito's words, or actions. That's when she realised it wasn't the cold making her shiver.

THE CLEANER

STEFANO DROVE TO WORK, dodging abandoned cars abandoned in narrow streets turned babbling brooks. He should have stayed home, but they needed food, and the museum would need him today. Detouring roads made impassable by flooded drains, meant it took him half an hour more to reach the museum but at least fate had provided a parking space across the road and he limped across the waterlogged street, and through the main doors. There was no likelihood the incompetent museum director would be out in this weather, so there was little risk of being reprimanded for using the front entrance.

Waving to Lucinda in the ticket office, where he knew there was a small heater pointed at her gouty feet, he limped past the early flow of tourists, his head down.

Stefano gathered his mop, bucket, cleaning cloths, and a toxic all-purpose cleaning spray, and limped back to the entrance, keeping his eyes on the floor to avoid any contact with the tourists. No one paid him to be a guide. If they were too uneducated to interpret the signs directing them to the toilets, he wasn't about to waste his time helping them. He had better things to do.

'Excuse me?' interrupted a dour middle-aged man.

'Sorry,' Stefano replied, walking off, mop and bucket banging against his legs.

'Show me to the office of the museum director,' the man demanded.

'Ask the front desk,' Stefano replied, moving away, putting the man from his mind, until a hand closed around his wrist.

Stefano looked up, taking seconds to discern the whiff of enforcement emanating from the crumpled man.

'The director's office?' Stefano clarified.

'That's what I said, or are you hard of hearing and incompetent at your job?'

Stefano chose not to reply or to call any further attention to himself, and without waiting for the policeman man to follow, he turned away, bucket and mop clanging as he navigated the wide halls, before opening an unmarked door. Here the corridor narrowed, functional in its simplicity, hiding the minions who kept the place running — the accountants, the guides, ancillary staff until he came to an office bearing a polished brass plaque declaring it the office of the director.

Stefano motioned towards the office, and without waiting to see if the man was in, shuffled away. He preferred being as far away from the police as possible. Not that he feared them, they knew nothing, but always it was best to keep to yourself. Besides, other things occupied his mind — one more day, then he would be free of this drudgery.

Ignoring the footprints in the staff corridor, Stefano returned to the entrance, stopping to remove a scarf draped around the marbled neck of a statue, slipping the scarf around his own neck until he could hand it in at the ticket office. If he sold even half the items he'd found, he'd be a wealthy man, the washrooms a prime source of jewellery discarded at the sinks by women rinsing their hands.

He came to a gallery filled with Renaissance era art by artists unknown. His favourite room, mainly because almost no one lingered here. They came for Cosimo's art and Michelangelo's sculptures, not for sweeping masterpieces rendered by names long lost to time. He wondered if they would remember his name after tomorrow.

THE SOUND REVERBERATED off the stone walls, amplified by the ancient tiles. Stefano's heart stopped, and he needed only to follow the hubbub of the tourists to identify the source.

There was something about a disaster which drew the crowds, and from the wave of excited gasps, he expected an absolute catastrophe.

Like shells on a beach after a storm, fragments of the fingers and toes of an ancient sculpture littered the floor. A polished arm lay at the feet of a crying boy, snot dribbling from his nose, his teacher tugging at his jacket. A squall of similar children tittered in delight at the devastation in front of them, the noise a crescendo echoing through the halls.

Tears sprung from the corners of Stefano's eyes. David lay broken on the floor. Not *the* David, but a lesser regarded version by Bernini. A sculpture Stefano had spent his entire adult life caring for. It was like losing a child. He...

no, he wouldn't think of that. Grief threatened to crush him.

The museum director arrived.

'*Merda.*' One all encompassing word, blanching his skin as he surveyed the carnage.

'That will be hard to glue back together,' the policeman said.

'Clear out this room, close it off,' Seuss commanded.

Stefano flicked his eyes towards the security guards who'd arrived slower than a sloth on heat, flinching as Seuss barked at them, gawping at the destruction. Would they still have a job after today?

The guards bustled into life, ordering the visitors to leave and placing inadequate velvet barricades across the doorways.

'Do you want to find out who was responsible?' Stefano overheard the policeman asking Seuss, recognising the reproach in the policeman's voice. Seuss wouldn't put any effort into finding the culprit, he'd had an unidentifiable number of artefacts go missing under his watch and hadn't lifted a finger, until today.

'There's no point. Unless someone admits to it, there is little we can do,' Seuss replied.

'But the cameras?' the policeman gestured towards the cameras Stefano had helped instal.

Seuss shrugged. 'Even if the guards were watching the screen, look,' he said, gazing around the hall, 'everyone has left. Even if we identified the person responsible from the footage, they are long gone. No, this is now in the hands of our insurance company to sort out. It is convenient that you are here. You can tell them that the museum was not negligent in its duties. We'll go back to my office and await their call.'

Stefano watched Seuss striding back to his office, the

policeman following. He stood like a lost soul amidst the devastation.

'I'm not sure if I can repair this,' said a voice behind Stefano.

A short woman moved next to him, her stubby fingers laced through her short hair. Karen Knowles, the museum's lead curator.

'Karen,' Stefano nodded to the curator with a grudging respect. When the museum had appointed a New Zealander, he'd raised his eyebrows at the decision to use someone from a country with less history than his furniture. But she had headed off the director's more outlandish ideas, and had put together several exceptional exhibitions, saving the museum's more obscure pieces from a slow decay in storage.

'I can't imagine what the papers will say about this.' Karen cradled a piece of David's foot in her hands, turning it over as if inspecting a fish for freshness.

A crowd of Karen's minions appeared, armed with tissue lined boxes, dustpans and brooms, and Stefano stood back as Karen took over, her brusqueness replaced by a level of compassion reserved for all things antique. She directed her team with an air of efficiency and piece-by-piece the dismembered statue disappeared into a variety of crates, leaving a young volunteer wielding a broom through the hall, sweeping up the last slivers from the marble floor.

'There is a piece missing,' Karen announced in her forthright way, her hands returning to their customary position, interlaced in her hair.

'One piece? How can you tell?' Stefano asked.

'He's missing a hand. It's not in any of the boxes, I checked.'

Stefano's head swivelled like a fairground clown. The hall was empty, the circus over. There was another thief in the building.

THE POLICEMAN

PISANI TRIED ESCAPING the museum director's clutches, but he called upon him to confirm the sequence of events, absolving Seuss of any responsibility for the sculpture's destruction.

He watched Seuss field phone calls from the media, pontificating and obfuscating his way through interview after interview.

Pisani interrupted as Seuss was about to answer yet another call. 'It is time I returned to my office. Call me when you've reviewed the security tapes, and we can discuss the thefts.'

'No, no, you must stay. The insurance assessors are coming over,' Seuss stressed.

'Director, have you seen the weather? No one is coming straight over, not even the newspaper reporters dare venture out. I shall wait to hear from you. *Ciao*.' Pisani left Seuss spluttering into his phone and walked out, shaking off the taint of personal ambition, oblivious to it clinging to his own aura.

Pisani headed towards what he thought was the exit —

the jumble of doorways and dead ends unnerving him — a literal death trap. Door after door led to offices or storerooms or straight into the display halls. Then he found himself in an unusually tidy workshop, made even more unusual by the sight of a woman extricating herself from underneath a bench.

Amused, he watched the woman stretch her limbs as she freed herself from the confines of the compact space, adjusting her dress.

'*Ciao*,' Pisani said.

On the cusp of middle age, she had a look about her which screamed housewife. Not the glamorous kind in magazines, but the sort you saw at the markets, weighed down by bags of fresh produce, children in tow, whose only role in life was raising her family and servicing a husband.

'*Ciao*,' she squeaked back, 'Hello.'

'Why were you underneath the bench?'

'I was looking for something,' she said in English, pulling her bag towards her, eyes darting every which way except towards him.

'What's in the bag?'

Her worry piqued his interest even more. 'I asked you a question,' he said, raising his voice

'I have to join my group,' she said, and rabbit-like, darted out the door he'd just entered through.

Cursing his slow reactions, he stumbled after her. What on earth was he doing, chasing after a middle-aged tourist like a fresh recruit? He stopped. It wasn't his job to patrol the museum; they had their own security staff, so he followed at a more sedate rate, following the direction he thought she'd gone until he emerged into torrential rain.

Pisani hurried to his car, the strange woman washed from his mind by the pelting rain and his uncoordinated fumbling as he clambered into the car. A tribe of frogs could have lived in the frigid water filling his shoes, and his mood was as dark as the skies above him.

Safe in his car, he missed seeing a team of officers from the Carabinieri Art Squad ascending the staircase of the museum, the rain no obstruction to their mission.

Pisani took a moment to congratulate himself for his personal diligence, secure in the knowledge he'd done his job. He drove home smiling. It had been years since he'd had such a productive day, and dinner beckoned with a glass or two of *vino*. If only he could shake this headache, his constant companion for weeks, always there, lurking behind his temples.

THE GUEST

When Carstone woke, he couldn't see his arm, or feel it. He wrenched his body away from the black behemoth next to him and fell down, landing hard on the wooden floor, knocking his memory straight back into him.

As he sat up, he whacked his head on the underside, reopening his head wound. He cursed, the blood running into his eyes.

'Hello?' he called out, his heart racing, the darkness adding to his anxiety. He had an irrational fear of being in an enclosed space with a dead body, and almost couldn't bring himself to check if the policewoman was still alive.

Reaching out, his hands encountered her still warm body. He tugged the rug tighter around her, all too aware that if she woke up with him crawling back under the rug with her, she'd be none too pleased. No, he should find a seat elsewhere.

With his arms outstretched, he cast about for something to sit on, before bashing his shins on a wooden chair.

The chair at least had a fabric base. He hugged himself

tighter, hands buried in his armpits, trying not to breathe too deeply, the frigid air digging into his bruised lungs. There'd be no more sleep tonight. And then he heard something — the policewoman.

'I'm coming.'

All he got back was a mumbled stream of Italian. He groped towards her foreign tongue, his fingers brushed against a wetness on her face. Tears.

Carstone had always worked better with his hands than his tongue, but he did his best to reassure her. Her grasp of English diminished in the accident, and she replied with an incoherent babble of Italian interspersed with sobs.

'Listen, you've been in an accident. You were badly hurt. I don't know where we are and there is no telephone to ring for help. Stay calm and don't panic, at least until the morning. Do you understand?'

She mumbled.

He leaned in, and she bit his ear.

Carstone screamed.

'Get away from me,' she yelled.

'You mad cow. I saved you, and this is how you repay me? It's the bloody apocalypse outside, there's no electricity, your car is a wreck, much like the guy who was driving—'

She tried sitting up, 'What happened to Ludo?'

'He wasn't wearing his seatbelt. Darwin's Theory, I guess…'

'I don't understand?'

'He didn't have his seatbelt on and we crashed, sending his head through the windscreen. I've got no idea where we are. Maybe in the offsite storage for a museum? You're injured, broken arm, suffering concussion with I don't know how many broken ribs, so we will wait here until the morning. Understand?'

That was the longest conversation he'd had with anyone for several years. Exhausted, he retreated to the chair. His ear throbbing where she'd bitten him. Her reaction understandable given the circumstances — disorientated, in pain, and suffering from shock, fighting against the bitter cold filling the room. His medical training suggested he should return to warming her with his own body, but the logical, stubborn side of him rebelled.

The thundering rain, and the dripping leaks lulled him back into an uncomfortable sleep, marred with visions of his brother, intermingled with the face of the dead man. At least he had not caused the policeman's death, only his brother's.

THE WIFE

CROWDS FILLED THE CORRIDORS, their chatter loosened by the rain. Their day trips to Tuscan vineyards cancelled, but not their holiday. There was still pizza and gelato and art.

Deep in the museum's heart, Rhonda soaked up the art adorning the walls. Even the chairs scattered around the walls were antiques. She wasn't sure if they allowed it, but she sat in one to rest her legs, shocked at how unfit she felt. Rhonda closed her eyes to enjoy the solitude without being badgered for sex, or listening to his snide comments about her hair, her weight, her style, her friends, her existence.

Above her head hung a painting as dark as her memories — the image of a fallen wolf, defending itself from a pack of hunting dogs, the frenzied attack rendered in perfect detail by the artist, Jean-Baptiste Oudry. Unlike the wolf, Rhonda planned on surviving.

A hundred different conversations swirled around her in a dozen unfamiliar languages, words flowing over each other, the laughter universal. A group of school children giggling at the naked statues, daring each other to touch the bare marble bottoms.

Smash

Pushed from its base by a pair of boys wrestling, the statue of David toppled over. Heads turned, onlookers gasped, children scattered, teachers ran.

A marble hand skidded to a halt under Rhonda's chair. In a daze, Rhonda scooped it up and slipped it into her handbag. And melted into the shadows.

In the melee, Rhonda tried the nearest door, unlocked. She slipped through into a narrow corridor, her heart racing. She had to leave before the police arrived, and padded down the cobbled corridor, the naked lightbulbs a sign this wasn't a thoroughfare for tourists.

She paused at an ancient wooden door, her hand on the banded wood. Who knew who'd walked through here in the past? And she turned the heavy metal handle, slipping into the darkened room moments before a cacophony of voices sounded outside.

As her eyes adjusted, she realised she hadn't found the exit, rather a caretaker's workroom with cleaning products crowding roughhewn shelves, and a battalion of buckets standing sentinel against a wall. Tins with hand-written labels crowded the shelves, filled with screws and nails and tacks. Across the room stood another door. Scared the voices were coming closer, she struggled with the latch but it wouldn't budge. No matter how hard she tried, it wouldn't move. The gaping hole for a giant key providing the reason. With her eye to the keyhole, she glimpsed the watery outside world. Freedom was so close.

The hallway vibrated with voices.

Like a frightened sparrow she searched for a hiding place and in desperation she crawled under a bench, her legs protesting at the flexibility she demanded. The door swung open, and she held her breath.

THE STUDENT

HELENA COULDN'T STOP her teeth chattering. For want of something to do, she wandered into the alcove Sim claimed as his own.

'I wouldn't go in there,' said Benito, the stench of his aftershave clawing at her throat as he loomed behind her.

'Did Feodor paint these?' she asked, confusion flooding her face as she examined the canvases stacked around the walls. They all looked so familiar, as if she'd seen them before, but not in a museum or gallery, somewhere else. In books, maybe? She couldn't pinpoint the familiarity.

Canvas after canvas belonged on the walls of the Uffizi instead of in their tiny restoration laboratory. As students, they worked on less important pieces, repairing items for regional museums or for collectors without the funds to buy pieces by the more desirable artists.

Benito shrugged, sliding his hand across a painting depicting a woman reclining on an elegant chair, her hair obscuring her face.

'Who is he restoring them for? Where did they come from? From Casadei?' Helena asked.

Benito lifted an eyebrow, and Helena shivered at the look on his face, knowing with absolute certainty that she'd said too much.

'He's not restoring them,' Benito said, rubbing his unshaven face.

'What's he doing then?' Helena's mouth dropped as realisation dawned. 'He's painting them. He is painting them onto used canvases to age them and passing them off as genuine? I'm right, aren't I?'

'It is not as clear cut as that.'

'He wouldn't do that,' Helena said, but questioned what she knew of her tutor. Feodor Sim, a forger? 'He doesn't need to paint forgeries, he's better than that.'

'Most of these went missing during the war and it suits the art market to have them back. You shouldn't be asking these questions. It is better to leave it. She's pretty, don't you think? Looks as though she just stepped off the street yesterday, straight into the painting.' Benito laughed, kissing his finger and transferring the kiss to the girl's face in the painting.

Helena tugged at the sleeve of her lab coat. She had no recollection of her life during the war. Her twin was the only reason she hadn't died. Her mother had also survived, immigrating to England as soon as the Allied troops rescued them, leaving behind the horrors of the war and abandoning any hope of recovering her father's art collection or any of their plundered belongings.

'These aren't the original pieces taken by Hitler?'

'Don't be so foolish, Helena. You're smarter than that. The Americans destroyed or stole most of those.'

'And you're selling them as genuine? You and Sim?'

'We can't get them out fast enough.' Benito smiled. 'It would be disappointing if news of our sideline got out…'

Helena's jaw tightened at the implied threat.

'I'm going home to change, I'm freezing,' she said, inching past Benito. 'Tell Sim that I'll…' She wondered what to say. Did she want to carry on studying under a forger? Swallowing her pride, she said, 'Tell him I'll be back tomorrow to help clean up. He's obviously not coming anymore, so there's no need for me to stay.' She only had one more semester of study to go. She could keep Sim's secrets till then.

Benito followed her down the hall, his breath hot on her neck. He pushed past, placing himself in front of the door, a sad smile playing across his face.

'Sim wants you to wait for him. I'm sorry, but leaving isn't an option. You shouldn't have come.'

Something crashed outside, and they both jumped back. Water gushed through a hole where the boards of the door had moved.

Panic reversed Benito's former threatening demeanour as the water around them rose even further and self preservation took over.

'Help me,' Benito said, leaning into the door, trying to push it open.

Helena pressed her body against the door and braced her feet. Nothing happened.

'Push harder,' Benito instructed.

They pushed together, Benito grunting with exertion.

'Why won't it open?' Helena asked.

Benito peered through the keyhole.

'What can you see?'

Benito stood up and closed his eyes, his bluster and bravado gone.

Helena shoved him out of the way and bent to peer through the keyhole herself. It took a moment to realise that something obstructed the door. Just enough light showed the edges of a car pressed hard against the lab's entrance.

Benito ignored her and walked back into the lab.

'Someone will come to move the car, won't they?' Helena said. She tried screaming for help through the keyhole. But if anyone was outside, the heaving water drowned out her cries. As she turned towards the lab, another horrendous blow hit the door from the outside, splintering the wooden planks, admitting a torrent of debris and mud-filled water.

THE CLEANER

THAT SOMEONE HAD STOLEN a piece of the damaged statue was so reprehensible that Stefano failed to see the irony. He'd been stealing from the Bargello for years, yet the instant someone else stole something, anger consumed him.

'Who would do this?' he asked.

Karen looked at him, her expression fleetingly displaying the pity she felt for his pain.

'Could have been anyone, Stefano. Get security to check the tapes, but since they've spotted no one stealing before, it's unlikely they'll see anything this time. Too many people there at the same time.'

'We could tell the airports to look for it?' Stefano suggested.

Karen laughed. 'Stefano, the security guards at the airports are more useless than ours. No, it's gone.'

Stefano watched her walk off to confer with a colleague, the frown lines on her forehead deeper than before.

Stefano ran his hand over the marble as if it were his

own flesh and blood. With no children of his own, not anymore, the statues were his family. With aching knees, and his heart broken with the loss of another son, he hobbled away. The conservators would do their best to piece him together again, while he, Stefano, would find the stolen hand.

'THE MUSEUM IS CLOSED, escort the visitors out,' barked the Carabinieri officer to the assembled employees.

At the back, Stefano decided the instructions didn't include the cleaning staff, and tried slipping away, but another officer barred his way.

The officer addressing the staff noticed the altercation and reworded his order. 'All staff are to help with evacuating the visitors. The only persons allowed to remain on site after that are the conservators, the security staff and management. The rest must leave.'

Stefano shook his arm free of the officer's hand and limped away. Despite the directive, he needed to find that hand, but as he sorted through the faces from today, none stood out as suspicious. The children he discounted. They broke the statue, so they were already in trouble and wouldn't have wanted to exacerbate things any further. So it wasn't a child. Someone with a bag, but who? A woman? A tourist with a backpack?

As he filled a bucket in his workroom he shuffled through his memory. His shoulder twitched, and he turned the water off. Something wasn't right, someone else had been in here. He kept his workroom immaculate and everything had its place, but two paint tins weren't flush under the bench where he kept them tidied away.

Stefano limped towards the shelf. Yes, he kept the

workroom tidy, but he didn't bother dusting the shelves. Yet underneath the bench was clear of dust. He bent down to straighten the tins, his confusion palpable.

Someone had been in here. His eye fell on his satchel, hanging from its customary hook. There was nothing of value inside, other than his lunch, and nothing worth stealing. His workroom only contained buckets and chemicals, mops and brooms, glue and paint. Even his assortment of hand tools appeared untouched.

The workshop door flew open, sending in leaves and rubbish, a torrent of rain and a uniformed Carabinieri officer, a ring of keys in his hand. Stefano froze.

'You are the Bargello's cleaner?' the officer asked.

'Yes.'

'How long have you been here?'

'All my life, apart from during the war,' Stefano answered. His father had been a restorer at the museum, and as a boy Stefano had accompanied him to work, running errands and doing odd jobs. School hadn't interested him, so his parents hadn't protested when he dropped out to fill a vacancy, a vacancy created when his future wife's father fell down a flight of the museum's stairs, breaking his neck — a fortuitous accident for young Stefano's employment.

'I meant here, in this room?'

'After the officer dismissed us.'

'Can anyone leave through there?'

'Not without a key,' Stefano replied, patting his pocket.

'We will question all the staff about the museum thefts.'

Stefano's eyes flickered towards his satchel.

'*Thefts?* I thought it was the statue's hand which was missing?'

The officer raised an eyebrow. 'Come now, you more

than anyone here knows what's been happening. You see everything, hear everything.'

His easy camaraderie rattled Stefano. This wasn't the natural order of things. He didn't trust the Carabinieri, too clever. Much shrewder than the policeman from earlier.

'People treat you as if you are invisible, yet you observe things that others miss—'

Stefano interrupted, his words tangling in his throat, but the officer held up his hand, his fingers tapered and manicured. A hand as unfamiliar to physical labour as Stefano was to the truth. All his life he'd told lies — to his parents, his wife, his employer, to the army, for the army. An impossible habit to break. He was so close to escaping, so close to leaving all his worries behind him, that his hands curled into fists. He had one more day until the buyer came for the art. One more day dealing with tourists who defecated in urinals and spat on the floors. Would this clever officer thwart his plans? Plans he had spent more than a decade preparing?

'Tomorrow you are to come to the Carabinieri station for a statement. And from there…' he shrugged. He wasn't an easy pushover.

The officer left Stefano surveying his workshop; the floor littered with debris trekked in. A woman's handkerchief lay behind the misplaced paint tins. But Stefano didn't see that, just his freedom slipping from his hands like an eel on a riverbank. He remembered that men worse than this one had interviewed him in the past. He'd held his tongue then, kept his secrets, the same as he'd do this time.

Stefano sloshed soapy water over his muddied floor, swishing the mop across the ancient flagstones as he considered his options and the loose ends which needed tying off. While the interview was an annoyance, it wasn't a disaster and the trade would still go ahead. After that, he could leave the shadows of the past once and for all.

THE POLICEMAN

THE TRIP TO work the next morning was a trial for Pisani, with every civilian he passed begging him for help. As if he had time to help the poor unfortunates rescue their belongings from the threatening flood waters. Nor did he have the patience to listen to their complaints about the lack of electricity or where their clean drinking water would come from. Those were questions for their utility providers. He was a policeman and far too busy and they needed to realise that. Pisani blasted his horn at the mob blocking his path. Laden with suitcases and empty-eyed, they moved.

With the station's underground carpark coned off, Pisani left his car outside, and squelched into the station, thin hair plastered to his mottled forehead by the never-ending rain.

'Why's the back entrance closed?' Pisani asked as he walked in. 'I had to park on the street.'

'Flooding. We're waiting for the fire service to pump it out, but…' the officer raised an eyebrow.

'Typical, it's always me that suffers for someone else's

incompetence,' Pisani sniffed, drying his face on the bottom of his uniform shirt, the only part still dry.

'You're wanted in Nucci's office,' said the officer at the front desk, ignoring Pisani's whinging, focussing on the mayhem of the waiting room, where dozens of hands waved around like branches on a storm-whipped tree, angry voices demanding action.

Pisani slipped through the side entrance, ignoring any members of the public who wanted him to help. Nucci could wait. He needed a coffee. The lights flickered, once, twice, before settling, the station's power running on borrowed time.

'Pisani!' bellowed Nucci from a room filled with four other officers.

The coffee was so close, but the expression on Nucci's face made Pisani abandon the thought.

'Fonti is missing. No one has seen her since yesterday, the same with Ludo Gallo. Not since they left to return the American tourist to his hotel. The Altavilla reports that they have not seen Fonti, nor the American. I want one team to go straight to the hotel, with another team tracing the routes they could have taken to or from the Altavilla. I'm not satisfied that the story from the hotelier is true—'

'You want me to go out in this weather? Have you been outside today?' Pisani said, his face reddening.

'I'm aware of the challenges facing us, but two of our own are missing, and the flooding won't hurt you,' Nucci said, malice dripping from his words. 'As I was saying, two teams. This is our priority. The rest of us will help those poor souls.'

The room emptied, and Pisani stood alone as if marooned on an island.

'Why are you still in my office, Pisani?'

'Which team am I leading?' Pisani asked.

'Neither of them, you're assigned to Romano. His team will drive to the Altavilla and work backwards from there,' Nucci said, shuffling through the files on his desk.

'You want Romano to lead the team? Romano, who couldn't even catch the underwear thief in his own building? He's leading the search for Fonti? She's probably shacked up with the American. You know Italian women, put a rich American in their sights, and they're worse than opium addicts.'

'That's enough, Pisani.'

'I can't help Romano, I'm dealing with the museum thefts. I presume you've heard about the ruined statue I'm investigating. Romano will have to search for the love birds on his own.'

'I wasn't going to mention the Bargello incident, given everything else, but now you've raised it. I sent you there to investigate the artefacts missing from their collections. Did you view the security tapes?'

'No—'

'Interviewed the staff?'

'No, I—'

'Have you photographed the areas where the thefts occurred?'

'Let me—'

'Did you search the premises?' Nucci paused. 'Did you?'

His headache dug its claws in deeper, crawling its way around Pisani's head. 'I'm working on it,' he responded, fingernails digging into his palms.

'You can work on it harder once you've helped find Fonti - your colleague, who was working on a case with you, until you abandoned her. Let that sit on your conscience. You think you're as good as *Duca Lamberti*, but he is a hundred times more competent than you'll ever be, and he is a fictional policeman. Now go.'

Pisani stumbled out the office. Museum thefts, Fonti and Gallo, a city drowning. He wasn't capable of handling any of it. Everyone knew it, even him.

THE RIVER

THE SCENE above The River fuelled her anger, and she flung herself at the foundations of the Ponte Vecchio. Like ants, the jewellers scurried above her, ferrying their gold and treasures to safety. How dare they? By choosing gold above the lives of their fellow citizens, they had chosen death. There was a darkness staining their souls the way oil slicked her shores and killed the life deep beneath her rushing flow. Let their gold-tarred lives grow dim as they struggled beneath her waves. She saw everything. She would have her revenge. Let heaven mourn them, she wouldn't.

With an inhuman howl, she ripped a pair of sculpted wooden angels from the walls of an antique shop on the riverbank, tossing them into the rising water. Punching them until they splintered unrecognisable into sharp gold-painted daggers of cypress. Let the angel's wings pierce the hearts of the unworthy.

And still her power grew. The River flowed at 145,000 cubic feet per second as she welcomed the melt from the Monte Falterona, shivering with delight. Then a sudden sadness tainted her joy. The River stilled for a moment as the bloated corpse of an Apennine wolf joined her flow, carried into her arms by the melting snow, a bullet lodged in its shaggy grey neck. Shot and left to die.

The River ferried the wolf's body to a copse of trees, where she let it drift into the undergrowth. A fitting resting place for the noble animal. Superior to humankind in every single way.

Anointing the wolf with her watery finger, The River returned her attention to the sinners in her midst. No praying to their gods of polished marble or gilt-framed icons could save them now. She whipped herself into a twenty-foot vortex of water and mud and hurled herself towards the heart of Florence.

THE GUEST

AN INSIDIOUS CREEPING light brushed Carstone's face, waking him. Every part of his body ached, and his mouth was as dry as sin. A crippling case of pins and needles struck him as he stretched, leaving him wondering if dying felt this way — with every limb stretched across a sharpened bed of nails, covered with a slab of concrete. He'd ruined his shoulder by breaking into the building.

In the half light he saw the outlines of furniture and ornate frames hanging on the wall, but devoid of form or identity, akin to being on a horror movie set. Any minute he expected to see Boris Karloff sweep into the room, his dark cape flowing behind him.

A rectangle of light surrounded the door, and Carstone stumbled towards it, hope infusing his odd gait.

He had wedged an antique chair under the handle the night before, and when he tugged the chair away, the broken door slammed open, bringing with it a torrent of water, knocking him off his feet.

Trying to shut the door was like trying to stuff an elephant into a refrigerator, and Carstone gave up as he caught sight of the carnage. There was no sign of the car. Even the road had vanished. Water pulsated everywhere, stabbing its way into every nook and cranny, creating a scene of devastation.

For as far as he could see, there was water — a river of mud-stained, debris-filled water, flowing faster than Bob Hayes in the 100 metres sprint final at the 1964 Tokyo Olympics. And it was rising.

They may have taken refuge in an ancient stone building, built tighter than a nun's proverbial, but there was no way the building would withstand the juggernaut coming their way. They weren't safe, not by a long shot. Even now the place moaned and shuddered as the water snagged at the foundations, weakened by centuries of smaller floods and nearby construction.

Carstone took a step into the flow, testing the strength of the flow, and almost lost his footing. It would be impossible to stay vertical in the current with the injured policewoman in his arms.

He waded back inside to check for any other exits or staircases, but found nothing other than dozens of cabinets heaving with someone's collection or stock and pieces of antique furniture. Against the walls stood freestanding panels dripping with art.

Carstone pushed aside one panel, revealing a window, paint covering its glass. Selecting a bulky marble bust, Carstone hurled it through the glass. The sharp-edged void showed an undulating slope in easy reach of the back of the building. Hectic water flowed beneath the window, but Carstone thought the narrow culvert should be simple enough to cross. He just had to get himself, and a woman with suspected internal bleeding, out of a window the size of a small coffee table, across an apocalyptic flood, and up the slope to safety, in the murky dawn light. Easy.

Carstone cleared the glass from the frame and considered the policewoman. It had been hard pulling her from the car, and that was with the benefit of adrenaline. He could leave her here to drown, or he could hoist her off the desk, lift her out the window, and carry her up a hillside.

'Hey, hey, wake up. I am going to pick you up and it will hurt. Sorry, but I can't make it any easier. We have to leave here. Come on, here we go,' and he scooped her up.

Like a caressing lover, the water slipped over the stoop and raced across the flagstones, making it hard to see where he was placing his feet. They were in trouble now. The water rising quicker than his pulse.

Slipping on the stones, he dropped her, and she screamed. After hoisting her back up into his arms, he leaned against a screen, catching his breath. He was so out of shape, there'd been a time when he been able to run ten miles without breaking a sweat, followed by a hundred pushups. Now he struggled to carry an average-sized woman ten paces. He was a walking heart attack waiting to happen.

'Come on, got to go through the window. Can't go out the door.'

She whispered something.

'What?' he leaned in, despite being close enough to smell the blood on her clothes.

'The oil painting,' she said.

'What? What painting?' Carstone spun to look. There were at least two dozen paintings hanging on the screens, and more in piles on the furniture, as if someone had expected the flooding and had made sure everything of value was up high.

'That painting,' she repeated, pointing towards an oil painting caught in the light from the glassless window.

The painting had as much water in it as there was surrounding them, except the people in the painting had a boat. He shifted her weight, conscious that the water was now past his waist, and rising, fast.

'It is just a painting, and we have got to leave before we're fish food.'

'Take the canvas too,' she wheezed with a manic intensity.

'You're joking? It's safe hanging there, but we're not.'

He balanced her backside on the window ledge, ignoring her cries.

'I am not saving a bloody picture.'

'You have to, it is *The Storm on the Sea of Galilee*,' she said, struggling to catch her breath.

Had she punctured her lungs?

'It's priceless,' she added.

Carstone had never heard of it, but its value made it suddenly very appealing. 'Fine,' he said through clenched teeth, 'I'll come back for it, but we've got to leave now.'

Water, which had lapped at his legs, now reached his waist, sending shivers of fear right through him as he wasted precious moments wedging the painting into the window frame for later extraction.

He clambered through the window, lowering his legs into the current, nearly losing his grip — the flood a hundred times stronger than he'd thought, but there was no turning back. The front door obstructed by furniture hurtling about like Russian missiles, lethal to anybody in their way.

'Come on, we have to get out, and up that hill.'

He tried ignoring the whimpers of pain from the patient, but every one pierced his heart. He'd once sworn an oath to not cause injury to anyone. Yet here he was, hauling a woman with serious injuries out a window, when what she needed was transportation to a hospital.

The current stole his legs out from underneath him, and Carstone only just managed not to drop the policewoman. She screamed in agony at the pull of the water. With superhuman strength, Carstone struggled to his feet, his eyes on the copse of trees at the top of the slope. They'd offer shelter, as long as the dumping rain hadn't loosened the earth, otherwise they'd be at risk of being caught in a mudslide and flung into the maelstrom at the bottom of the hill.

He got them to the trees and lowered the woman to the soggy ground.

'The painting, get the painting.'

Somehow Carstone nodded, before skidding down the muddy bank into the water. The flow had increased, as if the dam upriver had disgorged every gallon of water it held. Carstone didn't know whether it had burst, or if it had blown up, or had failed because of a black market deal on poor quality concrete. He had to stay upright long enough to rescue a priceless painting and get back to his patient. He hadn't been able to save the life of his brother, which might explain why he was wading back into the bowels of hell.

The freezing water clawed at him, trying to drag him under the surface. He tried planting his feet into the ground, the water whipping him into the side of the building, the rough wall stripping the skin from his arms. Scrabbling for purchase before his feet lost their grip, he hauled himself up into the window, foul water filling his mouth and nostrils. His stomach cramping as it tried expelling the unwelcome water from his stomach, the bile burning on the way up his throat.

With the dawn gloom lifting, the light revealed an

Aladdin's Cave of treasure, a room filled with antiques and oil paintings in the style of the Old Masters. At once both familiar but different. Although he didn't recognise any of them, their beauty was unmistakable. They gleamed in the dawn light. Exquisite. Perfect. Valuable.

This wasn't the time for an art appreciation class and he wrapped the sailing ship picture with a nearby rug and awkwardly clambered outside, the large frame under one arm.

There was nothing for it. He couldn't sit in the window like an Amsterdam whore, so launched himself into the water, praying he'd be able to withstand the current without being crushed against the building.

Scrambling up the hill, slowed by his sodden clothes, whilst carrying a piece of priceless art, was one of the hardest things he had ever done in his life.

'Is that you, Carstone? Richard?'

An umbrella of foreign plants hid the woman, sheltering her from the downpour.

'I'm here,' he called out. 'I'm passing you the painting.'

'You saved it,' she said, stroking the painting he'd unknowingly laid across her chest.

Carstone pushed his way into the confined space, lifting the frame from her chest, wedging it on a vertical slant against the undergrowth, the painting side facing down, before covering her with the old rug. He lay back in the dirt, exhausted.

'How bad is it?' she asked, each word broken by shallow panting.

Carstone fumbled for words, 'It's not great, but at least here we are safe from the flooding. We'll be fine.'

She made a sound, the sort women make when they don't believe you.

'This is awful, since we've just spent the night together,'

Carstone laughed, trying to lighten the mood, 'but I don't remember your name.'

There was no immediate response from the woman, but her eyes crinkled. 'I would laugh, but it hurts too much,' she wheezed. 'I'm Rosa, Rosa Fonti.'

THE WIFE

RHONDA DARTED from the cleaner's workroom like a fox fleeing from a pack of hounds on the hunt. Ducking past dawdling Americans and gawping Germans, she hid amongst a group of middle-aged Englishwomen tittering over the statue's destruction.

Her bag banged against her hip as she moved out of the way of uniformed men shoving their way through the crowds into the Bargello Museum. They didn't register her presence, except one of the group who threw an apologetic smile her way as she shrank against the wall to allow them space to pass.

Satisfied no one had followed her, she darted into the rain, rushing away from the museum. Where to from here? She couldn't wander around Florence with a stolen artefact in her bag. That might invite questions involving the police, and they would notify her husband. She should have left the hand at the museum. Now one moment of stupidity threatened to derail her life.

Head down, she stumbled through the Niagara-like puddles forming around her, oblivious to the rubbish floating in the overflowing gutters. She considered potential solutions, selling it to a vendor at the *Mercato Centrale*, or hiding it somewhere, to come back for it later... no one paid any attention to middle-aged women ambling through the streets.

A green space caught her eye, and pushing through the rain, she aimed for the oasis, making a solitary figure under the punishing sky. Marble-hued tombs filled the cemetery, the perfect hiding place for the orphaned hand.

Rhonda hurried further through the cemetery's grounds, dark cypresses casting shadows on the path as she passed the unkept tombstone of abolitionist Theodore Parker, that true believer in human liberty. But Rhonda rushed by, ignorant of Parker's famous words, "Never violate the sacredness of your individual self-respect." Perhaps if she had known, it would have given her the strength she needed.

After checking for onlookers, Rhonda pulled the disembodied hand from her bag, the stone colder against her skin than that of her husband. Rhonda shivered at the memory. She thrust the hand underneath the sodden bench, and turned to leave, and found herself face-to-face with Paul Tobias.

'Hello Rhonda, your husband sends his regards.'

Rhonda's world imploded, the man's words ice in her veins. This shouldn't be happening.

'Your husband has been very unwell, Rhonda, since you left. But you know that, don't you?'

Rhonda backed away, her legs hitting a toppled marble tombstone, snaking myrtle roots the cause of the tomb's demise. Every fear she ever harboured standing before her.

'It seems a fitting place for us to meet again, in the English Cemetery, or as the locals call it, the Isle of the Dead. Or did you not know the name of this place you've chosen for our rendezvous? So, Rhonda, you'll be coming with me then. Your husband is waiting for you to apologise for leaving. He has questions which need answers.'

Horror froze her. In the distance, a large-than-life marble skeleton stood sentinel above the other tombs, rags hanging from his skeletal form, a scythe clasped in his bony hands. But not even the Reaper himself could save her now. This wasn't the end of her nightmare, it was the start of a fresh one.

Rhonda swore at Tobias. Years of frustration and fear boiling over into filthy profanities.

'Your beloved husband said your mouth was filthy, but I assumed he meant in the bedroom,' her stalker said, taking a step closer, his feet leaving indentations in the lush grass that the rain hurried to fill. Now he stood close enough for her to smell his cologne.

Nausea rising, she turned away as if to lower herself onto the tomb in defeat, and bending a fraction further, Rhonda snatched up the marble hand, straightening just as Tobias loomed over her.

Thwack

Paul Tobias reeled backwards. The marble hand against his fleshy face as solid as a punch in a bareknuckle brawl. His tongue licked at the line of blood in the corner of his mouth and Rhonda stepped forward, backhanding him with the severed limb.

Reeling from the attack, and his cheek split from the force of the first blow, Tobias lifted his arms to prevent another strike. This time, with both hands, Rhonda swung the makeshift weapon towards the man who threatened to return her to a prison she'd called home for twenty years, a cage with gilded bars.

Crack

Tobias toppled to his knees, unconscious.

Rhonda ran as if her life depended upon it, and it did. He wouldn't stop hunting her now. What a fool she'd been to imagine she'd found safety. But no matter how far she ran, or where in the world she hid, he would find her. If only he'd stayed dead. She'd done her research, so didn't understand why her husband hadn't died. Everything she'd read pointed to an undetectable quick and painless death, more than he deserved. She'd collected the mushrooms herself, careful to wear gloves as she prepared them for the casserole, discarding the stalks and the gloves, leaving no evidence. How easy it was to confuse the common Caesar mushroom with the deadly Death Cap mushroom and cooking them was no different. Cooking the one skill he praised her for. She'd left the steaming beef and mushroom casserole on the table, claiming a headache and going to bed, only escaping the house after he'd collapsed into unconsciousness. Why hadn't he died?

Still clinging to the statue's white hand, Rhonda fled, panicking. She couldn't return to her hotel, Tobias knew where it was. She'd have to find somewhere else to stay until disappearing again. Would this be her life now, running until her husband found her? But she needed to go back for the rest of her money, and for the canvas hidden in her suitcase. That most of all.

Rhonda lurched through the oblivious locals. Not a single person noticed the crying woman, searching for somewhere to hide, to gather her thoughts. A cafe, or a quiet corner in a restaurant.

She should have killed Tobias. When he came round, he'd find her. Her husband only ever used the best men for the dirty tasks he wanted done, never dirtying his own hands, unless it was against his wife — his favourite sport. He didn't need to use anyone for that.

The war changed her husband, as it did many men.

Her husband had channelled his new skills and acquaintances into a successful business dealing in the lucrative antiquities trade. She was the first to admit that in the beginning she'd enjoyed the outward trappings of that life, but she'd never been able to tell anyone about what happened behind closed doors. And Rhonda's husband knew just how far he could go, aware of how far the veneer of civility stretched amongst their friends, his friends. Her friends were no longer welcome in their lives, invitations went unanswered, until he left her with no one on her side. By then it was simpler to smile and nod and agree to everything. Easier to take the backhand across the face. Easier to master applying concealer and feign a headache. Until one day, it wasn't.

Art filled their home. It was the only part of their marriage she enjoyed. It filled their walls with yet more stored in their attic, most of it pieces he'd shipped back from his time in the army. She hadn't meant to go up into the attic space, but she'd been looking for a box of parts for her sewing machine, and vaguely remembered it being packed away upstairs. When she'd climbed up to look, the stacks of art sparked something inside her. An idea, a way out.

So many times she'd screamed behind closed eyelids when he'd entered the room, wishing he'd disappear as he'd taunted her with his cruel barbs, and even crueller hands. The hands that justified this one act of rebellion. At first she'd sold a piece of art to a modest gallery near the market. A gallery stuffed with landscapes and portraits by bored housewives. Wonky pottery and macrame pot hangers filled the remaining space. The gallery owned paid her thirty dollars in three crisp ten-dollar bills, and she felt like she'd won the lottery. For the first time since her wedding, she had access to her own money.

Rhonda hid the cash at the back of the bathroom vanity, amongst the cloth menstrual pads she'd needed less and less. From the sale of that one small oil painting, her escape plan grew. Selling minor pieces of art was doable. By hiding them in her wheeled shopping trolley, no one noticed, least of all her husband.

And so she continued; every few weeks she'd appear at the gallery with another painting hiding in her basket. Until the only paintings remaining in the attic were too large for her basket. And every time the gallery paid her, she'd hidden the cash, the stack of notes growing larger and larger as the months passed.

Then the fates aligned with her husband travelling for work with a colleague, leaving his car behind. Although she had her licence, she hadn't driven in years. But she'd manoeuvred the vehicle out of the garage, driving it to a larger gallery in a nearby town, selling the art straight from the trunk of the car.

And then she'd bided her time, rearranging the art upstairs to hide the gaps in case he ever looked. She kept house, held her tongue, and squirrelled away her housekeeping money, a dollar here, a dollar there, sometimes two dollars, never too much, counting every cent the same way she counted the seconds between the blows which rained down on her when he was angry.

No, she had to return to the hotel, to her suitcase, which contained one last piece of art she was selling. The arrangements had taken months to research and organise, using the helpful gallery owner who she suspected understood the truth of the situation. She'd felt guilty removing the canvas from its ornate frame and packing it under her sweaters and toiletries. But her inquiries had shown that it was the most valuable piece in the house, worth far more than any local gallery would give her. An insurance policy for her future. She wasn't meeting the buyer until tomorrow evening, at his gallery, but she had his phone number back at the hotel, so would ring him to bring forward their arrangements, and then she could disappear.

THE STUDENT

HELENA SCREAMED, scrabbling for safety as the water tore at her feet, pummelling her into the wall.

Water filled her mouth, her ears, her eyes. But it wasn't just flood water which barrelled through the door. The water brought with it rats, both dead and alive, and chair legs and walking sticks and cane baskets and rotten fruit and handbags and hats and umbrellas and sodden posters searching for a missing girl...

Helena struggled to the surface, coughing and spluttering, fighting for her life.

A pair of hands grabbed her as she flailed in the foetid morass, foul water fingering its way into her mouth and down her throat. Spinning around, in tiny whirlpools were shoes, and paintbrushes, and a wooden mask, its eyes as unseeing as her own had been underwater. Breathing and blinking and gasping and shivering, she spied Benito crouched atop a desk at the opposite end of the room, his expression a mirror of her own panic. Who had rescued her?

Feodor Sim's inscrutable face peered into hers. 'Are you are okay?' he asked, his hands still grasping her arms.

Helena nodded. She had no words, her thoughts on his forgeries forgotten.

'Feodor, is it safe?' came a voice from the corridor, a voice she couldn't place.

'Thank you,' Helena said, wiping the foul water from her face, the overpowering stench triggering more coughing as she tried expelling what she'd swallowed, her mind still reeling from the shock of the flood.

Feodor waded deeper into the lab, towards his art as the stranger appeared, well-dressed and somewhat familiar. Helena recognised him, but couldn't place him. A client, or another artist?

'Is everything safe?' he called to Feodor, ignoring Helena and Benito.

'I'm checking, Leo.'

'We moved everything to safety,' Benito called out from his perch.

'You moved my art?' Feodor asked. 'You know the rules about entering my workspace.'

'But the water was—' Helena started.

'They moved it,' Feodor said to the stranger.

The stranger waded into the lab, his long black jacket billowing up behind him. He ignored Helena, joining Feodor in the alcove where Feodor's art lay in haphazard stacks safe from the water.

'We can't leave everything here, Feodor,' the other man said. 'Not now. There will be people searching, thieving.'

'Maybe they won't come here, and the water level won't rise any more?' Sim replied.

'We can't take the risk.'

'We won't be able to move everything,' Feodor said, swaying in the water's embrace.

While Feodor conferred with the stranger, Benito clambered across the tables to Helena.

'Go,' he said, leaning into her.

'What?'

'Just go, Helena, while they're occupied.'

'I don't understand?'

The room fell silent.

'You won't be leaving, at least not in the way you're expecting,' said the man called Leo.

Helena turned towards Feodor, who was shaking his head, his face inscrutable.

'Please bring her closer, Benito.'

'The water is rising, we should go while we can,' Benito replied, his arm snaking around Helena's shoulders.

'Then no one will miss her,' Leo replied.

'Benito? What's happening? What does he mean?' Helena asked, her blood turning to ice.

'You shouldn't have touched Benito's things, or looked through my art,' Sim said. 'And as for going to Casadei's gallery. You foolish, foolish girl.'

Benito's arm tightened around Helena's shoulders, as he inched backwards, closer to the exit. Not understanding his intentions, Helena fought against Benito's embrace, dragging her feet, making it difficult.

'You need not have worried about the art, Helena, we are art restorers. What does it matter if the water damages one or two paintings when the city has a surplus?' Feodor said. 'Besides, the damage adds a particular level of authenticity, yes?'

'I don't understand. I won't say anything,' Helena said.

'You don't have to understand but you have seen things you should not have, and for that, well, we are fortunate that my dear colleague, Leo Kubin, has a unique artistic talent. A talent awarded by many accolades from the art world.'

Kubin squeezed a blob of oil paint onto the back of his hand and dipped a fine-tipped brush in the thick black paint.

'I won't tell anyone about your art, I swear. I'll go back to England and that will be the last you will ever see of me,' Helena babbled, struggling against Benito's arms in the rising water.

'Life is not that simple, my dear,' Feodor said. 'After today, many people will be dead or missing. One more is neither here nor there, and it is what Signore Casadei instructed after your brief visit the other night. Nothing can compromise our business, not even a girl like you.'

'She's right though, we should get out while we still can,' Benito said, the water up to his waist.

'You haven't seen Leo work before, have you?' Sim asked. 'Watch and learn. It is fascinating, masterful. Has Kubin not been an effective tutor, Benito? It is a sought after skill and you should be proud to be his student, to carry on his work.'

'But Helena isn't like the other girls,' Benito said. 'You can trust her. Leo doesn't need to paint her.'

Kubin looked on with hungry eyes, staring at Helena. Without taking his eyes from her face, tapped his brush against the canvas, leaving a gash of black on the empty rectangle.

Helena threw her head backwards into Benito's forehead, howling, the pain intolerable. Surprised by the sudden jolt, Benito released Helena's arms, sending her tumbling into the water.

Kubin lifted his brush, before stabbing it against the canvas, shading the beginnings of a face, Helena's face.

Helena screamed again, tearing at her own features as if they were on fire.

'Stop it,' Benito yelled, his attention on Helena and the lines opening on her face.

'Keep watching,' Sim said, his eyes blazing.

Kubin ignored Benito, his gaze following Helena's every thrash, every splash, soaking up every anguished wail and transferring her agony onto the canvas with his brush.

Benito's head flicked between Helena and the artist, before lunging for Kubin, knocking the canvas from his hands, sending it spiralling into the chaotic waters.

'Get out, Helena, run.'

Helena needed no encouragement. Her cheeks bleeding, she struggled against the violent water into the outside world where the current snatched at her bleeding body, tugging her downstream with the dregs of the city, swirling and sinking and drowning and diving and struggling.

'Oh, Benito, what have you done?' Sim asked, as Kubin's ruined canvas floated facedown on the water filling the lab.

THE CLEANER

CHURCH BELLS WOKE STEFANO. The tolling wasn't unusual, churches surrounded them, but it was far too early with the sun not yet risen. When the discordant sound of honking car horns joined the bells, Stefano woke.

Stefano limped towards the window. His bedroom looked out onto the walls of his neighbours, so close he could reach out and touch them. But it meant he could see nothing of the road beyond the building. His wife's room had a better view.

He peered into Carmela's room; she appeared unbothered by the bells and horns; her face still in sweet repose, her dreams holding her captive. Stefano stepped over to the window overlooking the street leading towards the Arno. It was here she sat everyday waiting for the return of a boy who would never come, her mind betrayed by her all-encompassing grief. Twenty-five years and she couldn't move beyond the day she'd heard their son wasn't returning. She'd refused to believe, and so waited at her window, forsaking her husband, her friends, her life. Her silence his punishment.

The view delivered through her window was its own tragedy. It wasn't their son marching up the road to greet his mother; it was the river.

Neighbours filled the street below as the water rose. The local butcher stood in the street bellowing at the residents to get out. In life he was a giant of a man, but seeing him in the water he looked nothing more than average height, chopped off at the waist, moving through the churning black water.

Stefano should think of moving them both to higher ground, but logic said the water wouldn't reach them on the second floor. The Arno had never flooded that badly. No point waking her. That always made things worse. Better if she woke in her own time, and he'd be back by then. His priority now was his art. Not the museum's art but his private collection, the art he'd spent years squirrelling away for the rainy payday he deserved. Today was to have been his payday. Cashing up his extensive collection and disappearing with Carmela into the Tuscan hills they loved so much.

Stefano wasn't thinking straight, he had to get to his collection. It was too near to the Arno to escape the flood waters. Of the museum, he gave no thought.

Whilst dressing, he chose his old army boots, knowing the weathered leather would at least keep his feet dry. By the time he reached the bottom of the staircase, wet feet were the last of his concerns.

The water had pushed its way inside, filling every corner and pouring through cupboards and family albums, ruining decades of memories and wiping away the last remnants of their son.

Stefano hesitated, looking back towards Carmela's room. Their old bedroom, the one they had shared in happier times. Should he tell her? No, he'd let her sleep.

She wouldn't venture downstairs, and he didn't have time to worry about her reaction. For two decades he'd fretted, keeping his secrets, putting her safety first. But now he had to save his art. He'd be back soon enough.

Stefano smiled as he realised the flood was a welcome answer to his prayers. They would blame his disappearance on the deluge, leaving him to vanish like a mist, with no streetlights or neighbours to witness his flight. And he and Carmela would live the life he'd promised her after the death of their son.

His leg wasn't up to clambering over rooftops like other residents trying to escape, so instead he pressed himself against the rough wall, gripping onto doorhandles and window ledges as he manoeuvred his way against the current.

In utter disbelief, he saw one man riding a bicycle through the floodwaters, his clanging bell adding to the cacophony — church bells, car horns, the bellowing of the butcher, and even the baker leaning outside his window banging two pots together. Stefano spat in disgust. The baker should salvage what he could from his store, as food would be at a premium after today. But like the rest of the fools he lived among, the lazy baker seemed satisfied with his insignificant life and his insular circle of childhood acquaintances. Stefano wasn't like that. He'd lived, he'd seen things, experiencing a life outside the norm, even during the darkest days of the war when nothing was normal and people did things they never imagined possible. He had done things he tried to forget. But that life was his secret, festering beneath his skin like a devouring canker. He had waited years to escape that life and nothing would get in his way.

Blank-faced men stood everywhere, the hopelessness of

the scene writ clear in their eyes, but Stefano ignored them. None of them mattered.

He watched them retch at the foul stench of the water, but he remembered worse smells from other times, and pressed forward. This was nothing. At least bodies weren't filling the water, yet. The dead stink and pits of massacred men, women and children emit the peculiar stench of hell. The smell of this water would never be that evil.

He clung with an iron grip to the edges of buildings to avoid being swept away as a thousand other things washed past — beautiful things. Antiques, oven mitts and jars of olives. A china-faced doll with her head staved in, one blue eye accusing him of opening the gates of hell, sped past in a flash of lace petticoats soiled by the filthy overflowing sewers. Stefano passed a pet shop, the animals still in their cages. The lives of a pair of bright yellow canaries snuffed out by the waters, their tiny bodies pressed into the top of their cage, the water still rising.

Stefano encountered no one else headed his way as he floundered towards his workshop. Everyone else was focussed on saving the historic buildings and their contents. No one cared about the poor living nearer the commercial zone, left to fend for themselves — sacrificial lambs to the ineptitude of the government. The rich always prospered and the poor always died. But after today, he would be one of the lucky rich, wealthier than he had ever envisioned, as long as his collection remained safe.

Crossing the square to reach his workshop, the most dangerous hurdle. Stefano didn't want to risk being shunted by the debris hurtling through the open square, but there were no other options.

Stefano grabbed a floating chair, and using it as a shield, braced his good leg against the flow and edged away from the protective wall. The water tried claiming him, sucking him into its murky depths, tearing the chair from his hands. Something under the surface gashed at his leg. He stumbled, shuffling back several paces, hugging the safety of an abandoned doorway.

Pressed against the stone building, Stefano considered his options. He had to cross the square. He hadn't survived the war to drown in the river he loved.

More chairs surged past, hand-in-hand with boulders and tree trunks and cooking pots and clothing and the flotsam and jetsam of life, including a long-handled broom. Stefano lunged for the wooden handle like a drowning man reaching for a life preserver. Shoving the broom into the current, he hurled himself towards his workshop, using the broom the same way a gondolier navigates his craft.

Step by step, inch by inch, Stefano moved closer to his goal, alone in the square with a lifetime of other people's possessions surging around him. He heard the faint cries of someone calling for help, but had neither the time nor inclination to help anyone else. His collection all that mattered.

THE POLICEMAN

Pisani paced his office. It wasn't because of his negligence that the Fonti woman was missing. And they couldn't blame him for the city's poor planning for such foul weather. And it wasn't his fault a gang had chosen the American tourist to rob. It was more than unfair that Nucci was treating him like a criminal instead of as a highly decorated officer. He paused his pacing to sip his coffee, tepid but warmer than the reception from the rest of the team who clearly blamed him for Fonti's disappearance. If Nucci was so worried about Fonti, why wasn't he out there looking for her himself?

A post-war concrete monstrosity housed the police station — one they'd outgrown five years after moving in. But it boasted impressive windows, and Pisani had a view over Florence. He couldn't normally see the Arno from here, but that wasn't the case today. Today the Arno River crept towards him, a thief in the night, the slippery water weaving its way through the legs of foolish pedestrians, caressing tree trunks and power poles, peeking through letter boxes, climbing into cars. The Arno was everywhere.

Pisani swallowed the remnants of his coffee and, ignoring the questioning looks from the other officers, hurried downstairs and out the front door, grabbing an umbrella leaning against the front desk.

With the black circle above his head, Pisani splashed through the growing puddles, his trousers drenched in moments. He moved out of the way for a woman pushing a pram, an umbrella held above her head. As she passed, Pisani turned to see if the baby was dry under the pram's hood. There was no baby. Instead, the pram was full of tinned food, heaped in a pile covered by an embroidered blanket.

Before Pisani processed what he'd seen, the woman vanished, the moment lost. He shook his head and carried on. The officers manning the road closure had disappeared, their traffic cones too, although Pisani saw one being tugged down the hill by the water, rolling over and over, twisting this way and that, running roughshod over obstacles like a tank in the war.

Pisani's car spluttered into life and he headed toward the Altavilla. The hotel boasted of views of the Arno in its advertising literature, which didn't bode well for their guests today.

The route to the Altavilla took him past hordes of residents brandishing mops and rags, failing to hold back the water threatening their homes. A futile exercise for those in ground-floor apartments. Some streets proved impassable, blocked by cars whose engines had faltered in the rising tide, abandoned by their owners as they escaped the spiralling water. Would it ever stop coming?

After a dozen twists and turns, backtracks and detours, Pisani parked outside the Altavilla, and debated with himself what he should do. A natural disaster was unfolding within the confines of his beloved city. He should help. But Fonti…

The police radio squawked into life, informing every officer on the channel that the prison was flooding, and the guards were releasing the prisoners. Apparently letting them drown wasn't an option, despite that being the preference Pisani would have chosen if he'd been in charge.

At least he was here, well away from the released prisoners or anything else as distasteful. He battled to raise the umbrella, and with as much haste as his bulk allowed, entered the Altavilla Hotel.

'Hello?' he called out at the empty reception, water soaking the stained carpet. 'Police.'

No answer.

An air of abandonment lay on the place, increasing as Pisani walked through to the dining room — empty tables sat ready for breakfast, pastries protected under solid glass domes, a solitary fly bouncing from side to side inside the walls of one dome, trying to escape.

Pisani pushed through the swinging doors into the kitchen where the rank smell of old oil assailed his nostrils. A shadow caught his eye — a rat running along the counter, disappearing behind a stack of pots. Pisani's stomach turned, and he tried not to gag, the pressure in his temples increasing.

Through the heavy silence, Pisani made his way to the private quarters of the Altavilla management. They had spent even less money on this part of the establishment, stuffed full of retired lounge suites and wooden packing crates, old-fashioned dining chairs and threadbare rugs. Tattered photo frames of a family with too many children and little money for fripperies adorned the walls, jostling for space with nicotine-stained religious icons and poorly rendered depictions of Saint John the Baptist.

Pisani found a lukewarm cup of coffee on the bench. Not hot, but warm. Someone was here.

'Hello? Police,' Pisani said, advancing further into the apartment, the dark hallway leading to three other rooms.

He opened the first door — a bathroom with a filthy tide line adorning the white porcelain tub, three toothbrushes standing sentinel in a chipped mug next to a sliver of curled soap. The next door revealing a bedroom with a single bed and a small set of drawers, an obligatory crucifix nailed onto the wall above the bed. The windowless room felt unloved, a relic from decades gone.

Pisani hesitated outside the remaining room. He knocked once before turning the handle.

A gust of wind and rain greeted him as he stepped into a room dominated by a rumpled bed and an open wardrobe. Another crucifix held centre stage above the chest of drawers.

Mayhem reigned. Every drawer emptied and tossed onto the floor. The wardrobe stood open, clothes ripped from their hangers, strewn across the floor, joining the bedclothes pulled from the mattress. The bed itself sat askew on its base, as if someone had checked for cash under the heavy mattress.

Pisani peered out the open window but couldn't see anything. The ground-floor apartment opened onto a service alleyway which lead to the street. The miscreant had taken a chance whilst the owners were elsewhere in the hotel. Good luck to them. It wasn't his responsibility to report a break in at the hotel.

As Pisani closed the window, he noticed two passports on the floor below the window. Scooping them up, his back twinged. He was too old to be running around.

One passport had the name of an American called Chuck Tingle.

'Stupid name,' Pisani muttered.

The second also belonged to an American - Richard Carstone. Pisani lowered himself onto the bed as he examined the inside of Carstone's passport — the pages empty save for the immigration stamp from his entry into Italy two days earlier.

Pisani examined the room anew, wondering what the thief had been searching for. They must have dropped the passports in their haste to escape. He cursed himself for announcing himself as he entered the residence. He must have disturbed them.

Leveraging himself off the bed, he leaned out the window and spied another passport submerged in the water. Years ago he would have clambered out to rescue it, but he wasn't that stupid now. He'd retrieve it later, after locating the owners of the Altavilla.

As Pisani tucked the passports into his jacket pocket, he reminded himself that he was here for Fonti, not for the investigation into passport thefts. That could wait for another day. A day when the Arno River hadn't breached its banks, taking out the entire city's electricity grid. The thief had long since fled the premises.

Pisani wandered the halls, but the place was as empty as a priest's balls. Water squelched under foot as he searched the hotel. Someone had left their coffee in the kitchen, and it seemed inconceivable that it was the thief. Thieves didn't stop for a drink.

Just rattling the handles of every door wouldn't get him anywhere. He needed a set of keys. As he turned towards reception, someone hit him from behind, sending him sprawling to the ground, unconscious. In his unconscious state, Pisani was oblivious to the thief rifling through his pockets, removing the passports, including Richard Carstone's passport.

THE RIVER

Upon reaching Ghiberti's *Gates of Paradise*, The River paused. Destroying the gilded doors would strike at Florence's heart.

And at the height of her strength, she tore at the decorative panels, like a wolf tearing at the neck of an injured fawn, ripping five of Ghiberti's masterpieces from their bronze frames, flinging them eastwards down the narrow Florentine streets. The panels themselves prophetic of the flood, with one featuring the image of Noah stepping from his ark as the biblical floods receded.

The River mocked Ghiberti's audacity. She would leave nothing in her wake.

THE GUEST

CARSTONE SHIFTED in the damp ground, every part of his body aching, Rosa Fonti curled into his back, her meagre warmth almost enough to keep his shivering at bay, but still his teeth chattered.

Fonti had fallen silent. Initially, she'd wanted him to run for help, but everything ached and he couldn't think straight after their escape from the warehouse.

Of all the things they were sheltering underneath, they'd huddled beneath a painting thought lost two centuries ago, according to the policewoman. Carstone knew little about art. The art he'd owned when he was flush with cash was long gone, sold to pay the mounting costs of a practice he'd ruined by dropping his pants for the wrong people.

Pinned down by Fonti's sleeping form, and with old memories stirring, he tried moving away from her body. Of all the times to get an erection. Worse than the time at the pools when he was a teenager and Maggie Collins had worn a tiny bikini, he wasn't the only boy hurrying to wrap a towel around his waist that day. It didn't help matters that Rosa bore a passing resemblance to Miss Maggie Collins.

Fonti moaned, and Carstone put his hand to her brow — hot to the touch. He needed to get her to hospital, sooner rather than later. The rain wasn't letting up and the rushing water sounded much closer than it had been. Whether he liked it, they had to move, and soon.

'Rosa, can you hear me? The water is getting closer. We have to move.'

She stirred. 'I told you we should have moved before,' she wheezed.

Carstone's cheeks flushed at the implied criticism, but as he crawled out from under the foliage, the apocalyptic scene wiped away his frustration. The sun had finished rising, revealing a foreign world.

He couldn't see the window they'd climbed out — angry torrents of water concealed it, the building now half its former height, the rest under water. A car bobbed past, as if it were a cork on the ocean. Water surrounded them. Water filled with debris, hurtling past, crashing and banging, decimating everything in its path.

Carstone bent to help Fonti up, and she stood shivering next to him, one arm wrapped around her ribs, her face contorted in pain or fear or both.

'How?'

'I don't know,' Carstone replied, with no other words to describe the scene.

Fonti limped to the water's edge, jumping back as a rogue branch whipped past in the violent maelstrom.

'We're stuck here,' she said.

Carstone walked past the trees to check the other side of their hill. The scene was worse, and he returned to Fonti.

'We are,' he replied, his voice shaking. He'd seen a

body floating past, an old woman, her loose hair arrayed behind her as she'd washed by on the current, one side of her face staved in by god-knows-what.

'You should go back under the trees,' he suggested, 'and rest.'

'People will need help, trapped in their homes, scared of what's coming next.'

'You are in no position to help them,' he said.

'But you are,' Fonti replied, coughing, spittle laced with blood tinted her lips.

'I can't leave you here alone,' he protested. He wasn't venturing into the flood. Bravery wasn't in his blood.

'People out there need your help,' Fonti pressed, oblivious to the blood on her pale face.

'That's what the police are for. I can't help, I'm just a visitor. And besides, I have to stay with you.'

Fonti narrowed her eyes. 'You told me you are a doctor,' she said.

'I was an eye surgeon. I don't think anyone out there,' Carstone said, waving his arms towards the city, 'needs cataract surgery right now.'

Fonti snorted. 'You're a doctor. They need you more than I do.'

'I'm not going,' he argued. 'I've got a wedding I have to go to tomorrow.'

The likelihood of a wedding taking place anywhere in Florence was so low that his words made Fonti laugh, which turned into a cough, her body spasming with pain, followed by a look of surprise as she crumpled to the ground.

'Shit. Shit, shit.'

Carstone raced to Fonti's side, his medical training kicking in as he checked her vital signs. Unconscious, her breathing was shallow and bubbles of blood bloomed from her lips. Gently he moved her under the spindly trees and the priceless art and arranged her into the recovery position as best he could. He had to get help or she would die. Of that, he was certain.

'I'm going for help,' he whispered, positioning her head so that if she threw up, she wouldn't choke on her own vomit. He stroked her hair, his unfamiliar feelings making him reluctant to leave her. 'Just hang on a little longer.'

Teeth chattering, he backed out of the vegetation, and waded into the surging waters, wondering how on earth the old veteran from outside the cafe was managing with no legs.

THE WIFE

RHONDA SHOVED the statue's hand deep into her purse, which banged against her side as she lengthened her stride in her haste to return to the hotel. Drenched, she ignored the wide-eyed stares of the staff, praying that the elevator would move faster than the glaciers as she dripped onto the lush carpet in the iron cage.

With the privacy lock engaged, Rhonda sank to the floor, shivering as the adrenaline seeped away. She eased off her ruined shoes and massaged her feet, blisters puckered her heels and the thought of putting her shoes back on filled her with dread, but not as much as the terror of what her husband would do when he found her.

Spurred on by her nightmares, Rhonda needed to calm down before taking any further action. She'd come this far through meticulous planning. She couldn't ruin it now. Somehow he'd found her, but he wasn't here, yet. And until he stood toe-to-toe with her, she could still escape. She needed to think.

With her teeth chattering, a hot bath was the best

interim step. Rhonda poured a generous helping of scented bath salts into the steaming water, and leaving her wet clothes in a heap on the bathroom floor, climbed into the bathtub. The dress ruined with the taint of the man in the park, Tobias. If he located her once, he could do it again. She should have made sure he was dead. She'd made that mistake before, and that had come back to haunt her. What a fool she was, but she wouldn't make the same error a third time.

THE BATH DID little to cleanse Rhonda's fears. Every creak of the building, or drip of water widening her blue eyes, leaving her hands shaking and her heart racing.

This morning she dressed in a more practical skirt and cardigan and paged through her diary until she came to the pencilled phone number of the gallery owner.

She called reception, asking them to dial his number for her.

'*Sì?*'

'Hello, Mister Casadei?'

'*Sì.*'

'It is Rhonda Devlyn here,' she said.

If her call surprised Casadei, he didn't say, and Rhonda asked to bring their meeting forward to tonight. After hanging up, she realised her hands had stopped shaking, and that she felt in control again. Everything would be fine.

With several hours before the meeting, Rhonda packed up her room. She would have liked to have enjoyed the luxurious splendour for a few more days, but her husband had ripped that from her, the same way he'd stolen the best years of her life, leaving her nothing other than too many scars to count, both physical and emotional.

Opening her suitcase, she unwrapped the canvas and gazed at the piece of art she'd brought with her from America — a couple clinging to each other, their wrecked sloop splintered against a rocky outcrop in the empty ocean. The artist's signature, a black smear in the work's corner, originally obscured by the old frame she'd left behind in America. The frame had borne the title of the piece, *The Sloop* by German artist Carl Farber, part of a series long lost to history, destroyed by the Nazi's.

She'd been lucky that day she'd driven to the gallery out of town. The woman at the gallery recognised *The Sloop* and arranged for Rhonda to contact her fiancé, who could offer a much greater price for it in Europe. Julia had been the woman's name, and Rhonda was forever grateful for her help. Rhonda had envied Julia's story — a widow who had found love through her own love of art, although Rhonda recognised the hidden fear in Julia's unspoken words about her ex brother-in-law. Rhonda knew too well what it was like to be under someone else's control. She remembered Julia mentioning that they were having a winter wedding, partly because of her brother-in-law's relentless interference. Would Julia be with Casadei tonight? Julia was the closest thing Rhonda had to a friend, and it would be a shame to let that go. A shame, but a necessity.

Rhonda repacked the canvas, and stuffed the rest of her clothes around the painting, before rescuing the statue's marble hand from her handbag. Blood still marred the pristine white of the stone, so she rinsed it off in the cooling bath water. Her attempt at a Salvador Dali painting — the marble hand laying on the bottom of the bath, the water tinged pink by the blood. Leaving it to soak, she packed away her toiletries, wiping the sink and countertop, a lifetime of habit hard to break.

Satisfied that she'd packed everything, save the dismembered hand, she straightened the sheets on the bed, although they didn't need any attention. Her husband had always been so particular that she didn't think she'd ever break the habit. On an impulse, she ripped back the covers to expose the white cotton sheets, leaving the cover crumpled on the floor. It took every ounce of willpower to leave it there and not straighten things up.

Retrieving the hand from the bath, she wrapped it in a towel and jammed it into her suitcase, then closed the lid, tugging the leather straps taut. She wouldn't be coming back here tonight. After her meeting, she'd take a bus to obscurity and to a fresh start.

The hotel asked no questions about her early check out when she settled her bill other than to enquire if she'd enjoyed her stay. Rhonda asked the concierge to arrange a taxi for her, demurring when he asked where she was going. The fewer the people who knew, the better.

Outside the hotel the rain fell in sheets, the overflowing gutters gurgling as tidal-like forces sent the water hurtling along the cobblestone streets.

Once she was in the taxi, her suitcase in the trunk, she allowed her mind to wander further afield and imagined herself sipping wine on a patio overlooking an olive grove. Tending a small garden and baking her own bread. The villagers would describe her as the widowed American lady who lives on her own and dabbles in watercolours. Kind enough, but keeps to herself, except at Christmas, when she showered the local children with expensive gifts. That was the life she deserved.

The taxi pulled up outside a nondescript building, and Rhonda had to check with the driver they were in the right place. He double checked the written address, nodding and pointing to an old wooden door nearby.

Rhonda paid the driver from her ever diminishing stack of money, and with her suitcase in one hand, knocked on the ancient door.

'Hello.'

THE STUDENT

HELENA GAVE UP, the flood ripping away her will to survive, leaving her as nothing more than a log in the water, a lost shoe, an abandoned umbrella. Until the moment a man on top of a nearby car, with a camera slung around his neck, dragged her onto the roof of a blue Volkswagen Beetle.

Helena lay on the car's roof, clutching the legs of her saviour, scared that if she let go, she'd fall into Dante's hell. She couldn't help thinking of Benito, the deep gouges on both cheeks a physical reminder of what she'd escaped, the memory so real she was sure that Kubin had stolen part of her soul.

'It's not safe here,' the cameraman said. 'The pressure will rip this car away like the others. We have to get to higher ground. Can you manage?' he asked.

Helena pulled herself to her knees. She'd seen several cars swing into the current like rats following the Pied Piper. She wasn't ready to die, not yet.

'Keep hold of me, and we'll make our way over there,' he said, pointing to a nearby church, where dozens of men and women congregated, some with children in their arms, others with suitcases and baskets filled with their worldly possessions. 'Are you ready?'

'Yes,' Helena replied.

'Don't let go,' he said.

Together they dodged everything the river threw at them. His grasp of Helena's hand vice-like, and with his other hand, he held his camera as high above the water as he could. Helena was under no illusions which one he'd save if push came to shove, but he didn't test her theory, and the crowd surged forward to pull them both from the foul water once they reached the stone steps.

As Helena stood on the steps, her heart breaking at the devastation, her saviour the photographer climbed higher, snapping images of the destruction, recording the heartbreak on the Florentine faces, documenting the incomprehensible sights sweeping past them on the flood waters.

Helena didn't think she should have to bear any further disasters in her life. She'd started life with a number on her arm, and now she'd survived a flood of biblical proportions, and whatever it was at the lab with Sim and Benito. Someone had grand plans for her, her time wasn't up yet.

The flood churned around them, the roaring of the angry water drowning out the laments of the lost. A single red shoe floated past, leaving Helena wondering where its twin was. Was it lost like her sister, or was it still on the petite foot of its owner?

Helena moved closer to one of the sturdy columns to block out the wind. As her view changed, it brought into focus a pair of two men pressed hard against a building on the opposite side of the square. They were staring at her - Feodor Sim, and the artist known as Leo Kubin.

THE CLEANER

THE DOOR TO Stefano's workshop swung in the current, battered by waters too strong to resist. It made little sense to Stefano. Regardless of the water's strength, the lock should have withstood the pressure thrown at it.

With his trusty broomstick as a makeshift crutch, Stefano made it to the doorway. He couldn't dwell any further on the failure of the lock now that the floodwaters hid it.

Once inside, his hope vanished. The room a tortured picture of chaos with nothing escaping the wrath of the river. Priceless antiquities — pillaged over decades, destroyed. Artwork by Renaissance masters reduced to splintered wooden fragments. Delicate porcelain crushed to smithereens, left floating amongst the filthy debris from the city flowing in from the outside — unwanted guests, unworthy of mixing with the incomparable treasure trove assembled by Stefano and his associates.

Stefano trembled in the entrance, his arthritic hands clamped on the doorframe. He cared not for the ruined chinaware and furniture. Of the ancient pewter and delicate ivory ornaments, he gave no thought. It was the walls of art that he struggled to reach, the swirling waters doing their utmost to drag him under their dark oily depths.

The flood tipping several panels backwards, leaving them to rest against the walls, the art on the upper levels safely above the waterline. But of the pieces hung lower, only empty hooks remained.

A deep guttural cry emerged from Stefano - a bellow of grief, a cry by a father for a son. If any strength remained, he would have rent his clothing, lamenting the death of his legacy, but he could barely stand amidst the destruction. Artwork bobbed around him, ripped from their centuries of rest behind gilded frames, now splintered into hundreds of pieces.

Stefano truly cared about one item, one piece of art, and swallowing his panic, he searched the room. It was too big for the water to have swept it from the room. Stefano rationalised that if he got the door shut, he could salvage most of the contents of the room. But that one piece, *The Storm on the Sea of Galilee*, they had a buyer for that. A buyer you didn't upset. And not even an apocalyptic flood would release him from the arrangement. He had to find it.

Stefano had two employers — the museum, and Casadei - the man he'd first met during the war, as they'd scrambled to save Italy's art from Hitler's relentless quest to collect the world's best art for his private collection. Stefano's role morphing into retaining the odd piece for personal reasons, but it hadn't taken long for that to change. The war forcing their hands — self preservation, that's what Stefano told himself. Then Casadei introduced him to Feodor Sim. An exceptional talent, a master craftsman in his own right, sought after as a restorer of excellence. Together, Casadei and Sim turned Stefano into little more than a thief.

Now wasn't the time to remember his history. Stefano didn't believe that their particular crimes had any true victims. But there would be a victim if he couldn't find the Rembrandt Casadei's buyer wanted.

At the far side, he spotted the panel where he'd hung the Rembrandt. Stefano lost his breath. Above the waterline, the panel was bone dry, untouched by the surging waters. But the heavy hooks, which had borne the weight of the masterpiece, were empty.

Stefano scanned the room, still roiling with gurgling water, echoing with the crashing of debris outside and the weakening wails of a woman calling for help, he felt something amiss with the room. Ludicrous, given the annihilation of everything around him. Instinct told him that was the truth.

There. A gaping hole where the upper window once stood. Nothing natural would have knocked the window out like that, from the inside. And although his teeth were chattering and his skin prickled, and the water reached his chest, his blood chilled as he realised someone had been here, inside his warehouse.

The crying stopped. The absence of the sound noticeable over the roaring water. Was the woman the thief? No one else lived nearby. The primary reason he'd chosen this location.

Stefano considered rescuing the pieces floating on the water, but despite their value, that wasn't his focus. The woman outside had been inside his private museum, and in his heart he knew she had stolen his art. And he would do whatever it took to retrieve his painting. Carmela's life depended upon it.

THE POLICEMAN

PISANI LAY on the hot sand of Castiglioncello, his favourite beach, listening to girls squealing at the water's edge, daring each other to wade further than the breaking waves, their tiny bikinis revealing more than their parents would have liked. He smiled, the dream so lifelike, the gentle whoosh of the waves caressing him, the sound lulling him back to sleep.

The shrieking and screaming carried on and he tried ignoring it, the sound inconsistent with the tableau in his mind, increasing as the sand hardened beneath him. Pungent waves crashed around him as reality hit and he forced his eyes to open.

He was lying on the threadbare carpet of the Altavilla Hotel, a carpet which had once boasted a floral riot of colour now sodden with several inches of foetid water. The screams weren't coming from nubile bathers, but from heavy set tourists lugging suitcases from their rooms, crashing into each other in the unlit hallway.

Buoyed by the water, Pisani sat up. The thump to his head hurt like Hades, and it took a moment for his vision to settle. He probed his head with his fingers — a lump the size of Vesuvius protruded just above his left ear. Pressing on it sent a wave of nausea through his body. Someone had hit him before turning on every tap in the place and opening every window, inviting the squally rain inside to drench the decor of one of Florence's cheapest hotels. An insurance job. Just his luck to be in the wrong place at the wrong time.

Soaked through, he stood up, leaning against the wall for support. Everyone ignored him, barging past, suitcases slamming against the walls in their haste to escape the waterlogged corridor.

Despite being surrounded by water, Pisani's throat was as dry as sin, which made speaking a challenge.

He grabbed the nearest tourist. 'What's happening?'

'They let the water out of the dams,' the man's frenzied eyes revealing everything Pisani needed to know.

Pisani released him. It wasn't taps or rain causing the flooding; it was worse. For years the engineers warned this would happen again. And the politicians had done nothing to fix it. Instead they bickered, blaming each other for their own inaction, until they lost the next election, and the sheep voted new idiots in, and the cycle began all over again.

Pisani flicked the light switch, up, down, up again. The power was still out. Splashing to the end of the corridor, he peered into the murky light. He couldn't tell how long he'd been out, but staring into the watery nothingness outside, he realised that the water level was rising in the hallway. And it was rising fast. No wonder the guests were so keen to escape. He added to the chaos, yelling in Italian and in passable English, well enough to get his point across that everyone needed to escape, and that they needed to leave now.

He hammered on the doors in the rapidly filling hallway, screaming at the slackers packing their cases, but there wasn't time to strong arm them out. From experience he knew the Altavilla had an abundance of elderly guests who couldn't afford to stay anywhere more salubrious. They needed his help more. He was about to be the officer in charge of the watery grave of dozens of foreign tourists. The final nail in his career.

He doubled his efforts, ignoring his dry throat and raging headache. He'd worry about who hit him later, when he wasn't at risk of drowning.

An elderly couple wrestled with their bags outside their room.

'Leave them,' Pisani screamed, shoving the bags back into the room.

The woman began hitting him with her oversized handbag.

'Get out before you both drown,' Pisani yelled in Italian, holding her wrists until she stopped struggling.

The woman's husband tutted to his wife, and with his money belt in one hand, rescued his wife from Pisani's clutches before disappearing out of sight.

Pisani didn't know where they'd go to be safe, hoping that someone was outside helping them, but with a sinking heart he knew they were as much at risk outside as they were inside. He couldn't save everyone, he was just one man.

After debating his inner demons, Pisani exhaled before wading through the water, trying to catch their retreating backs. But despite their age, they had disappeared before he had taken five paces in the freezing water. If they didn't drown, they would die from the bitter cold.

A door opened, and another elderly woman emerged, clutching a large handbag and a battered backpack. In her threadbare cardigan and skinny arms, it didn't look as though she'd ever be able to move the backpack on her own. What was she thinking?

'Leave it,' Pisani begged.

The woman stiffened at his instruction, spinning her scarf-covered head towards his voice, before hoisting the backpack over her shoulders and scarpering down the hall faster than Pisani thought possible.

Pisani grabbed for the backpack to stop the foolishness. She needed to save her life, not her clothes. Her patterned headscarf slipped from her curler-filled hair in the melee. It wasn't just the scarf that moved, her curly grey hair slipped too. A wig disguising her correct age.

The fleeing woman wrenched the backpack from Pisani's hands, hurling herself towards the exit. The water kept rising, leaving a slight gap between the surface of the water and the ceiling.

There was nowhere to go but up.

The woman's headscarf and wig floated past, followed by her handbag, the bag leaking passports and cash as it sped past on the surging water.

'Stop,' Pisani instructed.

She didn't.

Pisani lunged for the wig and the passports, holding them in his hands, before connecting the dots — the thief. He took off after the imposter, the water and backpack impeding her escape. 'Do you want to die?' he yelled, fearful for his own life now that his feet couldn't touch the floor.

He'd been an excellent swimmer in his youth, one of the few things he'd excelled at. And although he wasn't fit, his body remembered what to do, and he struck out in a mutated overarm crawl through the frigid water. He saw the woman reach the fire exit, a heavy glass door barring her way. She kept sinking under the water in her efforts to hold the backpack out of the water.

'Let it go,' Pisani yelled, kicking harder towards the woman.

She surfaced for a moment, still clutching the bag as she tried opening the stairwell door.

With a final powerful kick, Pisani reached the struggling woman as she disappeared under the rising water, hauling up, yanking the bag from her hands.

'No,' she screamed. 'No, no, no.'

She fought him, weakened by her struggles, and the bag sank to the bottom. The thief dived after it, disappearing in the darkness.

Pisani panicked. They had to get higher.

With a deep breath, he ducked down, wrapping his arm around the woman's waist, hauling her to the surface. The strain almost killing him, his brain threatening to explode with the exertion. The stupid woman held her backpack in her arms, holding it above her head as if it were the infant Moses himself.

Pisani didn't have the power to open the door against the crush of the water on his own, not anymore.

'Please help,' he pleaded, hopeful that she understood his words. The water sucking the English from him, and he spoke in Italian.

She must have understood, because she placed one hand on the handle, just above his, pulling when he did, bracing her feet, her backpack precariously wedged between her shoulder and the ceiling.

The glass door budged a fraction.

'Again,' Pisani said, his face red with effort and fear.

Together, the policeman and the thief pulled, and it opened. With her backpack gripped in her arms, the woman was first through, pushed from behind by Pisani whose head was scraping against the stained ceiling of the Altavilla's hallway. He prayed the couple had escaped because he couldn't help them now. He drew a deep breath before ducking his head under water to follow the woman through the fire exit and up the stairs to the safety of the second floor.

Pisani broke the surface and stumbled upstairs, hitting his shin. His leaden shoes and heavy clothes making every step an exercise in mental perseverance. Somewhere nearby he heard the muffled cries of a baby echoing through the corridor. And with no conscious thought, he muttered a silent prayer for the babe and its mother. They'd all need divine help before this day was over.

Pisani wanted nothing more than to close his eyes for a moment, but to do that meant death. Death for the elderly couple outside, and death for anyone else still stuck in their ground-floor apartments here at the Altavilla, or any ground-floor apartment.

For all his personal issues, and shameful ladder climbing at work, he'd joined the police to serve, and the people needed him.

THE RIVER

The River slithered into the crypt below the basilica of the Santa Croce, her reverence tempered by her disdain for everything man-made. But these men were different, They'd never defiled her, focussing instead on beauty and science. Swirling around their bones, she tossed one up, its polished surface soothing to the touch. What would Michelangelo Buonarroti say if he knew she was in his tomb? Would he demand that she abandon her crusade or beg her to becalm, capturing her mood upon his canvas?

She pushed forward, bringing his bones with her, reluctant to abandon such worthy prey. His followers should have left his bones in Rome. The River giggled, splashing the walls of Michelangelo's crypt. Higher and higher she rose, filling the space until there wasn't room for anything else.

The next tomb was just as welcoming — the bones laid out with perfect symmetry. She expected Galileo Galilei, a man of science, to respect her show of strength, but if he did, he didn't deem her questions worthy of answers.

The River roared, her rage palpable as she whipped

Galileo into a maelstrom of bones and dirt and filth, mixing his remains with those of Michelangelo and Niccolò Machiavelli. Her fury implacable as she rushed through the empty tomb of Dante, screaming his name. Dante's vision of hell nothing compared to what she was unleashing upon Florence's population.

Then rushing through the storm water drains, The River shot upwards, sending iron drainage grills up into the sky, ricocheting off the walls of ancient buildings. As a geyser, she spewed filthy water tainted with heating oil into the streets, showering the desecrators in filth.

And still she rose, staining every building she touched. Five feet, six feet, seven feet high. Higher. Eight feet. And still her level rose. Ten and a half feet. 2.5 billion cubic feet of water passing under the evacuated Ponte Vecchio.

From here she saw dozens of people scurrying across the rooftops, trying to escape. One woman faltered under the weight of a giant telescope.

'Fools!' roared The River, surging through the streets, making the stones tremble under her howl.

A petrol tanker standing in her way stood no chance, and she scooped it up with everything else in her path, the tanker no more than a bath toy as The River hurled it downstream towards the bridge she'd destroyed twice before — once in 1117 and again in 1333. The bridge the Florentines kept rebuilding — the Ponte Vecchio.

The tanker careened into the centre of the bridge, where The River bashed it again and again into the central archways. Over and over, the sound echoing through the city, louder even than The River herself.

Again and again, she hammered the truck against the arches, until the stone arch gave way.

The River rushed past, crowing with triumph, her arms full of more debris to fling at the city, reminiscent of a priest on Saint John the Baptist's Day, throwing alms to the poor.

Smashing through the middle of the Ponte Vecchio had released the pressure she'd been building, and she wailed louder, her plans thwarted by a foolish mistake. Who was the fool now?

THE GUEST

Rocks the size of enormous dogs hurtled past at tremendous speed. How they were still on the surface of the water was beyond Carstone's understanding of physics, but two such missiles had missed him by mere inches in the first five feet he'd ventured into the maelstrom.

Above him stood a clock tower. He'd been watching it, and it hadn't budged from 5:00am. It must be later than that. His watch had stopped working hours ago — being submerged in frigid flood waters hadn't done it any good.

He didn't have the faintest idea where to go for help. Somewhere where there were people. With no Italian language skills to communicate his needs, he'd just have to hope he'd find someone who spoke English, and they could ring for help. Thank god the street signs were high on the building walls instead of protruding from lamp posts. He'd seen plenty of those being flung down the rapids he was now trying to cross. Every step he took bucked him further into the chaos, and as much as he was trying to stay on the edges, he expected to fail. He always did. His life was a complete and utter failure. His brother Scott knew that.

Scott had tried to help him and look how that turned out. It had killed Scott. Carstone almost allowed the flood to take him. That would solve his problems and wash away the weight of his guilt. Death reuniting him with his brother.

A scream.

Carstone looked up to see a woman with a child in her arms, perched on the apex of a nearby roof. Surrounded by water, nowhere for them to go.

'Stay there,' he yelled. They were safer on the rooftop than anywhere else. He should know. He was being battered from all sides, from things seen and unseen. His legs a riot of colourful bruises.

The woman screamed at him in Italian, but he carried on. He had to find help for Rosa, or she would die. The mother and child were safer where they were. They just needed to sit tight.

'Don't move,' he called back, miming his words.

The sound of the water had reached near eye-splitting decibels, joining with clanging church bells, shattering windows and pulverised buildings.

Another giant rock hurtled past, missing him by less than an inch. He pressed his back into a nearby wall, clinging to a yellow Kodak sign hanging above the window, the glass long gone and the photography workshop awash with water.

The shriek of splintering wood rent the air.

As Carstone searched for the origin of the noise, a tiled roof washed past, intact, as if a giant had plucked it from a playhouse, flinging it to the ground in a fit of rage.

The sight chilled him, and although he didn't want to, he turned to look for the woman and her daughter. They weren't on the roof, because the roof wasn't there, neither was the building. Washed downstream. Two lives crushed by rocks, and trees, and building materials.

'No!' Carstone screamed, scanning the churning water, splashing out towards where the building had been, but he was fighting against the current. He should have helped them, they had needed him. He gave up and let the water take him.

'I'm coming Scott,' he said, his tears adding to the river's flow.

A tiny wail reached his ears just as the water sucked him under. He kicked up with his feet, once, twice, breaking the surface.

A child's cry.

The girl was within reach, her mother gone.

With a surge of power, he grabbed the child, clasping her to his chest, the roiling water tossing them like ships during an ocean storm. Alive, but destined for death. How was it a man responsible for his brother's death now held the fate of two strangers in his hands? Fonti first and now this innocent child?

His arms tiring, he tried readjusting his hold, and the girl responded by clinging tighter to his neck, choking him. He couldn't let go, he had to persevere. He spied an old man inching along the side of a nearby building, making his way against the flow of water.

'Help us,' Carstone rasped.

The man glanced their way before trudging past, using an old broom handle as a walking stick.

'Mister, help!' Carstone said, trying to steer them towards the man.

'Bastard,' Carstone screamed as the man ignored them.

The tears on his face were nothing compared to the flood water, and on and on they flowed, until a floating thicket of trees and vines and crops and farm equipment impeded their progress.

Carstone clung to a log stripped of its branches, the girl wedged between him and the tree, his arms under her shoulders, holding her out of the water as much as possible. Did he have the strength to carry on?

'*Mama?*' the girl asked, her voice muffled in Carstone's shoulder.

He didn't have an answer for her, but felt her grief as much as the grief in his broken heart. He held her and hoped that keeping her safe absolved him of his crimes.

'What's your name?' he asked, trying to stop his teeth chattering.

She whimpered into his chest, her tiny fingers like bird talons around his neck.

'I'm Richard. My name is Richard. What's yours?'

Her fingers loosened a fraction, and without startling her, Carstone pulled forward to release the pressure.

'Lola,' she replied, interpreting his question.

'Lola? That's a charming name,' Carstone said. He rabbited away, conscious she wouldn't understand a single word, but he was doing it more for his sanity than hers. He didn't know how much longer he could hold on and wanted to conserve his energy whilst he decided their next course of action.

'*Dov'è la mia mamma?*' she asked.

'I don't know where your mama is, Lola. I'm sorry. But we'll find her,' he said, presuming she'd just asked where her mother was.

The bitter cold of the water sucked the life from his limbs, and soon it wasn't just his teeth chattering. The tiny girl in his arms a block of shivering ice, the grip of her arms around his neck becoming looser and looser. He didn't realise, not until her arms dropped away and she slipped from his arms.

'Hold on to me,' he yelled, shocked at how he hadn't even noticed.

Hoisting her back up, he examined her face, bruised and battered, with a gash on her forehead. He apologised for yelling, and tucked her back in the tiny protective hollow amongst the tangled debris.

'I'm sorry, I'm so sorry. Hold on, please.'

Carstone sank into silence, the girl clinging to him, pummelled by the surging water. And then they heard shouts. Voices. Men's voices, calling out in Italian. The little girl stirred in his arms.

'*Mama*?' She lifted her head away from his chest.

Carstone looked for the voices. Salvation appeared in the form of a small rubber dinghy containing two men and a dog. The dog barked, but the men were heading away from the mass of vegetation concealing Carstone and the girl.

'Hey!' Carstone called, releasing one arm to wave frantically at the men. 'Over here!'

The dog pricked its ears, barking from the dinghy.

'*Aiuto!*' the child cried. Help.

'*Aiuto!*' Carstone yelled, over and over.

With the dog running around in the confines of the small boat, barking wildly, and with the crashing of debris against ancient buildings, and the sound of the rushing rapids, and the creaking buildings and smashing glass, it was a miracle that the men heard Carstone shouting at all. But they did, pulling Carstone and the girl into the dinghy, leaving them shivering in the bottom of the boat, the dog licking the tears from their faces. Their rescuers had no time to check on their welfare, focussing instead on rescuing the other waifs.

With the girl still clinging to his neck, Carstone tried begging his rescuers to help him save Fonti, but the language barrier was one he couldn't cross no matter how much he wanted to return for the policewoman.

The water had swept him too far through the city for them to rescue her now. To turn back for Fonti meant abandoning others who were closer, and at just as much risk.

THE WIFE

Rhonda sucked on her bloody knuckle. She'd caught her hand on a splinter, and still had her knuckle in her mouth when the door opened inwards revealing Casadei, his black suit immaculate, his silk paisley tie the perfect shade of blue, with his hair swept back from his temples. A delicious lemon scent wafted towards Rhonda as he leaned forward to relieve her of her suitcase and to usher her in out of the rain.

The intricate parquet flooring gleamed, its warmth absorbed from the soft light coming from the altered crystal chandeliers hanging above the entranceway.

'How divine,' she said, taking in the muted wealth filling the room. She'd thought they were well off, in their palatial home with a formal dining room and two living areas, but that was nothing compared to Casadei's home and, she assumed, Julia's home to be. Some women were luckier than others.

Casadei smiled, his teeth impossibly white, giving a wolfish cast to his features.

'We think it comfortable enough for a home which has

been in my family for more generations than anyone can remember,' Casadei said, before noticing the puddle forming beneath her. 'Please, your shoes. These floors are delicate in their old age.'

That's when Rhonda noticed the pairs of shoes lined up against the wall. All women's shoes, with heels not designed for delicate parquetry floors.

Rhonda slipped off her shoes, placing them next to an elegant pair of red shoes adorned with large brass buckles, and felt embarrassed about her own well-worn pair of sensible mid size heels, scuffed at the toe and worn at the back. It was a rare occasion when her husband provided her with the funds to update her wardrobe, usually when he required her as a prop at an event — a living prop trotted out on the odd occasion, her bruises covered with long sleeves or longer hems.

'Thank you. The housekeeper, she is very particular, and I fear her more than anyone else,' Casadei's laughter warming the moment. 'Please, come through.'

Rhonda followed him through to another luxurious space, this one complete with a heavy leather lounge suite, scarred from at least a century of use. Art filled every inch of the walls, and Rhonda took her time studying the pieces closest to her — a mixture of modern and old and raw and complex and every other descriptor available to describe such an eclectic selection. There was no rhyme or reason to the art. No commonality she could discern other than most of them were portraits, and most of them women.

'It is not a normal collection. The taste of my family is… different.'

Rhonda stood in front of a charcoal sketch of a young woman. She'd learnt a little about art since she'd started selling her husband's collection, but the signature in the corner of this piece wasn't one she recognised.

'Is this by a local artist? I don't recognise the signature.'

'Hmm, the artist of that one? No, he is an American artist. He visits Florence to study, like many artists from around the world. Sometimes they hold exhibitions after their studies.' Casadei returned his attention to Rhonda. 'It is rare to invite clients into my personal space. The portraits unnerve other people, although I find them comforting, as if I am surrounded by old friends and acquaintances. Sometimes I see similarities to people I used to know,' Casadei added, staring at the charcoal sketch, the woman's hair loose around her face.

Even Rhonda fancied she recognised the girl in the picture. 'Is she someone famous?' she asked, pointing to the sketch. 'She looks familiar.'

Casadei leaned forward, examining the sketch, his finger tracing the line of the girl's jaw.

'No, no one special, not anymore, a student perhaps, I don't recall. So many beautiful girls come to Florence, for employment or to study. After a time, they blend into one.'

A memory stirred in Rhonda's mind at Casadei's words. His tone familiar, disturbing. Such careless use of words, and she wondered who the poor girl was, how she'd been part of Casadei's life. What was Julia getting herself into? Or was Rhonda reading too much into the wistful memories of a man in his middle age?

'Can I interest you in a drink before we discuss your art?'

Rhonda nodded, her unease quieted by the offer of a drink. Normal behaviour from a man well respected in his community, a supporter of both new and old artists. She shelved her disquiet, accepting a small glass of amber liquid.

Following her host's lead, Rhonda took a generous sip,

and tried to hide her surprise as the liquid burnt her throat. She rarely drank anything stronger than a *Prosecco*.

The gallery owner chortled as he knocked back the contents of his own glass. '*Grappa*, stronger than you are used to in America, yes?'

'A little,' Rhonda replied, coughing. She felt her cheeks beginning to glow as she took another sip, a smaller one, the alcohol creating a pleasant glow in the pit of her stomach.

'A refill?' Casadei asked, refilling her glass before she'd even answered.

'Do you paint too?' Rhonda asked, spotting a large easel standing with its back to the couch.

Casadei looked towards the paint-splattered easel and shook his head.

'No, it is not my talent. I have friends who sometimes use this space if they need the quiet for their pursuits.' He checked his wristwatch. 'One of them is due here soon. Have you heard of him, Leo Kubin? He has achieved a modicum of fame in your country.'

'Sorry no, it's not a name I know.' Rhonda didn't follow the art world other than for what she needed to secure her escape from her husband. The name Leo Kubin meant nothing.

'A shame, he has a way of trapping the essence of a person on his canvas, as you saw with that sketch you were admiring. That is Kubin's work. It's almost as if he captures the soul of his subjects within his brush strokes. You should stay, it's so rare an artist paints to an audience. He puts up with me. But your feedback would be welcome, yes?'

Rhonda shook her fuzzy head, the *Grappa* starting to take effect. She was here to sell the art, then she had a train to catch. There was no time to waste.

'Shall I open the suitcase for you?' she offered, stumbling as she reached for the suitcase Casadei had left on the couch.

'Thank you.'

Rhonda's fingers struggled with the taut leather straps and Casadei took over, his long fingers teasing the leather through the buckles with ease.

'These can be tricky,' he mused, flicking the latches with practised ease.

'It is at the bottom of the case, under my clothes.' Rhonda's face coloured as she caught sight of her undergarments, but Casadei folded everything into the lid with a flourish, revealing the wrapped canvas. Time slowed as he unwrapped the painting.

'It is not in its original frame, sorry,' she mumbled, taking a seat, the warm room leaving her woozy. 'But I can remember the details on the frame, if you need them?'

Casadei waved her apologies away as he held the painting at eye level, a beatific smile on his face.

'It is more exquisite than I imagined,' he said, propping it on his desk against a marble bust of the Roman orator Cicero. 'And to think I have only ever seen a copy before. Yes, I must have it. This calls for a toast,' he announced, refilling his glass until it overflowed before pouring the rest of the bottle into Rhonda's empty glass.

With the euphoria of selling the painting, Rhonda clinked her glass against Casadei's, her smile transforming her into the beautiful girl she'd once been. One worthy of her own portrait.

THE STUDENT

HELENA'S RESCUER, a photographer, grabbed her by the arm, breaking her connection with the artists. Gesturing with his hands, and shouting over the cacophony of the rushing water, Helena stumbled after him, nodding her agreement. And she launched headfirst into one of the world's greatest civilian-led rescue and recovery operations of priceless art, antiquities, and books. Tens of thousands of books and manuscripts, attacked by the unprecedented flood waters. Well, not so unprecedented. Centuries earlier Leonardo da Vinci had warned the Florentines that their flood defences were insufficient, with many others heralding a similar alarm in the years that followed. But progress is slow in Italy.

The mass of humanity inside the National Library was akin to the membership of the United Nations. Almost every country and continent had a representative covered in mud and exhausted to the point of being unrecognisable. Known as the Mud Angels, they were the heroes Italy deserved, and the safety net Helena needed.

With the photographer alternating between shooting

stills of the historic scene, and helping move piles of books, Helena launched into the melee, eager to be among others, to help. There was safety in numbers.

Hours passed, and she'd sunk well past caring about her appearance, or her empty stomach, or her tired arms. All that mattered was saving the art, the statues, the books, the icons. The laments of the pious rang out from nearby churches as the damage became unmistakable in the morning light. As the morning met midday and the death-filled water started ebbing away, the horror of the floods revealed themselves.

A colourful city reduced to a grey carbon copy of itself. Every building, every wall, every garden, every street, every car, bleached of its colour and dipped in the stinking, sticky grey mud left behind by millions and millions of gallons of water. Helena was hiding in a broken city left floundering, a fish out of water.

Exhausted, she stepped out of the chain for a moment's respite. With no electricity, and no natural light, the volunteers were operating in near darkness; the blackness lifting when a film crew arrived with lights used to shoot actors on set. The poor light and the stench and the perpetual damp almost drove them to despair, but they persevered. Their motivation to save the art a uniting force.

Perched on a ledge outside, Helena surveyed the callous damage, imagining the loss of life in the crowded apartments filled with multiple generations living cheek by jowl.

Crowds of volunteers flooded the ornate building, young and old, feeble and able-bodied. Everyone wanted to help. Pulled back into the chain, Helena carried on passing objects from right to left, her body aching with repetition, unable to appreciate the art they were saving, most of it unrecognisable covered in an oily grey filth which would take restorers decades to remove.

The surrounding faces were a blur, paired with a kaleidoscope of nationalities. And now there were cameras everywhere, when initially it was one man with a camera, shooting into the gloom. With the light of a flaming comet, the cavernous halls were lit by a film crew's giant spotlights, revealing the Mud Angels scurrying through the water like mosquito larvae, the sound of the rolling film reels loud in the confined space.

Helena turned from the light, the sudden brilliance all but blinding her. Blinking, the surrounding faces swam in and out of focus, and she thought one looked familiar, but with everyone covered in mud their identities merged into each other. She ignored the prickle of familiarity.

She probed the wounds on her cheeks, the memory of that moment surreal. Had she gouged her own cheeks? How? Her panic must have played tricks on her mind as she couldn't remember why she'd scratched her face, but the proof was there, deep wounds down each cheek. No one questioned her injuries, and she realised that they'd assumed the flood caused them. Everyone around her looked just as battered and bruised.

Helena shook her head. Worrying about Sim and Benito and what had happened in the lab was for another day. The three of them were running a forgery scam, and she'd stumbled right into it. Helena cursed herself for going into Sim's private room, and she couldn't believe she'd ever considered Benito handsome. What would become of her training? Her thoughts leapt over each other, every one of them rushing ahead, worrying her even more. But she just didn't have the energy to care, saving Florence's history far more important.

The weak sunlight warmed her enough for her to

return to the chain of workers, but as she turned, a rough hand clamped over her mouth, with another arm wrapped around her sodden waist, tugging her behind a decaying column, obscuring her from sight.

She couldn't scream or escape. The hands holding her stronger than iron bars. A frisson of light limped its way around the column, highlighting the face of her captor — the artist from the lab - Leo Kubin. Her memories flooded back.

Helena was no match for his strength. Bucking against him, she fought with every ounce of strength, clawing at his face, kicking out with stockinged feet, her mind registering that she'd lost her shoes.

The broken safety chain on her bracelet caught the edge of his mouth, and he punched her straight to the temple, rendering her unconscious. Leo Kubin carried her away from the crowd, dancing along the edges of the light, unnoticed by anyone else.

THE CLEANER

Stefano pushed outside the water doing its best to thwart him. He hadn't worked his entire life to let a minor flood stop him.

As he inched around the outside of the building, he had a flashback to a moment in the war, when he'd been underground, laying mines or destroying mines or something similar, and he'd stumbled across a cache of art. From his time working in the museum, he knew enough to know that this wasn't just any art. There were hints of Bordone, Otto Dix, Rousseau, Rubens and Domineco Fetti as he shuffled through the stacks of paintings. Stacks which in places were higher than he was tall.

He had been partnered with an Italian officer - Casadei. A man who'd fought tooth and nail to avoid being sent to the front lines, but as the war neared its end, it was all hands on deck, forcing Casadei to dirty his hands in battle. Stefano knew of Casadei and his family's connections to the art world. He knew of their wealth and their unsullied reputation, but he never expected what happened next.

Casadei had pulled out his sidearm, shooting their colleague in the temple, before firing at the fourth member of their team. Stefano remembered freezing on the spot, his hand hovering above live explosives. His last thoughts of his wife at home, and his son, deployed god-knows-where, all gangly teenage legs and arms too long for his uniform shirt.

But his expected death hadn't come. Casadei had shouldered his sidearm, nodding at him, before rolling the dead men into a corner of the underground cavern.

'No one knows what's in this cave other than the men who put it here, and now you and I. And the people who put the art here are on the losing side, that is obvious, is it not?'

Stefano remembered nodding, the blood of the other men still warm on his skin.

'If you want to keep your boy and your wife safe, you'll keep quiet. Help me now, and you'll make a decent life for your family. Say nothing of what happened here.'

For twenty years, Casadei had kept his word, supplementing Stefano's meagre salary, asking little more from him than to ease the movement of art, occasionally delivering a piece, or holding artworks in storage, even swapping out an artwork for a replica, the original going to one of Casadei's wealthy clients. And he wasn't the only one doing Casadei's bidding. He knew there was a network of minions, a few he colluded with, others he didn't know their identities. He'd kept his secrets, and banked his money.

But Casadei still held Stefano's life in his hands - Stefano's life, and that of his dutiful wife.

Stefano shook away his anger at the situation, pushing through the flood water with a new determination, the tree-filled hill his target. He stabbed at the hidden ground with his makeshift walking stick, daring the water to attack him, and aimed for the higher ground.

He could still hear the faint sounds of the woman's cries above the rushing water, giving him the boost he needed to traverse the last several feet of flood water before grabbing handfuls of grass to pull his aching body onto the saturated hill, wriggling earthworms curling into themselves at the sudden exposure to dawn's light.

Stefano had a simple goal in mind — a small crop of spindly trees and low shrubs, their leaves forming a natural canopy of sorts, under which he could see a simple pair of black women's shoes.

He called out, oblivious to the chill seeping into his bones. He hadn't been warm for a long time now, but nothing would be as cold as the winter of 1944. This flood was nothing more than a minor inconvenience, despite being the worst flood in Florence in a century.

The woman stirred, her feet disturbing the vegetation, a soft moaning reaching Stefano's ears. It reminded him of the sounds his wife used to make. Oh, how he missed those. He thought of her now, as he limped towards the bush, his beautiful, clever wife. His parents had warned him she was beyond his reach, suggesting he lower his sights to someone more pliable, someone equal to his intellect. They didn't trust anyone educated beyond what they considered normal. But he'd loved her, and her appreciation of the art she surrounded herself with. And she'd admired the education he'd gained through his work at the museum. He'd never realised how much he'd picked up just from cleaning the exhibits and listening to snippets of the guides' patter as they escorted the tourists. Together they'd been a formidable pair.

'Help. I'm in here.'

Stefano paused, the exertion straining his face, resting for a moment on his makeshift walking stick. It had been a long time since he'd killed a person, but it wasn't a skill you forgot.

He pulled back a handful of foliage, revealing the pain-ravaged face of a woman partially dressed in the distinctive black uniform of the Italian police. It wasn't the uniform which shocked him, but the callous disregard for the piece of art she was sheltering underneath.

By being this close, he could hear her laboured breathing, and smell the remnants of her perfume, and see the relief in her eyes. She thought he was here to rescue her, but that was the farthest thing from his mind.

'I know you,' she wheezed, staring at his face, 'from the Bargello Museum, you're the cleaner.'

Stefano's face paled. How could she know him? No one ever notices the cleaner. He was invisible, always had been, always would be. He leaned in, tugging on the frame covering the woman, and it came away in his hands, the policewoman in no condition to fight him. She still thought he was there to save her.

'Keep it dry,' she said. 'It is more important than I am.'

Those words. He'd heard them once before, a long time ago, from his wife after she'd discovered his secret deal with Casadei. She'd begged him to keep their son safe, protesting that he was more important than her. That he should sacrifice her. Stefano disagreed, believing that he could persuade Casadei that his family would stay silent. But he couldn't, and he could still hear his son screaming for help in Casadei's private apartment. There'd been two other men there that night — the two artists Casadei used for the forgeries. They'd been there the night his son died, and for the next twenty years he did what he was told, meeting regularly with the witnesses to his son's death, protecting their secrets, and storing their art. He'd told his wife about their son, their beautiful boy, and she had never recovered. Now she sat at the window waiting for their boy to return, her heart turning to dust. It was better that way. At least Casadei's secrets were safe.

A flock of pigeons took to the sky, screaming at each other now that the heavy clouds were empty. The pigeons filled the sky with their noise, wheeling away from the flooded city in search of greener pastures instead of the mud-caked city below their furious wings.

'Where is Carstone? Is he there with you?'

Stefano wasn't listening. He had to get the painting, undamaged, ready for sale. The client coming to buy the Rembrandt wasn't buying just *The Storm on the Sea of Galilee*, but several other pieces Sim had prepared. This was their payday.

'Carstone?'

The woman wouldn't shut up. Stefano closed his eyes. He'd lost everything. He wasn't prepared to lose this.

'Be quiet, or I'll shut you up. I am thinking,' Stefano replied, overwhelmed with everything around him. He surveyed the ocean lapping at the walls of his building. Everything he'd built, everything he'd collected, swallowed by six-hundred-thousand cubic metres of water.

Stefano limped toward the water's edge, judging whether he could make it back to his workroom to salvage his collection. The art still on the walls had looked untouched by the flood. The water level would recede, so waiting was sensible, and from here he could watch for any signs of looting, and be close enough to deal with them if needed.

'Carstone? Richard, are you there?'

But the lady officer had seen him, and that wasn't

good. After leaning the painting against the mossy trunk of a tree, Stefano turned back towards the woman. He had nothing to lose and everything to gain, and brandishing the de facto walking stick above his head, he swung towards her head.

THE POLICEMAN

Pisani and the thief gasped for breath at the top of the stairs, waterlogged and exhausted by their struggle, the thief clutching the bag to her chest. Pisani didn't have the energy to do anything other than to ask if she was okay. He'd arrest her later.

The thief ignored Pisani's question, dragging herself and her bag further up the stairs.

Pisani berated her, but lost the will. He had more important things to worry about.

A pitiful cry reached his ears. The bleat of a faraway newborn lamb. Puzzled, Pisani cocked his head. He'd been hard of hearing in one ear since a childhood bout of measles, and sometimes his hearing played tricks on him. It wasn't too much bother, but with water in both ears and the relentless sound of surging water, there was no way of locating the noise.

'Can you hear that?' he asked the thief, turning his head to the other side.

She ignored him, focussing on the flap on the top of

her bag. Pisani gaped as she pulled a mewling infant from the wet rucksack.

The image swam in front of Pisani's eyes. He'd wrenched the bag from her hands, allowing it to sink underwater. He'd almost murdered a baby. Pisani swallowed the bile filling his throat. 'Is the baby okay?' he asked, shuffling closer to the woman and child.

'She is fine, just hungry and cold, like me,' the woman replied in perfect Italian.

'We need to go up,' Pisani said, pointing upwards. 'The water is still coming.'

The thief returned the baby to the rucksack before slinging the straps over her skinny shoulders.

Pisani recognised that the time for questions was later, but for now, he still feared for their safety, and the safety of everyone else in Florence.

From the windows of the Altavilla Hotel, Pisani surveyed the scenes of devastation. Everywhere he looked, he saw people perched on rooftops or hanging from windows doing the same thing he was — staring in shock at the inundation. The noise of the surging water overwhelmed the city. Hundreds of people needed his help, and he didn't know where to start.

'What should I do?' he asked himself from the safety of the second floor.

'Help them,' replied the thief. She stood behind him at the window, the baby back in her arms, a warm bedspread wrapped around her shoulders.

'Yes, I should,' he replied. 'You stay here. It's safe enough, I don't think the water will rise this far. But if it does…'

The thief nodded. Pisani thought they'd reached an understanding, the two of them. Now he needed to descend back into the swirling waters. Other women and children needed him, grandmothers and grandfathers, injured veterans who didn't deserve to die in their apartments. And Fonti, wherever she was.

Pisani climbed down the external fire escape, the ancient metal struts groaning under his weight, the water tugging at its base. Pisani prayed it would hold him. He took it one step at a time until he felt the water lapping at his feet. It was then that he realised he'd lost his shoes. He paused on the bottom rung, hesitant. He couldn't fix that now.

Splashing into the waters, the gagging smell of raw sewage struck him, as if the gates of Dante's hell had emptied a lifetime of human faeces into the streets of Florence.

Pisani may have been a slow learner who'd turned into a lazy policeman, but he was still a dutiful man and everywhere he looked, people called for help. He began yelling at the nearest able-bodied men, cajoling them to help. This mess would take weeks, if not months, to clean up, and he worried what they might find in the poorer parts of the city most affected by the flooding. The elderly, confined to their apartments by age and physical impairment.

'The ground-floor apartments, check those,' he yelled at the closest group of men trying to negotiate their way up the street.

With Pisani's uniform soaked through, his personal dress and bearing worse than it had ever been before, but they still obeyed him. Pisani hammered on doors, his voice hoarse with the effort, his bare feet ripped to shreds. The water swirled around him, although he imagined that the pressure was dropping, that the waterborne missiles weren't hurtling towards him with as much intensity.

He watched the men carry an elderly woman out of

her apartment, her long white hair trailing in the water, their raucous voices silenced. They carried her up the submerged steps of the church on the corner, laying her body next to the priest for his ministrations. The first of many deaths that day.

Pisani blinked back tears. He should have helped sooner, then maybe she wouldn't have died. How could he explain himself to her family? He pushed through the muddied water, hammering on doors with such intensity not even the dead could withstand his pleas to open up, to get to a higher point.

A child's shoe floated past, bobbing in innocence in the foetid stink. Pisani grabbed it before it disappeared. He stared at the tiny red patent leather shoe. Where was its owner? Was the girl another soul he hadn't saved through his laziness, his ineptitude?

'Help, we need help.'

Shaken from his melancholy, Pisani tucked the shoe into his pocket and turned towards the voice.

A boat filled with survivors navigated its way towards the church. Riding low in the water, the boat appeared close to sinking with its human cargo. Pisani struck out for the church, helping the exhausted survivors up the stairs. Someone passed him a child, her head lolling to one side. He held her for a moment, praying that she wasn't dead. She shuddered in his arms, a tiny sob escaping her blue tinted lips. Another pair of hands plucked her from Pisani's arms and passed the limp package up to the church. Pisani had for that one brief second considered giving up on life himself. If God saw fit to strike down an innocent child, what right did he have to carry on living?

'Hey, you, Mr. Policeman, you speak English, yes?'

Like an apparition from a nightmare, the American tourist leapt from the boat onto the stairs. Covered in muck and oil, with scratches down his face and a gash on his forehead, Pisani almost didn't recognise the man.

'You're the American,' Pisani said in English.

'You have to tell them to go back for Rosa,' Carstone said, grabbing Pisani's arm.

'Rosa? You mean Fonti?' asked Pisani, confused, unable to comprehend what he was seeing, or hearing. What had this American done to Fonti?

'She's injured. I left her on an island. If it's still there.'

'Injured? There's no island in Florence.'

'Are you going to repeat everything I say? There was an accident, injuring Fonti. Then we woke up to this flood, and I carried her to an island, up a hill. Then I went for help. We have to go back to help her. Tell these men we need their boat.'

Although Pisani's English was passable, he couldn't understand the American's words. There was so much to do. Surely Fonti was busy helping the other survivors wherever she was?

'She will die, you idiot, unless we get her to a hospital.'

The men in the inflatable dinghy pushed away from the steps of the church, continuing on their quest to rescue more survivors.

'Look what you've done now,' the American yelled at him.

'Calm, be calm,' Pisani said, 'I am thinking.' He wasn't stalling for time, but processing his options. He'd never given Rosa Fonti a fair time. She was a woman, and women shouldn't be working as police officers. It wasn't safe, but for all his arguments against women in the workforce, Fonti had shown she was a class above most of the men in their division. He owed it to her to save her.

'We will find another way, they need that boat. There's no one else coming to help them here,' Pisani said, knowing that the bulk of the city's resources would go to the monuments which made Florence so famous. They always left the poor till last. It was a fact. 'We will find a boat by the Arno,' Pisani directed, striking out from the relative dryness of the steps. The American tourist followed.

THE GUEST

OF ALL THE people to bump into in an apocalyptic Florence, it was Carstone's lousy luck to find the bumbling Italian policeman. Was it just yesterday he'd reported his wallet being stolen? Now his missing wallet and passport were the least of his worries.

Carstone wiped the blood from his eyes. His head wound wasn't serious, but cuts to the skull were notorious bleeders, and it needed somewhere dry with a nurse to stitch the gash.

'What direction?' the policeman asked.

'Against the flow of the water,' Carstone replied. 'On a hill with a copse of trees.'

The policeman looked confused.

'With many trees,' Carstone tried, 'and old buildings.' He twisted his mouth. Every building in Florence was old, older than the pilgrim settlements of America. How would he find his way back to Fonti? How to describe the place where he left her? The floods had washed away the crashed police car, and the body of the dead driver, making it difficult to pinpoint Fonti's location. 'We broke

266

into an old warehouse, just one level. Across from a small square, a small *pizzeria*?'

'*Pizzeria*? Or do you mean a *piazza*?'

'Does it matter if I've called it the wrong name? Surely you know what I mean?'

'You're describing most of Florence, or Venice, or even Rome. I need more,' the policeman said.

'She's dying. Think, a hill, trees, a row of warehouses, all one level, an open square, near to the river,' Carstone cried.

'All one level, no apartment buildings?'

'On the opposite side of the square. With warehouses backing onto the hill.'

'Okay, I understand the place,' the policeman said, recognition on his face.

'We have to hurry,' Carstone said.

But sourcing a boat was as hard as staying dry, impossible. After much posturing and yelling, the policeman secured them a grubby tender, barely watertight, but solid enough to withstand the onslaught of the debris swirling in the muddied waters.

With an oar each, the men struck out against the pulsating waters, avoiding the furniture bobbing on the water's surface. The boat scraped against an unseen obstacle, and Carstone held his breath, waiting for them to sink.

Carstone thought they'd never get there as the policeman paused to help every Tom, Dick and Harry, until Carstone couldn't stand it any longer.

'Jesus Christ, she's your colleague and you're letting her die.'

'We can't leave these other people to perish either. They need us.'

At every corner, the policeman forced Carstone to dock

the boat against another building to rescue a woman and her dog, or a man with a bundle of belongings, or a child and his mother, a pair of women, their arms filled with suitcases and hatboxes.

Carstone wanted to scream. Why was he so worried about Fonti? Deep down he suspected it wasn't just about the woman, and he hated himself for that. It was the art she had with her. Selling it would wipe his debts and allow him to start again. A new life, under a new name. Unfettered by scandal, or bothered by whispered glances, the undercurrent of anger towards him never far from the surface.

With the policeman back in the boat, Carstone hefted the oars and pulled. Although the rain had stopped, water still filled the air, dripping from every roofline, seeping into every crevice, soaking everything.

'Stop!'

Carstone ignored the policeman and increased his efforts.

'Stop, we go over there, to the *bibliotheca*.'

Carstone didn't know what a *bibliotheca* was, but saw a building nearby, inundated like every other building around them, save for a chain gang of people moving the contents to higher ground. They were so close. He could have rowed the tender towards the impressive building, but he had no intention of doing that.

'Whatever is happening, they have got enough people helping,' Carstone responded, subtly angling the tender away from the building.

He chanced a look at the policeman's face, a picture of abject misery. For a moment Carstone felt a pang of guilt, but abandoned that thought as an errant piece of concrete slammed against the side of the tender, nearly throwing them both from the craft.

'Hold on,' Carstone yelled, as the tender spun around, the air pierced with the sickening splintering of the oar.

'Christ, that was close. No more side trips to help anyone else,' Carstone said, repositioning himself on the sodden seat. With one complete oar, and the remains of half an oar, paddling towards Fonti now an impossible task.

'If we'd stopped to help at the *bibliotheca*, that would not have happened,' Pisani stated, staring back at the library.

He could ignore the barb, but Carstone couldn't avoid the thoughts surfacing in his head. He'd only needed the policeman for requisitioning the boat. What difference would it make if he dumped Pisani on the steps with the rest of the Italy?

'I'll take you back,' Carstone said, the idea of the heavy oar connecting with Pisani's head suddenly appealing.

The policeman hesitated. 'No, they have enough help. I pray they can save the books.'

That wasn't the answer Carstone wanted. Pisani might be a problem further down the track. With the devastation in Florence, what was one more death? From the edge of his vision, he saw a man carrying a woman away from the library steps, her head lolling to the side. No one cared. So he doubted anyone would notice if Pisani died in the floodwaters whilst saving the civilians. They would call him a hero, a title he would never receive in any other reality.

Carstone erased the blackness from his mind, and nodding at Pisani, leaned forward, pulling with their one remaining oar and struck out towards Fonti. And the painting — the answer to his financial woes.

THE WIFE

THROUGH HER HANGOVER, Rhonda thought she heard an avalanche. She'd heard one once, on her honeymoon, and she'd never forgotten the sound of certain death. Flinching from the sound, Rhonda couldn't understand why she couldn't move. With a pounding headache threatening to split her skull, she didn't want to open her eyes, but snow from the avalanche was melting around her, soaking her.

'Wake up, Rhonda.'

Rhonda moaned.

'I said, wake up, Rhonda.'

The voice was louder now, more strident.

Rhonda forced her eyes open, but wished she hadn't. It wasn't an avalanche. It wasn't melting snow. But she wasn't any safer.

'Hello, Rhonda. Remember me?' Paul Tobias stood before her, one eye fully closed, the gash to his temple still swollen.

If Rhonda's head had ached before, now it screamed with pain and fear as the realisation of who she was with became obvious. 'You.'

'That's not polite, Rhonda,' Tobias said. 'Old friends' are usually more polite towards each other. And we are old friends, aren't we? We have a friend in common. Someone who misses you. Do you know who I mean?'

Rhonda shook her head, although she knew well who he meant.

'Our mutual friend will join us soon and he has an important question for you. What do you think his question is?'

Paul Tobias leaned forward, his damaged face gleeful. She had spent a lifetime living in constant fear of stepping out of line and suffering the consequences. And just when she thought she'd escaped, she realised they'd been playing her for a fool and giving her just enough rope to hang herself.

'He wants his wife back, and his paintings. It's difficult to sell paintings as originals, when more than one is on the market. You have made life problematic for your husband and his business partners.'

'I've no idea what you're talking about,' Rhonda ventured, summoning a modicum of backbone.

'Don't play with me, Rhonda. Your husband hired me to find you and find you I have. What a merry dance we've had, yes? It's a shame I'm not permitted to repay the damage you did to me,' he said, pointing to his blackened eye, 'but I'm told your husband will punish you. I am surprised he never told me how delightful you are. In fact, after he shared the horrible stories about your behaviour, I was expecting to find someone monstrous, a veritable Medusa of a woman. Yet here you are, complete with some very appealing assets.'

Although Tobias scared her, he didn't scare Rhonda as much as her husband did. And until he arrived, a chance of escape existed. She had to try.

'My husband will bury you ten feet underground when he sees what you have done to me,' she threatened.

'Self defence, my dear. Self defence.'

Trying a different tack, she asked, 'Where am I?'. But after leveraging herself up from the worn leather couch with exposed horsehair stuffing, she guessed she was still in Casadei's palazzo, her glass from the night before in pieces on the parquet floor. Everything fell into place. Casadei's insistence of celebrating with another drink, the euphoria of selling the art, her exciting new life. A con with her husband's sticky fingers over the entire thing. Was Julia in on it too?

'Ah, you must recognise where we are,' Tobias said. 'Now you understand that the art world is not as big as you imagined it to be, hmm? You have put your husband in an embarrassing position. There are specific pieces which cannot be, shall we say, released into the public eye just yet. Not the originals, the copies yes, but not the originals, and you have upset the apple cart. People are asking questions. Do you remember how much your husband despises questions?'

Rhonda stared at the man's face, the fuzziness of the alcohol wearing off as she tried to understand what he was saying. The originals?

'Confused?' Tobias laughed. 'I don't think it's complicated, but you are a woman so maybe it is. Do you know what your husband did in the war? No? He was part of the team hunting Hitler's art collection. Your husband was good at his job, everyone said so. He has the medals to prove it, yes? As well as a talent for finding things, he excelled at reallocating the art his team found, sharing the cultural wealth. And shipping it back to the States turned out to be as easy as apple pie, after your husband recruited like-minded colleagues who shared his views on culture and profit.'

'You stole that art?'

'You wound me, Rhonda. Is it stealing when someone else stole it first? As far as the world knows, the war destroyed the art. But for those in our trusted inner circle, certain pieces can become available, like *The Sloop* for example. Or more desirable pieces, for the right price…'

Rhonda's plans of disappearing with the proceeds from selling *The Sloop* melted away. Casadei, her husband, Paul Tobias - they were in on it. She would receive nothing from the sale of the painting. Tears streamed down her face.

'No need to cry, at least not before your husband arrives and you are both reunited.'

Rhonda watched Tobias examining the portraits on the walls. There was nothing left to say. She didn't have to say anything, Tobias kept a running patter, enough for both of them.

'Fine examples of Kubin's work, don't you think? Watching him work is a visceral experience. It is a shame your husband said no to Kubin painting your portrait. Casadei was very disappointed. He'd taken a shine to you and likes to keep mementoes of the women who entertain him. Mementoes like your wedding rings.' Tobias opened his palm, revealing two circles of gold. 'I suspect your husband will want to put these back on your finger himself. I will just leave them here to remind you of your wedding vows.'

Tobias positioned the rings on an elegant silver tray, next to the empty bottle of *Grappa*. Rhonda swallowed the bile threatening to erupt, when a distant bell rang, the echoing peals like the sighs of a dying woman.

The face of her captor lit up.

'Guess who that is?' he said in his Texan drawl,

rubbing his hands together. 'Such fun we will have. Just like in the war. I miss those days,' Tobias elaborated. 'Now you stay here while I greet our guest.'

Without a backward look, Tobias left.

Rhonda didn't need to imagine what would happen next. Her husband's repertoire followed the same playlist, every time — a backhand across her face, then a sucker punch to her stomach. A kick to the ribs next, followed by a slow choke hold until she passed out. He would wait until she woke up, then start again. For an entire year he'd given up smoking, which meant sparing her the cigarette burns he had been so fond of in the early days of his abuse. But his nicotine habit proved too strong, and he'd returned to smoking a packet a day, sometimes two, meaning the discrete burns were her constant companions once again. She would not surrender to his violence any more. She had to escape.

Her body refused to obey her brain, leaving her motionless on the couch as she wrestled with her plan. Another door stood at the far end, leading to where she didn't know. But that was the only other exit. Faint voices were coming from the direction Tobias had gone. Rhonda stood up, her decision made.

Unable to rescue her shoes from the other room, barefoot, she bolted for the exit. Then everything moved, as if an errant train had crashed into the building. The room shuddered and portraits leapt from the wall, smashing to the floor. Wood splintered, and a glass-fronted cabinet keeled over, the glass spilling onto the wooden floor, throwing Rhonda to the ground. Screams filled the air, and she heard her husband calling her name. That was enough to launch her to her feet, stumbling forwards, until a gush of water hit her legs, propelling her towards the door.

With the torrent inching up her legs, she focussed on the exit, pushing through into another receiving room reminiscent of the Hall of Mirrors at Versailles. Rhonda forced her way out into an open courtyard and waded into the flooded space.

The gloomy, rain-drenched dawn left little to see, but the noise was overwhelming. Like a thousand trains pulling into the station at once, amplified by the screams of unseen hordes of victims wrapped in the arms of the flood. With her husband's voice ringing in her ears, Rhonda half swam half waded through the churning water into an alleyway plugging with debris, giant trees ripped from the sodden earth, cars plucked from their dormant parks, shoes, baskets, a redundant mop, a chair still with its chintz cushion tied to the seat. And still she kept going, running, wading, swimming, tripping, climbing upwards, towards higher ground. She kept going, not to escape the surge, but to escape her husband, his voice still echoing in her head, his guttural cry for help when the flood slammed against the building. It was a cry for help or a cry of utter rage. She didn't know and didn't care. She prayed for his death but knew she'd never be that lucky.

Rhonda paused on the steps of a church, her hands shaking. She'd just thrown up, heaving until nothing remained in her stomach. She'd run so far, paying no attention to where she was, the water washing away any signs of the roads she should have remembered. Water surrounded her, crashing debris against buildings and cars and lampposts and telephone boxes. She'd seen upturned prams and discarded umbrellas become dangerous missiles. With any luck, her husband and his cronies had become floating corpses.

As she caught her breath and calmed her racing imagination, Rhonda noticed a stream of people fighting their way towards a gracious building. Tall people, short people, young, old, well-dressed, dressed in rags, wading through the chest-high water which was still rising. A woman rushed past and Rhonda reached out to stop her.

'What's happening?'

The woman wriggled from Rhonda's grasp.

'Quick, come and help,' the woman said, her American accent taking Rhonda by surprise.

Perhaps it was the safety of being with someone else, or the possibility of reaching a refuge from the flood, but Rhonda followed her, and together they stumbled through the current, holding onto each other for support until they made it up the worn stairs and into the grand old building. That's when Rhonda realised where she was — the Uffizi Museum - the repository of Italy's treasures, treasures now inundated with the surging flood waters.

Rhonda stood in water up to her knees, unfazed. She shivered, but didn't let it affect her. She couldn't understand a word anyone said, but didn't care.

Everywhere she looked, she saw the ruination of art, and a human chain trying to save the priceless artefacts housed within the walls of the Uffizi.

A man bumped her from behind, apologised, and carried on, his arms full of manuscripts. To her left, a middle-aged couple were carrying a wooden Madonna, feet first, up the marble steps. A multilingual chain gang of students passed books and gilt frames and manuscripts up the winding staircase.

Another man pushed her forward. She couldn't understand his words, but understood the meaning — he wanted her to help. Rhonda splashed towards the human chain, and two bearded youths made room, the links in the chain spreading out to accommodate the newcomer. Moving the treasure was relentless. At one point old gilt covered Rhonda's hands, sloughed off the frames they were rescuing. She had no time to dwell on the potential damage. They were doing their best, and their best was better than leaving the art under the oil-laced water.

At first glance someone could have mistaken their activity for pillaging — looting ancient artefacts. For some statues, it wasn't the first time. Seized as the spoils of war, or changing ownership during a revolution, a war, fratricide. Or robbed from graves or deconsecrated churches. But she didn't think anyone had ever moved them to save them from a flood.

Women in headscarves stood shoulder-to-shoulder with shabby youths and wizened old men. Everyone was filthy, covered head-to-toe in mud, working as one to save Florence's treasures. Everything needed moving to higher ground, up stairs made perilous by slippery mud and muck.

Someone pulled her from the line, pressing a cup of coffee into her hands. The chain contracted to fill her space, then opened again to admit a new volunteer — a fresh pair of hands and a clean face, another Mud Angel.

Rhonda checked her reflection — hair plastered to her scalp, streaks of mud across her forehead and cheeks. She'd lost an earring and was still missing her shoes, yet couldn't be happier. They needed her. She might be a tiny cog in the scheme of things, but she had a worth, and that made up for a lifetime of abuse.

Being so close to the art was like having an out-of-body experience. Even in the gloom, with everything covered with filth and excrement, their glorious colours shone bright. The genius of the artists unmistakable and their religious fervour unquenchable. She hadn't believed in God for a long time, but felt His presence today.

The water kept rising, the torrent echoing around

them. Injured people appeared, seeking aid, their blood diluting the unforgiving waters.

Rhonda peeked outside, the steaming cup clasped in her hands. The world had become a violent ocean where cars were like icebergs and tree trunks and uprooted vegetation formed floating islands. Furniture shot past — giant wardrobes and three-legged stools, followed by a body, and then another one. Rhonda dropped her cup, the coffee adding to the vile concoction.

She ran inside, grabbing a volunteer from the chain.

'There's a body,' she shouted, the noise swallowing her words.

He shook her off, replying in Italian.

As he tried rejoining the group, she pulled on his arm, the utter hopelessness of the bodies being swept away giving her strength.

'There are bodies outside,' she repeated, her voice rising.

With a confused shrug, he followed her. They stopped in the doorway because they could go no further. The water now a raging torrent and an iron bed head caught by the maelstrom almost took them both out.

With her hands over her mouth and her eyes wide, Rhonda watched the two bodies being hurled against the side of a building, before being dashed into the carcass of a floating car, becoming entangled in a mess of tree branches, their unseeing eyes looking into the heavy clouds, rain pelting their pale cheeks. A child's shoe rushed past the bodies, a red patent leather shoe. Someone's Sunday best. It bumped into the back of the corpses before the river tore it away.

Rhonda cried out, and the stranger put his arm around her to comfort her. There was nothing anyone could do.

She shrugged off the man's arm, and sank to her

knees, her mind in disarray. She'd seen dead bodies before, weeping over the graves of her parents, and that of a friend lost to cancer. But there were deaths she'd never cry over, despite the expectations of society. Some people were better off dead. Her husband, for one. It had been his body she'd seen slammed against the car. Him and Tobias. And she started laughing.

THE STUDENT

THE PAIN in each of Helena's fingers nothing like she'd ever experienced, as if an anorexic needle was being threaded through each of her knuckles, sewing her fingers together. She tried moving her hand, but nothing worked. Nothing would move. Nothing except her eyes, which allowed her to look around.

That wasn't the balm she'd hoped for. The last thing she remembered was taking a breather from helping salvage the books and manuscripts at the National Library. What happened after was a blur, hands grabbing her, covering her mouth, cutting short her screams. Then, nothing. Darkness. The cold. And wet. So wet. And the stink of death and decay seeping into her pores. A smell which awakened memories long since repressed — that of abject hopelessness.

'It is so much more enjoyable when the subjects are awake,' came a voice from beside her, as the man loosened the gag around her mouth, the cloth falling into her lap.

Helena swivelled her eyes towards the voice. It was the artist Kubin. She watched him take a seat behind an ancient artist's easel, where he sat observing her, a slender paintbrush in one hand and a burning cigarette in the other. A deep scratch marred the side of his mouth, the dry blood making it look like he'd tried sewing it closed himself.

'Where am I? What's happening? Where's Benito?'

'So many questions. It is more an accident of fate that you're here. Sad, though, when you have been through so much. But the pain, ah, now that is such a joy to paint.'

He flicked his brush on his canvas, and Helena screamed. Pain travelled up her finger, opening her bruised skin. Blood bloomed, dripping onto the naked wooden floorboards.

'Where you are is a place I use sometimes. Although the damp can be a problem. It is annoying that I have to start a second canvas, after I lost the first one to the floodwaters. Although they say that practice makes perfect. Shall we see?' Kubin laughed and slashed his brush again across the canvas.

Helena screamed again as the base of her thumb opened. She pulled against her restraints, her bare feet barely able to move more than an inch either way. Abstractly she realised her thin gold bracelet was also missing. The one her mother had given her on her eighteenth birthday, which she never took off. The last remaining gift her father had given her mother. And although its worth was negligible, it meant the world to Helena.

Struggling against the pain she asked, 'Where is my bracelet?'

Surprise flashed across Kubin's face.

'This?' he said, pointing to a thin chain dangling from the top of the easel with his cigarette, before taking a deep drag from the half-smoked cigarette. 'You should get that safety chain fixed.'

Through pain-clouded eyes, Helena saw her bracelet and renewed her struggles.

'I collect souvenirs, they help to keep the subject in situ. I'm sure you can understand that?'

Helena understood nothing, apart from the pain he was inflicting.

'Please let me go, I won't tell anyone what I've seen,' she begged. 'Benito will vouch for me, just ask him.'

'Hmm,' Kubin replied, a cigarette clamped between his thin lips, his attention focussed on squeezing tubes of oil paint onto a palette until it resembled a seething nest of poisonous vipers — coiled and ready to strike. 'Sadly, it turns out that Benito wasn't the right calibre of student. And he had been so promising. He cannot continue classes with Feodor, or with me.'

Kubin gestured towards a canvas leaning up against the legs of his easel, drawing Helena's eye towards a perfect likeness of Benito. His wide mouth open in surprise, the strong lines of his face a perfect match to the one she had imagined caressing every night for the past three years. Parts of the painting looked smudged, as if completed in a hurry, the artist using only the most basic of techniques to capture the image.

'Benito won't be coming to rescue you this time. But I am grateful that he has once again, in a manner of speaking, provided me with another beautiful subject. As I get older, it has become so much more difficult to attract the right girls to sit for me. But with Benito assisting… well, they flocked to the studio for him. Like bees to honey.' Kubin turned his attention to his palette, squeezing tubes of colour, mixing them carefully, consumed by his task.

It was impossible for Helena to imagine Benito being

part of this artist's world. Impossible, but also believable, and that hurt the most. Helena stared at Benito's portrait, her feelings as complicated as the emotion Kubin had captured on his canvas.

Helena used his inattention to try wriggling free of her bonds, loosening the ties against her ankles. The restraints holding her wrists immobile trickier, but she felt a little give, so renewed her efforts.

'It is always most difficult getting the eyes the right colour. I'm tempted to do it in shades of black and grey, but where's the fun in that?' Kubin asked, swirling the pigments around the palette with a wooden stick. His board now resembling a molten rainbow after a storm. 'Your eyes, how do you describe them?'

Helena refused to answer, clamping her mouth shut.

Kubin stubbed his cigarette on the edge of the easel, lighting up another one, the flare of his match adding a surreal hue to the room. He was painting in half gloom, the only light from a grubby skylight above them, which showed it was long past dawn, the rain gone, washing the clouds clean.

'Shall I try the eyes?' Kubin asked her, peering at her through the nicotine-filled smoke.

Helena closed her eyes, turning her head away.

'Don't turn away, how am I meant to paint the fear in your eyes? Open them,' he ordered.

Helena squeezed them tighter.

Pain exploded through her temples. She screamed. Her burning skin joining the filthy tobacco miasma. The pain hit again and again. With her eyes open, Helena screamed as Kubin applied his lit cigarette to the painting, tiny burning dots adorning the canvas.

'Stop, stop, stop,' Helena cried, tears falling.

'Tears, perfect. Shall I paint those as well?'

Entranced by her tears, he opened a second box of paints, sorting through the array of half-finished tubes, muttering to himself.

'How are you doing this?' Helena sobbed.

'You ask too many questions.'

'But you have answered none of them. How is this possible?' Helena cried.

Kubin laughed, turning away, pulling a handful of brushes from a jar behind him, testing their bristles against his thumb before settling on an even finer brush than the one he'd been using. 'It is a talent I have. You wouldn't understand. Art is pain and only genuine artists can harness that pain. It is exquisite, isn't it, how you feel each stroke of my brush? Tears should be blue, don't you think?' he asked before smearing a dab of blue onto his brush and transferring it to the canvas.

It was as if someone was holding a handful of snow against her face, freezing her to the core. And with one last tug against her bonds, Helena wrenched her hand free, the intense pain magnifying every movement.

Kubin's laughter rebounded off the walls until there were a thousand tiny replicas of the artist laughing in circles inside her head, taunting her from every angle.

Helena scrabbled with the last tie around her left wrist, trying to block the artist's mad cackles.

'Oh, I see your tattoo. Such a delicious colour,' Kubin's voice danced with glee. 'Casadei told me about it. You should have kept it hidden, then you might not be here and none of this would have happened.'

Helena felt, rather than saw, the artist sorting through his paints. For a fraction of a second, she closed her eyes to draw on a reserve of strength she hadn't needed for a very long time. Strength left to her by her sister, her father, her uncles and her aunts. A strength bequeathed to her through the deaths of her family at the hands of other men. Nothing Kubin could do to her would be worse than the monsters who had tattooed her arm and tortured her twin. Even Kubin's unnatural artistic talent was nothing to what she had endured, and survived, in the war.

At the precise moment Kubin uttered a cry of delight at finding the precise colour he needed, Helena's fingers untangled the last knot.

Kubin's hand darted across his canvas, the flick of blue oil paint from the top of his brush a bee sting, leaving a bubble of blood blooming from the middle of the number seven on her arm.

Ignoring the pain, Helena launched herself towards Kubin, crashing into the canvas, crushing the grinning man beneath the easel. Grabbing the nearest thing at hand, an artist's palette knife, Helena plunged the knife into the fleshy part of Kubin's shoulder. He cried out, his hand releasing the slender brush still covered in blue oil paint.

Helena twisted the knife, digging it deeper into Kubin's shoulder. The laughing man wasn't laughing anymore, bucking beneath the heavy easel. Helena scrambled backwards.

Kubin roared, the violence in his voice propelling Helena towards the door. The locked door.

Helena rattled the handle, pulling and shoving and kicking and screaming.

There was a crash as Kubin heaved the massive easel off himself, followed by a guttural cry as he yanked the knife from his shoulder. Blood gushed from the wound, drenching his shirt in the most perfect shade of red.

Helena screamed as the now familiar pain gouged her arm. She turned to face Kubin, her back against the wall. There was nothing she could do.

With the canvas clutched in the crook of his damaged arm and his brush clenched in his right hand, Kubin advanced upon Helena, his brush darting across the canvas, devouring her face with his eyes. 'You can't escape,' he repeated, stabbing at the canvas with his brush.

Helena began praying, using prayers she hadn't uttered in years, the words as much of a comfort as the faces of her sister and father, faces which had been so ethereal for much of her life turned whole, welcoming her to the other side.

As Kubin painted, Helena prayed. Her eyes open, staring at her father and her sister. Behind them stood a hundred other people, hints of who they had once been. Gone but never forgotten, and still Kubin painted. Her shoulder, her neck, a hint of her dark hair tucked behind her ear. And slowly she vanished until Helena herself was as ethereal as her memories.

Her likeness now fully transferred to the canvas, leaving nothing of her mortal self behind. One more missing girl for the police files.

Leo Kubin painted the last of Helena using the blood from his wound, finishing her lips and garnishing her cheeks with a dark blush, the perfect artistic flair. The haunting look of pain on her face the perfect accompaniment to his collection of portraits stored at Casadei's home, waiting for shipment back to his home. Wedging Helena's delicate bracelet into the back of the finished canvas, he took a key from his pocket and unlocked the door. They always tried to escape.

And he wondered who he would paint next.

THE CLEANER

STEFANO STRUCK THE WOMAN. His feet slipped in the mud as he swung, leaving him off balance and ruining his aim.

The woman screamed. Vile words spewing from her mouth. Women should never speak that way. If Carmela had ever raised her voice, he would have... but no, she never had. She was an honourable woman, an obedient wife. He'd never raised a hand to her. His wife was his life, his whole heart, and he needed to return to her. She was on her own in this terrible flood.

The policewoman reached towards him as he tried hitting her a second time. Why was she screaming at him? What had he done? She had plundered his art after breaking into his warehouse. If he let her go, she'd turn him in, then everything would have been for nothing. Years of servitude, a lifetime of menial labour, the death of his son... No, this woman, this policewoman, who should have been at home looking after her family instead of interfering in his life, had to disappear.

Stefano screamed at her, unleashing decades of frustration as he struck again. Once, twice, three times.

The woman twisting away, her arms fending off the blows from his stick, his broom handle.

Rage filled his ears. As if the flood itself was rushing through him. The fury of the water translating to a violence he thought he had controlled. Stefano was incapable of hearing anything else. His unshed grief for his son louder than the tidal wave of muddy water.

His son had returned from the war a different person. As damaged as Stefano was himself, but angrier. Angry at the officers who'd lead them, angry at the Germans and the Americans. Bitter towards the people who'd stayed behind, who wanted to move on, pretending nothing had happened. And indignant at those who'd prospered during the war, growing rich from the deaths of his friends. People like Casadei.

Stefano tried keeping the truth from his son, getting him a job at the museum, keeping him busy. But his son was too curious. And curiosity has a habit of killing the cat. His son threatened to go to the authorities, raging that forgery was a crime, as was selling stolen artworks, that Casadei was a criminal, and that Stefano was just as guilty. His son's rage spiralling out of control, allowing his accusations to reach Casadei's ears.

'You will not take my wife. I will kill you, and the others. Crawl back into the hell hole you came from,' Stefano yelled, missing the confusion on the policewoman's face. He was making no sense, his anger crushing the carefully constructed facade he'd lived behind.

Spittle flew from Stefano's lips. Why wouldn't she die? Then he could throw her into the floodwaters, rescue his painting and be free. That's all he wanted, freedom from living under Casadei's threat.

'Die, damn you, die,' he cried, his words whipped away by the flood's roar.

'Get away from her, you bastard,' said a voice in English behind him.

As he turned towards the voice, Stefano slipped, losing his grip on the splintered wooden broom handle.

From his knees on the soaking ground, Stefano looked up into the twisted face of a monster, his clothes covered in mud and muck. Behind him was another man, bent over at the water's edge, his once black uniform in tatters, his shoes missing.

'Get away,' Stefano howled, struggling to his feet, his arthritic limp hindering his efforts.

'Rosa, are you okay?'

The American ignored Stefano, trying to rescue the policewoman under the trees.

'Leave her alone. She's a thief, a thief.' Stefano placed himself between the man and the policewoman. 'Get away.'

The American pushed him out of the way, and Stefano tumbled over, the fall knocking the wind out of him.

'Help me with her,' the American man said to his companion.

With no breath left in his lungs to stop them, Stefano lay gasping for air on the ground, his life crumbling around him. It couldn't end this way. It couldn't. He had promised Carmela a new life. He had promised her.

As the American and his friend pulled the woman into the open, her handgun dropped from her belt into a puddle, the splash happening in slow motion, each droplet of water showing Stefano what he needed to do.

On his hands and knees, dragging his leg behind him like an injured mutt, he crawled towards the handgun. It had been twenty years since he'd last fired a gun. Done then out of necessity, changing his life for ever. He'd thrown his army issue pistol in the Arno after that, the feel of the recoil haunting his nightmares every single night.

His memories threatened to drown him. The arguments with his son. Casadei's anger. Carmela begging him on her knees, pleading. Their son refusing to stay quiet. Their handsome boy, who always played by the rules. The child who followed the teacher's instructions, and who lived his life in pure shades of black-and-white. Their son who wouldn't permit his father's involvement in Casadei's forgery scheme.

After hours of toying with the boy, Casadei had forced Stefano to shoot his own flesh and blood. In the head. The shot killing his boy instantly. An irreversible, necessary, life-changing decision.

With the pistol in his hands, Stefano steadied his breath as he watched the men carrying the policewoman to the boat, with Stefano's painting lodged atop of the woman. Would the thieving never end? Stefano took a deep breath, released it, then pulled the trigger.

THE POLICEMAN

'*ATTENTO!*' Pisani screamed before ducking, knowing full well the American wouldn't understand him, but there was no time to trawl his mind for the right English word. The American got the drift of his instruction and ducked just as the boom of a firing gun rent the air.

'He's shooting at us,' Carstone screamed, almost dropping Fonti.

Pisani had dropped Rosa, apologising to her as he pulled his own gun, praying that his lack of attention to the handgun's maintenance wouldn't come back to haunt him now.

'Drop the gun,' Pisani yelled at the man holding Fonti's gun. The man looked familiar, but with everything else happening, he couldn't remember the details. 'The gun, drop the gun.'

'That's my painting, you can't have it,' the madman replied.

Pisani turned to check what the guy was going on about. Carstone had loaded Fonti into the small boat they'd commandeered and was handing her a painting of a ship in a storm. The sight of the painting nudged Pisani's memory.

'You are from the Bargello, the cleaner,' Pisani stated, turning to point his gun at the man. He recognised him now. What was a cleaner doing with a valuable painting on a hillside so far from the Bargello Museum? The mist in his mind cleared — those thefts from the museum. Carstone had told him about the car crash and sheltering in a building filled with art and antiquities. This man, the cleaner, must be the thief.

Pisani took a moment to imagine the glory coming his way when he recovered the Bargello's stolen artefacts. What a coup. He should arrest the cleaner now, or he could shoot him. An arrest was preferable, but problematic given everything happening. What a miraculous day. First, he'd found the passport thief, and now this.

The cleaner fired his gun again.

Pisani toppled over, his ears ringing. On his back, staring up at the grey clouds, he blinked away the light from the sudden spray of sunshine from a break in the clouds.

'Get up, you fool.'

Someone was yelling at him, but in English. Did they speak English in heaven? What was happening?

'Get up before he shoots you again.'

Pisani's head was on fire, one ear burning brighter than the sun. His hand came away wet from his earlobe — a nick. The shot had only nicked his ear. Pisani laughed. Who was the fool now he thought as he aimed at the cleaner and pulled the trigger.

Nothing happened. The mechanism jammed. Years of inattention and halfhearted cleaning coupled with a lack of interest in ever using the thing had come home to roost.

Pisani tried again, and again, and again, the hammer clicking uselessly.

Like everything else in his life, he'd failed at this too.

'Get her to the hospital,' he yelled at Carstone, whilst still pointing his handgun at the cleaner. At least he could protect Fonti with his body and give the American enough time to push the boat off and get Fonti to safety.

The American didn't need to be told twice. From the corner of his eye, Pisani watched the American shove the boat away from the edge before leaping into it, screaming at Pisani to get in to the boat.

The Bargello's cleaner screamed at the retreating boat, the anguish in his voice obvious even to Pisani.

'I have to arrest you,' Pisani called out, his useless gun still in his hand.

The cleaner sat on his heels, tears streaming down his face, Fonti's gun abandoned on the ground.

'He will kill my wife.'

'No one is killing anyone,' Pisani said automatically, deciding the man was deranged.

'Save my wife. I will wait here, I promise. But my wife, he will kill her if you take the painting. The flood took everything else, don't let him take my wife. Carmela will die, then me.'

Pisani tried to placate the man while his brain processed the cleaner's words. He didn't know what he was on about, but whatever it was, it terrified the cleaner.

'We will save your wife, I promise. Tell me where she is.'

THE GUEST

CARSTONE SCREAMED at the policeman to get in the boat. The idiot would get them shot. Bloody country. He didn't know whether to leave or return for the fool. They had to get out of here soon either way. The boat was being hit left, right and centre with chunks of concrete, giant trees and the entire contents of a furniture factory.

'Get in the boat,' Carstone screamed.

Pulling on the oar, he rowed him and Fonti out of range of the gun.

'Help him,' Rosa said from the bottom of the boat, *The Storm on the Sea of Galilee* painting resting against her twisted body.

'Help him? Are you mad? His gun is useless, and the other guy thinks he's fighting the war. Look at him.'

The boat juddered as another concrete missile hurtled into its side.

'Christ,' Carstone swore. He hadn't come here to swap out injured police officers. It was their job to keep him alive, not vice versa.

'Please, Carstone?' Rosa Fonti asked.

Carstone saw the effort she'd made to say those words, draining the last of her energy, injured more than she was letting on. The original goal of rescuing her was to take her to the nearest hospital before helping himself to a priceless piece of art. Now that was in jeopardy.

'Hell.'

Closer to the shore, Carstone assessed the scene. The two men, separated by less than nine feet, were still facing off, guns wavering in the air.

'Pisani, get in the boat,' Carstone yelled.

Both men turned to look at him, Carstone's voice carrying above the rumble of the water.

'Take us both,' Pisani called back.

Carstone's mouth dropped open, and he shook his head.

'You can't leave him there,' Rosa said, pulling herself up, making space in the small boat.

'You're joking.'

'It is our job to help people,' she wheezed

Carstone stiffened as she leaned against his legs, her body wracked with shivers.

'Fine.'

Bumping the boat into the shoreline, he held the boat steady with the oar, and waited for the men. Swearing, he battled to hold the boat steady, the cords of muscle in his neck straining under the effort. The flood was throwing everything it had at the little vessel, and every time he moved, Fonti flinched or uttered a muffled cry. He knew she was hurting.

'Get in the bloody boat now,' Carstone yelled. 'Hell.' He didn't care whether they understood his words, his intent was crystal clear.

Pisani was helping the other man to his feet — the idiot who'd just shot at them. Carstone shook his head. Letting that man into the boat with them was like inviting a wolf into bed with you, hoping it wouldn't get hungry in the middle of the night.

'He's dropped the gun,' Rosa said, panting.

'Thank god for that. I wasn't going to let him in otherwise,' Carstone replied, shifting, trying to make her more comfortable.

The weight of the extra men lowered the boat in the water, sending waves splashing in over the sides. They'd need a miracle to stay afloat. One decent strike and they'd all be in the murky waters, battling those monsters instead of just the one with the gun.

At the other end of the boat, the madman had taken grip of the painting, holding on to it for dear life. The painting which would solve Carstone's financial woes. Problems which had grown beyond all expectations since his brother's death. Marrying Julia had been one way out. But she'd rebuffed him the same way she had before she'd married his brother, the golden child. The child who could do no wrong. Everything Scott touched turned to gold, everything except Richard. He'd tried persuading Scott to bail him out, which would have solved everything, and then he wouldn't have found himself in this accursed country, sitting in a sinking boat with a dying woman, a fat policeman and a deranged gunman. If Scott had just lent him the money, Scott would be alive and this wouldn't be happening.

Carstone struggled with one oar. He hadn't rowed since high school and even back then he hadn't excelled. To be fair, he hadn't excelled at anything, but the basics came back with every stroke. Rowing with the flow of water, the easiest option. There was no point in fighting against the strength of the water, not without capsizing them. Carstone kept one eye on the water and one on the painting.

Relying on directions from Pisani, Carstone rowed as if his life depended upon it, all the time working through the scenarios open to him. Save Fonti, grab the painting, leave the city. They each seemed to cancel each other out. Doing one meant forgoing the others. He had to shake himself out of it. He needed the painting. Pisani could look after Fonti. She was nothing to him. But was that true? Maybe once, but now?

Carstone was oblivious to the surrounding devastation, but every time something careened into the side of the boat, it forced his attention back to their immediate predicament.

'Where now?' he called to Pisani, who looked like he was going into shock himself. His face pale save for his bleeding earlobe.

'Straight ahead,' Pisani replied, waving his hand loosely in an easterly direction.

'Straight ahead where?'

'To Carmela, my wife,' the madman replied, his English belaboured, his tongue struggling over the words.

'What the hell? We're not going to your house, we're taking Rosa to a hospital. Damn your wife,' Carstone swore.

'We will get his wife first,' Pisani said, his voice more steel than defeat.

'Like hell we are.'

Now wasn't the time for the damn policeman to find his balls, so Carstone rowed towards a set of steps full of folk scurrying about like ants.

'Hey, help, we need help here,' he yelled, hoping find someone in charge. Someone to relieve of his responsibilities.

'We go to the house first, the hospital second,' Pisani repeated, clamping his hand on Carstone's arm. 'Fonti will be fine, won't you?'

'This might kill her, you know that?' Carstone said, shaking off Pisani's hand before checking Rosa's pulse. Rapid, too rapid, as fast as the water flowing around them.

'His wife, or I'll arrest you for her injuries and theft and whatever else I can think up,' Pisani threatened. 'And you'll spend your last days in an Italian cell. Is that what you want?'

There was nothing Carstone could do, apart from comply as mayhem flowed around them, Pisani directing him with slight hand movements based on murmured directions from the other man. And still Carstone rowed. There was no other choice.

For most of the journey, Carstone let the water take them, conserving what little energy he had. The memory of the stale pastry he'd had for breakfast long gone now. If he was suffering from lack of food, he suspected Rosa was just as hungry. Resting the oar across his knees, he stroked Fonti's forehead. It was hot to the touch. His moment of affection overtaken by his clinical analysis. This mission to rescue the cleaner's wife would kill Rosa.

Just as Carstone contemplated his options, but this time putting Fonti front and centre, Pisani announced that they'd arrived, gesturing towards a skinny building with bars over the ground-floor window, the front door hanging open in the swirling water.

The cleaner wailed. Without warning, he leapt from the boat into the water, thrashing out towards his house and his wife. As he jumped, the boat wobbled and Carstone struggled to hold on to the oar and protect Rosa. The abandoned painting teetered on the side of the boat.

'Get the painting,' Carstone yelled at Pisani.

With their attention distracted by the art, they missed the sight of a giant tree barrelling towards their tiny boat. The flash of panic on Pisani's face made Carstone turn at the last second.

The tree was one of hundreds ripped from the earth by the water released from the dam, and hurled down the valley, gathering speed and debris on their violent rampage towards Florence.

Carstone cried out a warning, abandoning the oar and covering Rosa's body with his own, a futile effort as the tree exploded against the side of their boat.

Devoid of emotion, the tree cared not one whit for the jewelled tones of the masterpiece in the prow. And gave no thought to the years of service of the policeman, just as it didn't hold his former missteps against Pisani. The tree had no memory of Carstone shaking the ladder his brother stood on as he pruned another, healthier tree back in America. It didn't know or care that Richard Carstone had caused the death of his own brother beneath a similar leafy canopy. The tree held no judgement, and for that reason alone, the tree was more lethal than judge or jury.

The boat splintered, an ear-piercing sound of wood against wood. Water gushed through the gap, filling the small boat within seconds. The impact threw Pisani from the boat, the priceless painting ripped from his arms by the turbulent water, water echoing the storm in the painting. Life imitating art.

Through pure chance, or through the dance of fate, the tree pushed the boat against the side of the building the cleaner had desperately tried to reach.

Thump

Another tree walloped into the first, deafening them. Of Pisani, there was no sign. Carstone searched for the painting. Gone. Only one choice was open to Carstone now.

With a silent apology, he hooked his freezing hands under Rosa's arms, and launched them both through the open doorway, splashing into the roiling waters desecrating the cleaner's home.

He'd been cold before, but never like this. Exacerbated by the fear coursing through him, Carstone panicked, Rosa's body heavy in his arms. Heavier than anything he'd ever carried. He loosened his grip, just for a moment to rest. He lost his grip. Rosa sunk beneath the water, leaving no sign of her existence, of her hopes, of her problems, or of her dreams.

In that second, he realised he had a choice. A choice he'd never given Scott. He could shrug off his tiredness and save the policewoman, or allow her to sink to the floor and vanish and return to America, where no one would be any the wiser. There would be no one to blame for the car crash, no prosecution for the supposed assault at the hotel. He'd be one of hundreds of tourists, his possessions swept away in the floods, trying to escape the disaster.

Richard dived, the foul water filling his eyes and ears, and stretching out with his arms, he yanked Rosa back to the surface, gagging at the taste of the filthy water in his mouth. Rosa spluttered in his arms. Carstone felt Scott looking down upon him, washing away his sin, forgiving him for the terrible mistake which had cost his brother his life. He'd never meant to kill Scott. Shaking the ladder in anger, never for a second expecting his brother to fall, he'd gone into shock as Scott lay twitching on the ground. Fearful of losing what little reputation he had, he'd run away. No one had seen him. They couldn't link the accident to him. There was nothing he could have done for his brother. He knew that. But he couldn't escape from his guilt, which sat on his shoulders like Atlas carrying the weight of the world. By saving Rosa's life, he felt that guilt evaporating. Scott's death had been a terrible accident, an accident he'd initiated, but still just a terrible accident.

Carstone spied a staircase at the end of the short hallway, and bumping through floating frames and chopping boards and onions the colour of clay, he gently pulled Rosa over to the stairs before hefting her into his tired arms.

Carstone carried the unconscious woman up the narrow stairwell, ignoring the priceless art still hanging from their hooks. None of it meant anything to him anymore.

A sound of weeping reached Carstone's ears. Coming from the end bedroom, the pang of loss as transparent as the film of winter ice on a transitory puddle. Were they too late? Had someone killed the man's wife?

Carstone staggered towards the noise, a black smear of water trailing behind him.

Scott dying was the worst thing he'd ever seen. Until today. Until he peered into the cleaner's bedroom.

It wasn't the sight of cleaner on his knees beside a chair at the window, crying, which chilled Carstone, but the sight of the cleaner's wife. An ivory-white skull sporting a complicated twist of wiry hair, with a strand of dull pearls around her neck, wearing a filthy shirt and knee-length skirt, her shoes filled with nothing more than sagging silk stockings and slender white bones.

After placing Rosa on the floor, Carstone took a step into the room, a delicate crunch under his foot pulling him up sharp. A stray finger bone, crushed to a fine powder beneath his ruined shoes. He wished he had imagined it.

Despite the emptiness of his stomach, bile forced its way up Carstone's throat. He backed up, choking on the vile liquid. The woman was dead, more than dead, for twenty years at least. Probably at the hands of the man on his knees, his head in the bony lap of the skeletal woman, a tray of food at her side, peppered with rat droppings.

Carstone pulled the door closed, shutting the monster away.

'Let's find you a hospital,' he said to Rosa Fonti. His only priority now.

THE RIVER

When the tree barrelled into the boat, flinging the policeman overboard, The River wrapped her watery arms around his failing body. She caressed him, and cooled him, carrying him like a mother, safe in her flow.

Like all children, the policeman tried fighting with her, bucking against her rules and discipline, pushing himself to the surface, stealing a breath, fighting against her embrace, begging for release.

The River persisted. She'd been here before, many times. They tried stopping her by building walls and dams and stop-banks. But she was stronger than all of them.

She carried the policeman in her watery arms past galleries and bakeries, past museums and fishmongers, past tourists and tailors.

Around the steps of a church she paused, spinning in a circle, enjoying the freedom from the path mankind had designed for her. When would they learn that nature wouldn't stay corralled?

Standing at the top of the steps was a girl, one who'd escaped her clutches. In retaliation for the girl's escape,

The River sent a violent wave halfway up the marble steps. The girl stepped back, a baby hugged tight to her chest.

The River paused in her anger, she'd meant for the wave to reach the top, to tangle the girl's legs, pulling her and the babe downwards to their watery death. She could feel her power ebbing. It was too soon. Her fun had only just begun.

In the lull, the policeman called to the girl, begging her for help, but The River laughed, her gurgles and bubbles as indecipherable as the baby's cries.

The River saw the flash of recognition on the girl's face, and twisted away in anger. She would not give up her prey, not today. Not for a pretty dark-haired girl on a step. Not for anyone.

Again The River threw a wave of water towards the girl, drowning out her shouts. Foolish girl for trying to save the policeman. He belonged to The River now, not the girl. The River tossed the policeman about, swirling him round and around, like a merry-go-round.

Giving up on her revenge, The River dragged the policeman away from the girl's cries for help, away from salvation. Like a jaunty sail on a summer's day, The River steered the policeman away from the devastation she'd wrought on the city of Florence until he joined the flotsam and jetsam already caught in her flow.

The River enjoyed the weakness of his struggles. This was the part she loved the most — the peaceful acceptance of her victims in their final moments, their last breath taken underwater, filling their lungs with her sweet, sweet liquid.

She clasped him tighter, relishing his fear until he suddenly went limp.

No.

No.

No.

It wasn't his time yet.

The River shook him, jerking him backwards and forwards within a foam-lipped eddy near the foot of the bridge. A tiny red patent leather shoe slipped from the policeman's pocket and The River toyed with it for a second, before losing interest. The shoe raced away, its owner long since claimed by The River.

Enraged by the lack of response from the man, she threw him at the bridge, wasting her anger. She couldn't have known that the swollen blood vessel inside Pisani's head — the reason for his worsening headaches, had burst, killing him seconds after he realised the girl and her baby had made it to safety. The girl he'd saved from the flood at the Altavilla. As Pisani died, he smiled. He had done his job. He had saved her. He had saved the thief.

The River abandoned him. There would be someone else for her. There always was.

REVIEW

Dear Reader,

Thank you for reading *The Forger and the Thief*. If you enjoyed the story, you may also enjoy reading *Painted*, where you will once again meet the artist Leo Kubin, this time at his house...

READ PAINTED

Reviews help spread the word, and I would love it if you could post a rating or a review on your favourite digital platform.

POST AN ONLINE REVIEW

Thank you

Kirsten McKenzie x

AUTHOR'S NOTE

In November 1966, the River Arno burst its banks and flooded Florence, Italy killed 101 people and damaged or destroyed millions of masterpieces of art and rare books and manuscripts.

It wasn't the first time the Arno had flooded. Historical records list fifty-seven devastating floods since the 12th century. Notably, most of them occurred in November...

The combined effort of Italian and foreign volunteers, known as *Mud Angels*, saved much of Florence's treasure in the days following the flood. From their efforts, restoration laboratories were established and new methods in conservation were devised. However, decades later, much work remains to be done.

This story revolves around the Arno River as a central character to the story. She is real. The rest of my characters are entirely fictional.

Of the artworks mentioned, some are real, some are fictional. Some are still missing, and some never existed.

It is true that both Leonardo da Vinci and Michelanglo

put forward flood mitigation plans for Florence. They were ignored. The sketches da Vinci prepared still exist today.

The cemetery Rhonda finds herself in is also real. Known as the English Cemetery, it is the final resting place of Elizabeth Barrett Browning, and a number of American abolitionists. The statue of the Reaper sits above the tomb of a child in the cemetery.

The book *Dark River* by Robert Clark was an invaluable research tool, as were the documented accounts of the Mud Angels. The book *Art Crime and its Prevention*, edited by Arthur Tompkins, was also very helpful.

CAST OF PLAYERS

THE GUEST
Richard Carstone
Julia Carstone, Wife of Scott
Scott Carstone, Brother of Richard

THE CLEANER
Stefano Mazzi
Carmela Mazzi, Wife of Stefano
Marco Seuss, Museum Director
Karen Knowles, Curator

THE STUDENT
Helena Stolar
Feodor Sim, Tutor
Benito DiMarco, Student
Oona, Student
Marisa, Student
Vitali, Student
Alfonso Casadei, Gallery Owner
Leo Kubin, Artist

THE POLICEMAN
Antonio Pisani
Rosa Fonti, Policewoman
Ludo Gallo, Driver
Fausto Nucci, Chief Inspector
Bianca Zito, Suspect
Lucia Nicastri, Missing Girl

THE WIFE
Rhonda Devlyn
Paul Tobias, Private Investigator

ACKNOWLEDGMENTS

As always, thank you Emma Oakey for your editing services, and probing questions. What would I do without you!

To Andrene Low and Madeleine Roberts. It is magical having you in my life. Thank you for steering me down the right track, and always being on hand for a virtual hug or drink, sharing advice or commiserations. I look forward to my embroidered sampler which says, "Don't ever let me do another preorder…".

Thanks also to my family - Fletcher, Sasha and Jetta. The last four weeks before publication were rough, and you have been amazing. Thank you for all the time and space you gave me, and the dinners and the hugs and the kisses. Thank you.

On a separate note, this book would have been finished a lot sooner if a/ I wasn't such a terrible procrastinator, and b/ We weren't all suffering under a world-wide pandemic.

During New Zealand's seven weeks of lockdown, I found I was unable to write a single word. Some people exercised, some people wrote twenty novels, I did neither. But I did bake one loaf of bread and went for plenty of walks with my family. I struggled.

So, if you are reading this in lockdown, or quarantine, or if you are self isolating because of age or medical concerns, please know that I wish you the very best. I always answer my emails, so I'm here if you want to chat.

Thank you for reading *The Forger and the Thief.*

I hope you enjoyed it.

Kirsten

xxx

ABOUT THE AUTHOR

For years Kirsten McKenzie worked in the family antiques store, where she went from being allowed to sell postcards in the corner, to selling Worcester vases and seventeenth century silverware, providing a unique insight into the world of antiques which touches every aspect of her writing.

Her historical time travel trilogy, *The Old Curiosity Shop* series, has been described as *Time Travellers Wife meets Far Pavilions*, and *Antiques Roadshow gone viral*. Audio books for the series are also available.

Kirsten has also written the bestselling gothic thriller *Painted*, and the medical thriller, *Doctor Perry*. Her latest novel, *The Forger and the Thief*, is a historical thriller set in Florence, Italy.

Kirsten lives in New Zealand with her husband, her daughters, and two rescue cats. She can usually be found procrastinating on Twitter.

You can sign up for her sporadic newsletter at:
www.kirstenmckenzie.com/newsletter/

Printed in Great Britain
by Amazon